HIS CAGED WOLF

By
Alex McAnders

McAnders Books

Official Website: www.AlexAndersBooks.com
Podcast: www.SoundsEroticPodcast.com
Visit Alex Anders
at: Facebook.com/AlexAndersBooks & Instagram
Get 6 FREE ebooks and an audiobook by signing up for Alex Anders' mailing list at: AlexAndersBooks.com

Published by McAnders Publishing

HIS CAGED WOLF

Chapter 1

Quin

I can't believe Lou talked me into doing this. At one point he's talking about how I'll go feral if I don't get out and meet somebody. And the next thing I know I'm yelling at him about how that's not how going feral works. He then tells me that that is exactly how it works and makes up a story about a dog that went crazy because it was tied up all day.

As insulting as it was to compare me to a dog, I have to admit that he's not entirely wrong. I've struggled figuring out who I am. Am I my father's miracle son as my father always say? Or, am I the thing that the rest of the world sees me as and that I'm always trying to suppress?

Either way, my life sucks. I mean, I have everything in life anyone could ask for thanks to my father's wildly successful genetics research company. But, it comes with a trade-off that makes it not worth it.

My father thought he was doing the world a service by curing infertility. And since my mom was infertile, she became the first test subject. I'm proof that it worked. But it had a side effect that no one could ever have imagined.

I lock myself away because of that side effect. And, because of it, I'm scared as hell of the full moon.

It's not that I think anything is going to happen to me during a full moon. There's been a lot of full moons since the first time, and I believe in science.

What terrifies me about it is what other people think will happen. If they've heard of me —and who hasn't heard of me thanks to my showboating father — and they see me out in a full moon, every crazy story they've read turns me into a monster in their eyes.

I don't want to feel their judgement or terror. What's more, I don't want to smell it. I've been told that I'm the only one who notices it, but people's scents are overwhelming. That's part of the reason I lock myself in my dorm room when I'm not attending class. Well, that and fact that no one at East Tennessee University has recognized me yet and I want it to stay that way.

The only one so far who knows about my condition is Louis, my roommate and first actual friend. I told him after the University matched us and I decided that this was the year I would attend.

Lou also happens to be the gayest guy I've ever met. Not only that, he has skills. He can scan a room full of boys with their girlfriends and have a date in 20 minutes. I thought I liked guys, but he is boy crazy.

I was far from that. Don't get me wrong, I wanted sex. During a certain time of the month, it is all I can think about. The full moon might not turn me into a snarling, half-human beast. But, it makes me think of sex like I need it to breath. The older I get, the worse it gets.

Is there a chance not leaving my dorm will make me go feral like Lou casually suggested? I don't think so. I've had a lot more control over things compared to when I was a kid. If this was an alcohol problem instead of what it is, I could say that I haven't had a drink in years.

But, whether Lou was joking or not, I didn't want him thinking that me going feral was a possibility. So, after some yelling and fighting, I looked up the only party on campus happening tonight, and dressed for it.

"Finally," Lou said as I headed to the door.

What killed me was that after all of our arguing, as I left he had a smirk on his face. It was like this was his plan all along and I was the only one who actually got upset. He had manipulated me into going out and getting a life. That sneaking little bastard!

"And I want proof that you didn't just go to a park and chase squirrels or something."

"I don't chase squirrels!" I protested strongly.

"Whatever! But, when I get back from my date, I want to see a naked guy in your bed and I want to see some shame, Mister. Plenty of it."

"There will be! There will be plenty of shame, for you. Because of how wrong you were about me... and stuff."

"Good."

"Good."

"I mean it, Quin."

"Me too."

So now, here I am marching across campus to the only party that my last-minute research turned up. East Tennessee University's football team won against West Tennessee University their cross-state rivals earlier in the day and the football fraternity was throwing a party. Nothing about any of that sounded fun, but I'm going... because Lou tricked me into it.

Fine. I'll go. I'll get proof that I was there. Then I'll go to a coffee shop and read a book on my phone.

I know he mentioned that thing about finding someone naked in my bed, but there's no way that's going to happen. I couldn't lose my virginity in a pool full of dicks. Believe me, I've tried. But as soon as anyone gets a good look at me and realizes who I am, they either talk about leashing me in case I turn on them in the middle of sex, or they run for the hills.

Nope. It looks like I'll just have to spend the rest of my life as a sad, lonely virgin. Did I just bum myself out? I think I did. Now I'm really not in the mood for a party.

Rounding the corner, I could hear the music before the fraternity house came into view. It was intimidating. I had to tap into my anger at what Lou had said to keep me going.

Face-to-face with my impending doom, I almost froze. I'm just not very good at human stuff. There is no way I was going to be able to mingle or cohort or whatever it was that people my age did.

New plan. I wasn't going in. I would get my proof that I was here, though. I was going to walk up to one of the half dozen people standing outside, ask to take a selfie with them and then get out of there as quickly as I could.

Looking around, I saw people smoking, people talking in a circle with red cups, and one guy standing by himself. That made the selection easy. All I had to do was walk up to him, ask to take a selfie, snap it, thank him and go. I could manage that. I wasn't a complete freak. I could talk to one person.

Tightening my lips, I hardened my resolve and charged over. I wasn't going to overthink it. I was just going to do it and be done.

"Excuse me, can I get a selfie with you?" I asked the guy with his back to me.

"You want a selfie with me? Why?" The guy said with an edge to his voice as he turned around.

Woah!

Do you know that feeling when you see something that takes your breath away? Warm prickles start at the back of your hands and shoot up your arms before settling in your face as the heat makes you lightheaded? That was what happened when our eyes met. The guy was beautiful.

His creamy skin contrasted with his jet black hair and pool-blue eyes. His jawline was carved out of marble. There were dimples, so many dimples, in his cheeks, underneath his bottom lip, on the tip of his chin. They were everywhere.

He was also big. He was inches taller than me and twice as wide. That isn't saying much considering how slight I am. But his rippling muscles looked like they had muscles. God, was he gorgeous.

More than that, he smelled amazing. There was a sweet musk to him that I had never smelt in my life. It made me drunk just standing there.

As his scent wafted off of him, it stripped me of my will. It was like he had leashed me while at the same time awaking the part of me I fought so hard to restrain.

I couldn't speak and he was clearly waiting for me to. He had asked me a question. What was it? Oh yeah! It was why I wanted a selfie with him, and he seemed upset about it.

Had I made him angry? Was it weird to ask to take a selfie with a complete stranger? It probably was? Shit! What the hell was I thinking?

"Sorry," I sputtered before forcing my legs to move in the opposite direction.

I got two steps away before he spoke again.

"Wait! Don't go."

I stopped.

"I'm sorry. I didn't mean to be rude. If you want a selfie, I'll take one with you."

"No, that's okay," I said wanting to look at him again but scared that if I did I wouldn't be able to breathe.

"No really. It's fine. You can get one. I don't know why anyone would want one. But, it's fine. I'd be happy to take one with you."

That was when I looked at him again. I recognized what he was saying. He was talking like a guy who was used to people asking to take pictures with him. I knew a little about that. That was in part why I chose a university in the middle of nowhere. I wanted to be where I wouldn't be recognized as Quin Toro, the only wolf shifter in existence.

That was me, though. Why did people ask him for selfies? He was the most amazing-looking guy ever. Did random strangers approach him dazzled by his beauty? It wouldn't surprise me if they did.

"I, um, wasn't asking for a selfie because I know who you are. I don't recognize you. I don't know who you are," I explained.

The guy jutted his head back startled. As I stared, his fair skin turned pink.

"Oh! Okay. Then..." he shook his head as if trying to shake something loose. "I'm sorry, why do you want a selfie with me?"

"It wasn't you. It was anybody," I told him.

"You wanted to get a selfie with anybody? Why?"

I huffed as my predicament reentered my mind.

"It's my roommate. He told me that I needed to get out and have fun. He said he needed proof..."

"And the selfie was going to be the proof?"

"Yeah."

"So, after you took the selfie..., what? You were gonna go?"

"Yeah," I admitted suddenly deflating.

The gorgeous guy looked at me like I was the freak that I am. A smile crept across his face. It would have made me feel bad about myself if it didn't make me want to melt into a puddle in the grass.

"This is going to sound crazy, but you're here. Why not go in and actually have fun?"

"I'm not good at this type of thing. You know, the social thing."

"Luckily, that's something I'm very good at. How about we make a deal? I'll give you your selfie as proof for your roommate, but you have to come in and actually try to have a good time. I'll introduce you to a couple of people. That way, when your roommate asks you about the night, you won't have to lie," he said his face exploding into dimples.

I stared at him. "Why would you do that?"

He looked at me twisting his head in confusion.

"Maybe I'm just being nice. Maybe I think you're a cool guy and that it would be cool to hang out. Maybe I'm flirting."

A chill shot through me upon hearing the word "flirting". What was going on? Did this guy like me? Was there something happening between us? Was there going to be a naked guy in my bed full of shame when Lou got home after all?

Wait, was I getting hard? I think I was. No, I definitely was.

"Um, okay," I said sure that I was turning beet-red.

"Cage, by the way?"

"What?"

"My name." He stared at me. "And your name is?"

"Oh. Quin."

"Cool. I like that name."

"Thanks. My parents gave it to me," I said losing control of my tongue.

Cage laughed.

"I mean, of course my parents gave it to me."

"Not of course. My parents didn't give me the name Cage."

"Who did? An uncle or somebody?"

"No, I did."

"So, what's your birth name?"

Cage looked at me with thoughts rushing through his head. "How about I take you inside and show you around?"

"So, I guess we're going to let that question go?"

Cage chuckled uncomfortably. "You don't have much of a filter, do you?"

I froze. That wasn't the first time I had heard that. The previous time was with the last guy I fell for.

"I guess not. Is that bad?"

"Actually, it's kind of refreshing."

"Oh. Okay," I said falling for him more.

"You have a nice smile."

"I didn't realize I was smiling," I told him.

"You are," he said looking at me with a smile of his own.

"You too. It's very nice," I said feeling my heart thump and not knowing what to do about it.

Cage led me up the stairs, onto the porch, and then into the frat house. It was hard to take my eyes off of him, but when I did I was surprised by what I saw. I didn't know what I was expecting, but it wasn't this. The large living room was sparsely furnished but full of people. Everyone had red cups in their hand and they spoke to each other like they were friends.

"It's still pretty early," Cage explained.

"What do you mean?" I said raising my voice over the country-pop music.

"There'll be more people later."

"More than this?" I asked looking around at what felt like a horde.

Cage chuckled. "Yeah."

"Damn. Okay."

"Cage!" A thick guy said throwing his arms around Cage spilling some of his drink onto Cage's shirt. "Oh, did I get you?"

"That's okay," Cage said casually. "Dan, this is Quin."

Dan turned to me and stared. "Quin!" he finally said removing the awkwardness. "Is he trying to recruit you?"

"What?" I asked confused.

"Is he trying to get you on the football team?"

I stared at him unsure what was happening. Was he being serious? I wasn't exactly built like a guy who ran full speed into 200-pound men.

"Football team?"

Dan turned to Cage confused.

"We play on the football team," Cage explained.

"You do?"

Dan threw his arms around Cage again. "Cage doesn't just play for the football team. He is the team."

I looked at Cage for an explanation.

He smiled with humility. "I'm the quarterback."

"This man isn't just the quarterback," Dan said mockingly. "He's the guy who is gonna lead us to a national championship, and then he's going pro."

"Ohhhh! Now I get it. The selfie. You thought I was asking for a selfie because you're a famous football player."

"I'm not a famous football player," he said quickly.

"Hell yeah, he's famous. There ain't anybody who doesn't know who he is," Dan said proudly.

I looked at Cage for his reaction. Cage looked back at me and chuckled uncomfortably.

"Not everyone knows who I am."

"Name me one person who doesn't," Dan challenged.

He gave me a knowing smile. "Quin, you want a drink? I think you need a drink. Follow me."

"Good meeting you, Quin," Dan said before wandering off.

"So, you're a quarterback?"

"Didn't you hear? I'm not just a quarterback, I'm the team," Cage said with self-deprecation.

I laughed. "I heard. Are you going to go pro? I have a couple of uncles who played in the NFL."

Cage looked back at me with surprise. "Do you?"

"Yeah. I mean, they're family friends. So, you know, "uncles"," I clarified.

"Did they like it?"

"Playing for the NFL?"

"Yeah."

"I guess so. You excited about getting drafted?"

"Sure," Cage said half-heartedly before turning to pump beer into two red cups.

"You don't sound excited."

"No. It's great. I can't wait for it. It's, ah, everything I've been working towards," he said handing me a cup and holding up his to cheers with mine. "To new friends."

I touched his cup and took a drink. "This beer is awful," I said looking down at my cup.

Cage laughed. "No, tell me what you really think."

"I mean that it's not very good," I explained.

Cage laughed louder. When he stopped he stared into my eyes. God did I want to kiss him.

"I suppose if I ask you if you're having fun yet, you'll tell me the truth."

"I'm having fun," I said moving closer in case he did want to kiss me.

Cage watched me with a devilish look in his eyes. I could have sworn that he was about to move his lips towards mine when he said, "Why don't I introduce you to a few more people."

"More people? I've already met two. How many more people can a person meet in a night?"

"Haha. A few more than that," he said slipping his hand around my shoulders and leading me away.

Feeling his touch made every part of me tingle. I felt like such a little guy in his arms. He was so big and strong. I couldn't believe that I had met someone like him. I couldn't believe that he was acting like he was into me. Could a guy like him be into guys?

Thinking about it set something off in me that I could barely control. It was the part of me that I fought to repress. It was fighting to get out. I knew I should have been doing everything to resist it, but I didn't want to. With it came a sense of power I had never felt before. I liked it. It made me feel... strong.

In spite of how much I wanted to let go, I did my best to stay with Cage in my present form. He was leading me around the party introducing me to people. He wasn't kidding about being good at social stuff. Everyone he introduced me to hung on his every word. And, when it was my turn to speak, they hung on my every word, too.

I couldn't tell if they were all just being nice, or if being with Cage had turned me into a more interesting version of myself. Whatever it was, I loved the feeling. These types of interactions had always been so hard for me, but at Cage's side, I was a different person.

What was even better than that was how he took every opportunity to touch me. He touched my shoulder when he introduced me. His pointing finger lightly rested on my chest when he was emphasizing a point. And, standing shoulder to shoulder as if we were already a couple, he would bump his shoulder against mine when he laughed.

I was on the verge of shifting by the time he was done with me. I knew that should have freaked me out. But instead I thought about what Lou had suggested. What would Cage look like naked in my bed?

With one of his teammates waving his arms around telling a story, I couldn't take my eyes off of Cage. With his full attention on his friend, Cage subtly retrieved his phone from his pocket and peaked down. Slipping it away quickly, he waited for the arm waving to die down and then looked between his friend and me.

"Guys, I have to head out," he said wrapping his large hand around my bicep.

"Yes, me too," I said quickly.

"Yeah? Where you headed?" He asked enthusiastically.

"Back to my room."

"Where's that?"

"Plaza Hall?"

"Really? I'll go with you," he said squeezing my arm.

My heart stopped. He was coming with me? Was this it? I couldn't believe it might finally happen. I prayed no one looked down because there was no hiding my excitement.

I swallowed and forced myself to speak.

"Cool."

After saying a few goodbyes, the two of us exited into the night. I was giddy from terror and arousal. As the silence between us drew out, I wondered why he wasn't saying anything. Wasn't he the one who was supposed to be good at stuff like this? I was about to mumble something when he finally spoke.

"It's a clear night."

"What?"

"You can see all of the stars," he said turning to me.

I looked up. He was right. The night was perfectly clear. There was nothing between us and the light of the full moon. How had I not remembered that tonight was the full moon?

It's not like it mattered. I wasn't a hollowing monster enslaved by it. I hadn't shifted in years. I had long ago gotten control over myself, over my body. I was Quin Toro, human, not some mindless wolf...

"You cold?"

"What?"

"You're shivering."

I was shaking. "I guess I'm nervous," I admitted.

"What are you nervous about?"

My face got hot. "I don't know."

Cage stared at me. "You're a good-looking guy. Do you know that?"

"So are you," I told him shaking even more.

"Thanks. Are you happy you came out tonight?"

"Yeah, definitely," I said fighting not to show him how much.

"We're here," he said as we approached the door of my building.

"We're here," I repeated my heart pounding. "Do you want to come in?"

"Come in?" Cage asked caught off guard.

"Yes," I replied struggling not to pounce him right there.

"Ahhhh," he murmured before the door popped open and a girl came out.

"Cage!" She said before wrapping her arms around him and standing on her tiptoes to kiss his lips.

My mouth dropped open in shock. What was going on? What had just happened?

The petite, blonde with angular features turned towards me. "Who's this?"

"Ah, this is Quin. Quin this is Tasha."

Tasha looked at me suspiciously while Cage became uncomfortable.

"Tasha is my girlfriend."

"How do you know Cage?" Tasha asked me.

I was too shocked by everything to speak.

"Quin had asked me for a selfie."

Tasha turned to Cage surprised. "Oh. Did you give him one?"

"Not yet," Cage said with a smile.

"I can take it," Tasha volunteered. "Give me your phone," she said approaching me with her hand out.

Still speechless, I handed her my phone and stood next to Cage.

"Say cheese," she said.

"Cheese," Cage replied while I stared back stunned.

"Here you go," she said handing me back my phone. "Check it."

I looked down and saw my full humiliation on display. "Yes."

"Okay. Let's go. I'm hungry," Tasha said entwining her body with Cage's and pulling him away.

"It was nice meeting you, Quin," he said looking at me as he left.

"Yes. It was nice meeting… you," I mumbled sure that he could no longer hear me.

I watched as the perfectly suited couple walked off. Of course, he had a girlfriend. And, of course, she looked like that. My heart hurt watching them go.

I can't believe I thought he was interested in me. No one's ever interested in me. How could I have been so foolish? How could I think a guy like him could be interested in a guy like me?

Once the two had disappeared into the darkness, I entered the building. Ascending the stairs in a daze, I felt like I was going to explode. Why didn't anyone ever like me back? Why didn't Cage like me?

I couldn't take this anymore. My skin vibrated with a ferocity I hadn't felt in years. When I finally realized what was going on, it was too late.

"Oh no. No, no, no, no, no," I said in a panic.

As I bound up the stairs, the world around me drifted further away. I needed to lock myself up. I couldn't believe this. It had been years. Why now? Why here?

Approaching my dorm room door, I smelled the last thing I wanted to smell or expected. Lou was home. Why was he home? Didn't he say he had a date?

I didn't want him to see me like this. I didn't want to terrify him with the truth of who I was. I didn't want to accidently kill him.

Was this how my mother died? Had I lost control and ripped out her throat? I was too young to remember. But a three-year-old child and a three-year-old wolf are different. If I let it, would the beast inside of me hurt another person I cared about?

No, I couldn't let it. I had to get behind closed doors as quickly as I could. Scrambling for my keys I flung open the door and charged in.

"Aren't you supposed to be out finding yourself a date?" he said as I rushed by him for my room. "Quin, what's wrong?"

As my bedroom door closed behind me and I searched for the padlock for the latch I installed, I finally lost control and did what I prayed for years that I wouldn't do. The feeling was torture. It all came rushing back.

A prickly feeling washed over me igniting every nerve in my body. My muscle clamped into the worst cramp you could imagine. And as my muscles pulled apart and ate itself, my bones snapped under the strain of it.

Mercifully, that was when I passed out. This was how it happened when I was a kid. At least it started that way. Because as a kid, I would black out in one location and wake up naked and covered in blood somewhere else.

My father often tested the blood to make sure none of it was human. It never was. But, every so often pictures of missing cats would end up posted around our upstate New York home.

Our neighbors knew what I was so they had their suspicions but they would never know for sure. The only person to ever see me shift was my father. And it wasn't until he determined that I, and my wolf, weren't a threat that we moved back to Manhattan.

This shift wasn't like any I had had when I was a kid, though. This time I woke up in my room in the dark. It felt like one of those instances when you wake up to learn that you can't move your body. I was conscious, fully conscious. But I was pacing in my room very close to the ground and it felt like I was being taken for a ride.

As much as I tried, I couldn't stop myself. My dresser whipped by me in rapid succession and as I entertained the sounds around me, I heard a wild panting. Oh no, I was in it. I was the monster.

The only way I had been able to come to terms with who I was was by convincing myself that I wasn't it and it wasn't me. I wasn't the one who killed my mother. It was. It was dangerous and brutal. I was not.

Yet, here I was disproving everything I held onto for my own sanity. I was awake, though not in control, and I was experiencing the world around me as if it were my own.

"Quin, are you alright?" a faint voice said just outside my door.

As if set on fire, my wolf went wild. It bulleted to the door and attacked it as if fighting to break through.

"Oh no, the latch. I didn't lock it," I remembered flooded with dread.

As soon as I said it, my eyes turned towards the door handle and it clawed at it. It heard me and it was fighting to get out. If it got out it would kill Lou. I was sure of it. It would kill everyone in its path until someone put it down or it ran away.

This was my greatest nightmare come true. It was why I locked myself away never wanting to come out. It was everything I had feared.

Wait! It heard me! That's how it knew to go after the lock. If it heard me say that, then...

"Stop it! You will not attack my friend. You won't do to him what you did to my mother!"

As if frozen in place, it stopped. Standing still, sadness washed through my mind. It wasn't me feeling it. It was the wolf. It was thinking about what it had done to my mom.

Regret filled it. Somehow I knew it hadn't meant to. And as if calmed by the tragedy, it slowly backed away from the door and whimpered.

My wolf was crying. It knew as well as I did how much it had lost that day. It also knew that it had been his fault. Both of us had grown up without a mother because of it. Death hadn't been my wolf's intention. It had acted impulsively and unexpected things had happened.

Without asking it to, the wolf walked in front of my full length mirror. It was dark, but the wolf's eyes were more sensitive than mine. I could make out his reflection clearly. I was 20 and just approaching adulthood. The wolf staring back at me was much older than that.

I had only seen video of it before. Back then it was of a much younger wolf. This one looked calmer and maybe even a little wiser than the one pacing back and forth in my father's safety room. Was it different than the one that had terrorized my world all of those years ago?

Maybe it was. Maybe I didn't know this wolf at all. Maybe I didn't know myself. Who would I be if I wasn't so scared of what I would become?

Chapter 2

Cage

Wow! I have never felt anything like that in my life. Looking at Quin I could barely contain myself. I couldn't keep my hands off of him. I could have stayed with him at the party all night. For the first time in a long time, I felt alive.

Returning to reality was a hard pill to swallow. When I got Tasha's text, it felt like the rug had been ripped from under me. I wanted to stay there with Quin. I wanted to see how far it would go. But, I had promised Tasha that I would take her to dinner whether or not we won the game. I always keep my obligations and I had made one to Tasha.

"So, I wanted to talk to you about something," Tasha said breaking the silence as we walked.

"What's that?"

Tasha looked at me excitedly and blushed. Seeing her display of emotion was an unusual sight. A dark cloud usually followed Tasha infecting everyone around her.

I had to assume she wasn't happy with her life. I was clearly a part of her dissatisfaction. But whenever I tried to talk to her about it, she accused me of trying to ruin the good thing we have going.

What good thing was that? She wasn't happy. I wasn't happy. And we never had sex.

"You know Vi, right?" Tasha asked bubbling.

"Your best friend Vi who you spend all of your time with. Yeah, I know her."

"You don't have to say it like that."

"You asked me if I knew the girl you always talk about."

"Why are you trying to start a fight? I'm trying to do something nice for you."

I caught myself and took a breath. I was feeling tense. I hadn't want to leave Quin, but I did because of Tasha. I couldn't even ask him for his number when we got back to his place. That was probably for the best, though. The way he made me feel could only lead to me making decisions I would regret.

I had larger things to consider. I had worked my whole life to play for the NFL. Being with a girl like Tasha helps sell the pack of me as the face of a franchise. At least, that's what my father says. And it had been his dream that I play professional football longer than it had been mine. I couldn't let him down.

"I'm sorry. I guess I'm still feeling beat up from the game. It's making me a little cranky."

Tasha smiled. "You're forgiven," she said wrapping her arms around mine. "And, I think I have something that will make you feel better."

"Okay," I said mustering a smile. "What is it?"

"Well, remember how we've been talking about spicing things up in… the bedroom?"

I looked at Tasha suspiciously. Spicing things up was something she had brought up and when she did, it felt like she had something very specific in mind that she wouldn't mention.

"I remember."

"So, I talked to Vi…"

"Okay," I said confused.

"I spoke to Vi and asked her if she would be interested in joining the two of us when we were… together. And she said yes," Tasha said crackling.

I stopped walking and stared at her. It took a second to wrap my head around what she was saying.

"You mean, like a threesome?"

"Yeah," she said turning bright red.

"Tasha, why would you do that?"

"What do you mean?"

"Why would you invite someone else into our bed… and without talking to me first?"

"I thought you would like it. Doesn't every guy want to be with two beautiful women at the same time?"

"Not every guy. And, if you would have asked me, I would have told you that I'm a one-guy, one-girl sort of man… if you would have asked me."

"I thought you would like it," she said heartbroken.

"Well, I don't. And, I don't know why you would even suggest it."

"Maybe it's because we never have sex anymore."

"And that's my fault? You're the one who spends all of her time with Vi."

"What are you saying?"

"I'm saying that I'm not the one who doesn't want to have sex."

"Well, you could have fooled me."

"Then, if you're so unhappy, maybe we shouldn't be together."

Tasha froze staring at me. "Why would you say that? Why would you say that?"

"Isn't that what's obvious?"

"No. We were meant to be together. I would make you the perfect wife. You know that. You're going to get drafted and become the starting quarterback for a big NFL team and I'll take care of the house and start a charity. We talked about this, Baby. Our futures are set."

She was right. We had talked about it and that was exactly what we had said. But now that I was in my senior year and I couldn't put off entering the draft any longer, I was starting to have my doubts. That wasn't her fault, though. And I shouldn't be taking it out on her.

"You're right. I'm sorry, Tasha. I'm just in a mood today. But, please, no more talking about threesomes, okay?"

As soon as I said it, I saw the light in Tasha's eyes blink out.

"Okay," she agreed before the two of us continued our walk to the restaurant in silence.

"I told you not to take that class, Rucker."

"Coach, it was something I was interested in," I tried to explain for the thousandth time.

"Intro to Childhood Education? What does a starting quarterback for the Dallas Cowboys or L.A. Rams need with a class on childhood education?" my coach asked more than a little pissed off.

"Look," I said finally losing my cool. "I took every class you told me to whether I wanted to or not. I attend every practice you schedule and I work hard enough to puke..."

"And look where you are because of it. A top prospect in a competitive draft class. You should be thanking me for how hard I've pushed you."

I caught myself and took a breath. "And I am. But Coach, I needed to take at least one class that was for me."

"But why that one?"

"It's what I'm interested in."

"Yet you haven't attended a single class since the beginning of the year?"

"That's because it starts 20 minutes after the end of practice. I thought I could just run over when I was done. But sometimes practice runs late, or I have to take an ice bath. Sometimes I'm just too tired."

"Well, you should have thought about that before you chose the class because this professor isn't as sympathetic to the challenges of student-athletes as the others are. This one thinks you should have to attend and take the tests to pass. And if you don't pass this class, you won't be allowed to play spring quarter. That means this team won't win and no one will scout you."

"I got it. I'll start going to class."

"Not just that. You're getting a tutor. I'll have one of my people find you someone. When's your next class?"

I looked up at the clock on the wall of Coach's office.

"Right now."

"Then get your ass over there."

"Coach, it's across campus. By the time I get there, there will only be five minutes left."

"I guess that means you'll have to run, doesn't it?"

"Coach, we just did 20 minutes of wind sprints."

"Don't talk back, just run. I mean it. Go, go, go!"

Backing out of the office, I did what I was told and ran. I had taken off my chest padding, but I was still in my cleats, compression shirt, and padded pants. The class was on the third floor of a building clear across campus. I didn't have time to change if I was going to make it.

I didn't know how I had gotten into this mess. Actually, I kinda did. It was my act of rebellion. Yeah, I knew that it would butt up against practice, but I thought it would give me an excuse to leave practice early. I was wrong. And now my entire future hung in the balance.

Entering the building and the stairwell, I was completely out of breath. Luckily no one could hear my panting over the thunderous noise of my metal cleats echoing off the concrete. There was no quietly sneaking into the back of the class. By the time I had opened the classroom door, everyone had already turned to look. There were 50 students and one angry professor all staring at me.

"Sorry. Please continue," I said between struggling breaths and plenty of humiliation.

Taking the first open seat, I rested my head on the desk to quietly catch my breath. I again felt like I wanted to throw up, but that wasn't happening here.

Gathering myself I sat up realizing that I hadn't grabbed my book bag from my locker. It wasn't like I had the notebook for this class in it or anything. I had given up on attending a long time ago. But it would have been nice to have something in front of me so I didn't look like an idiot.

Pulling out my phone, I did my best to seem like I was taking notes on it. I wasn't because I had no idea what the professor was talking about. It looked like everyone else did, though. They were all laser-focused on the woman standing in front of us. That is, everyone was paying attention except one person. And when I saw him, I couldn't breathe.

It was Quin, and he was looking up at me. Our eyes connected for a second but then he looked away. Everything inside of me tingled. I could immediately feel myself breathing harder.

Just seeing him did something to me. I had been given a second chance with him. I wasn't going to let him slip out of my life again.

"And, that's it. Next class will be a quiz on what we covered over the past two weeks. Be ready," the professor said before turning her attention to me. "Mr. Rucker, can I see you a moment?"

I wasn't expecting that. Worst still, Quin was seated on the opposite side of the room which had a different exit. He wasn't looking my way and he would be gone before I could ask him to wait for me.

"Mr. Rucker," the grey-haired, Asian woman called again.

"Coming," I told her keeping an eye on Quin as he approached the door.

Quickly swimming upstream past the flood of people, I approached the professor as she erased the board. She was taking her time with it and it was killing me. When Quin disappeared, my heart sank. He was gone again and I felt like crap.

"Coming in five minutes before the end of class isn't considered attending. At least not in my book."

"I know. And I'm really sorry about that. I ran over from practice. But I promise I won't be late again."

"I'm told you need to pass this class to remain eligible to play next season."

"That's correct, Ma'am."

"Then I would think you would take this class a little more seriously."

"And I promise, I will… moving forward."

"If you don't want to be here…"

"I do want to be here."

"Why?" She asked sincerely.

"Because it's a subject I'm really interested in. Teaching kids is something I've always wanted to do."

"What about football? I hear you have a promising professional career."

"Football is what I'm good at. It's a blessing. But it's not…"

I didn't finish the sentence. That was a box I didn't want open right now.

"Well, if you are serious about this class, you're going to have a lot of catching up to do."

"I realize that, and I'm willing to work. I'm getting a tutor."

"Are you?"

"Yes, Ma'am. In fact…" I said suddenly getting an idea. "Could we pick this up next class? I promise I'll be on time for it."

"You better be. Remember, attendance is mandatory."

"I got it. I'm on it. I'll be here. Promise," I said clomping my cleats on the carpet as I trotted to the door.

As soon as I was in the hall, I scanned both directions looking for him. He wasn't there. Where had he gone so quickly?

Most of the students were entering the stairwell headed downstairs. I jogged over and joined them. Craning my neck over the crowd, I couldn't see him. I was about to hate myself for not leaving sooner when I saw the back of someone who could only be Quin exiting the stairwell onto the main floor.

"Excuse me. Excuse me," I said squeezing past everyone.

It only got me down a few seconds sooner and by the time I was there, he was again nowhere to be seen.

Looking into every classroom as I ran past them, I didn't see him. I was about to give up hope when I popped open the door to the building and spotted his sexy frame walking away. Warmth washed across me. It felt like a spot of sunshine on a cloudy day.

Jogging towards him, I slowed when I was a few feet away. I couldn't lose my cool just because I was about to talk to the best-looking guy I had ever seen. I had to at least pretend like kissing him wasn't the only thing I could think about since the moment we met.

"Quin?" I said trying to be as casual as I could.

He stopped and turned around. He did not look as happy to see me as I was to see him. It triggered a twinge in my chest but I pushed past it.

"I thought that was you. How have you been? Hit up any big parties since I saw you last?" I said with a smile.

When he didn't reply, I said, "Cage. Cage Rucker. We met at the Sigma Chi party."

"I remember," he said coldly. Ouch! There was that twinge of pain again. "How's Tasha. That was your girlfriend's name, right?"

"Tasha? Oh, yeah. She's good. She's fine. Ah, did I do something to piss you off? If I did, I'm sorry," I said desperately wanting to see him smile again.

Quin stared at me with a look of frustration and then relented.

"No. You didn't do anything wrong. Don't mind me. I just had a rough night."

"Didn't sleep well?"

"Something like that. Or, maybe I'm just being stupid. I don't know."

"You? Being stupid? I find that hard to believe," I said with a smile.

He stared at me again. This time he looked like he was searching my soul.

"Why would you say that?"

"I don't know. I guess you strike me as being someone really smart."

He softened the intensity of his gaze.

"I'm not smart about anything that matters," he said before continuing his walk.

I caught up to him.

"I don't think that's true. In fact, I'll bet you're pretty smart at Intro to Childhood Education. I bet you're at the top of the class."

Quin looked at me when I said that.

"You are, aren't you?"

Quin looked away.

"I'll be damned. Okay. Then that will make the next thing I say less awkward. It turns out that I need this class to stay eligible for football and ultimately, the NFL draft. And, since I haven't been attending classes, I'm a little behind. I kind of need a tutor. The football program is willing to pay you for your time."

"I can't tutor you," he said dismissively.

"Why not?"

"I just can't. Sorry."

"Okay. Then how about if I make the pot a little sweeter?"

"What do you mean?"

"When we were at the party you said that you weren't good at being social, which I don't understand because you seemed perfectly comfortable with it."

"I was only comfortable because…"

"Because of what?" I asked hoping he would say because of me.

"Nothing."

"Well, if you're willing to tutor me in what you're good at, I can tutor you on what I'm good at."

"You mean being a football star that everyone wants a piece of."

"First of all, ouch. Second of all, there's a little more to me than that."

"I know. I'm sorry. See, I'm not good at this," Quin exclaimed.

I took his hand as casually as I could. I tried to pretend like this was just something I did when I talked to people, but the truth was I had been dying to hold it.

"You are good at this. At least, you can be. Let me help you. I know I can help you with this. And once you're done, you'll be a star football player who everyone wants a piece of like I am," I said with a smirk.

Quin laughed. I tingled so much I thought my teeth would fall out.

"So, what do you say?"

Quin stared at me considering it. As he did something weird happened. It felt like his eyes gained depth and then pierced through me.

It felt like he was searching my soul. As he did, something in me lit up. I can't explain what was going on.

Was he feeling it too? Was he doing it to me? What was going on between us?

Whatever it was it took my breath away. When he finally relaxed his gaze, I inhaled desperately. Quin pulled his hand from mine. He wasn't subtle about it. I think he was trying to send a message about boundaries. Fair enough, I could respect that.

"Okay," Quin said with a smile.

"Okay?" I repeated melting in his eyes.

"Okay," he confirmed to my absolute joy.

"I hear there's a quiz in the next couple of days."

"It's in two days and it covers two weeks of material."

"That sounds like a lot."

"It is," he confirmed.

"It sounds like your tutoring should start right away," I suggested wanting to spend every waking moment with him.

"How about tonight? I'll set up a lesson plan and we'll go from there."

"A lesson plan? You don't play around."

"I don't. You can't either if you want to pass the quiz."

"I won't."

Quin hesitated. "And you don't have any plans with your girlfriend or anything, do you?"

Being reminded of Tasha was a bucket of cold water on my runaway excitement about spending the night with Quin. My smile diminished.

"Even if I had something, I would cancel it. Passing the class and playing football comes first. She would understand."

"Okay. Then I'll see you tonight."

"Should I get your number?" I asked him not missing the opportunity this time.

"Yes. Give me your phone."

I handed it to him and he typed it in. A second later I heard the phone in his pocket ring.

"You know where I live. I'll text you the time and my room number," Quin said professionally.

"So we'll be doing this at your place?"

"Unless you have somewhere better. I guess we could go to a library but I don't know how much talking they'll allow."

"No, your place is great. I look forward to it."

"You look forward to studying?" He asked reminding me that this wasn't a date.

"Of course. Intro to Childhood Education is what I live for. Ask anybody."

Quin laughed. It melted my heart.

"See you then, Dimples," he said with a smile before turning and walking off. Man, was I in trouble.

Chapter 3

Quin

'See you then, Dimples?' Did I actually say that? What was I thinking? What was I thinking agreeing to any of this?

To say that the night before had been rough was the understatement of the year. I was trapped helpless in my wolf's body for hours. It didn't end until we both feel asleep.

In the morning, I wasn't covered in blood and I hadn't woken up in an unfamiliar location. I was in my room on my bed. Yeah, the door was thoroughly gouged from its claws, but it hadn't been opened.

It had been close to getting out. If it had given one more attempt, it would have done it. It would have freed itself and who knows what would have happened after that. But, it didn't. It hadn't even made that final attempt.

More than that, all morning I couldn't shake the feeling that he wasn't completely gone. It felt like he was lingering over my shoulder watching everything I did. It was him who told me that Lou had left in the middle of the night. He could even tell me the time he did it. I didn't know how, but my wolf knew.

Seeing Cage when he entered the classroom, it felt like his ears perked up. He seemed to like Cage even more than I did.

I wasn't a slave to his desires, though. And I was the one who had been introduced to his girlfriend, not him. So, there was no way I was going there, especially considering what he and his girlfriend had brought out in me.

I was willing to walk away from Cage and never see him again. Then he chased me down, and made that offer. The reason I said yes, had nothing to do with what my wolf wanted. It also didn't have to do with that weird connection I felt with him staring into his eyes.

I accepted his proposal because Quin Toro had come to the middle of nowhere Tennessee for one purpose, to figure out how to have a life. Sure, I couldn't have one with Cage. But, as I walked through the party with him was the most relaxed I had felt in a social situation in my life.

I needed to know how to feel that on my own. And, when I was looking into his eyes, something told me that he could bring it out of me. How did I know that? I don't know. But I was sure of it.

Could it have been my wolf playing with my mind for its own nefarious purpose? That was always a possibility — I had only just met him. He was something I only heard stories about before. — But, I didn't think so. There was something more going on with Cage.

Whatever it was, it was drawing me to him. It wasn't just how hot he was. — Don't think I suddenly got over that. He was still a gorgeous god. — But... I don't know.

There was more there that I couldn't put my finger on. It was telling me to accept his offer. And, once I did, my wolf went wild. Not in a way that felt dangerous. In way that made me smile.

"Lou, you're back?" I said reentering our apartment and finding him looking frazzled.

"Should I not be?"

He was seated at our dinner table terrified but trying to look brave. Sadness washed over me as I witnessed how much I had freaked him out. For the first time I had witnessed what my wolf sounded like when he was trying to get to someone. It was horrifying.

If I were the one who had listened to the scratching on the door as the beast tried to get to me, I probably would never have returned. Yet, here he was. Why was he back? Why would anyone return after seeing that part of me?

"No, you should be back. This is where you live… Should I leave?" I asked realizing that he might only have returned to stake his claim on the place.

"Should you leave?"

"I don't know. Should I leave?"

"Okay, I don't think we're getting anywhere here," he said handling this a hell of a lot better than I might have. "Look, I know you told me about your condition. But, you said that you hadn't had an episode it years. You said it had passed."

"I thought it had," I said easing myself into a chair facing him.

"Then, what was that?"

"I don't know."

"Did it happen because of the full moon?"

I heard my wolf growl at the suggestion. "No!" I snapped. As soon as I said it, my mind wandered. "At least, I don't think so."

"Well, you've been living here for months and that wasn't the first full moon."

"It wasn't. Was it?"

"Then, what was the difference this time?" Lou asked as if he was concerned about me instead of his own safety.

I thought about his question. What had been the difference? I couldn't be sure, but I had an idea. I pulled my phone out of my bag and found the picture from last night. I placed it on the table between us.

"Who's the guy?"

"His name is Cage. I met him at the party I went to."

"Why do you look so... devastated?"

"Because his girlfriend took the picture."

Lou's eyes bounced up meeting mine.

"Oh, I'm so sorry, Quin. I did this, didn't I? I manipulated you into going to that party and you ended up getting your heart broken and... relapsing."

"None of this was your fault. And, even if it was, nothing happened. No one was hurt."

"But, someone was hurt, Quin. You."

I didn't know what to say to that. I wanted to deny it but it was true. Was that why I shifted? Did he come out to protect me? And, if he did, what would he have done once freed? I didn't want to think about it.

"Can you not be here tonight?."

Lou's fingertips pressed into the glass with fright. "Is it gonna happen again?"

"No! At least, I don't think. No. I have someone coming over."

"Who?"

"Cage."

Lou's mouth dropped open in confusion.

"It's just to study. I'm tutoring him in a class we're both in."

"You have a class with him?"

"Apparently. Today was the first time he showed up. He was wearing his football gear," I said unable to stop the smile that was creeping across my face.

"You mean the very tight ones that football players wear."

"Ah-uh," I said feeling my face heat up.

"Oh! He's not just coming over to study, is he?"

"No, he is," I said bringing things back down to earth. "He needs to pass the class to play football next semester, and he asked me to tutor him."

"So, you're holding his life in your powerful, yet delicate hands?"

I looked down at my hands wondering what he meant.

"I mean, not really. But, kind of."

"Oh my god, you two are so gonna make out."

"What? No, we're not." Even as I said it, I felt my wolf run with excitement. "No! He has a girlfriend," I said making it clear to everyone listening.

"Maybe he wants you to join the two of them. Would you be into that?" he asked with a smile.

"To be honest, I don't think I would be."

"So, we're going to have to break the two of them up?" Lou asked with a devilish look in his eyes.

"No, we're not!"

"You're not going to eat her, are you?" he asked hesitantly.

"No! Just no, to all of it. If she is who he wants to be with, then… fine. I'm okay with that."

"How much did that hurt to say?" he said suddenly looking at me with sympathy.

I took a moment and allowed my words to settle in. "A lot. But, it will have to be true. I don't want to be with someone who doesn't want to be with me."

"You're a better man than I am," Lou said giving up.

"I don't know about better, but I am a lot more alone."

"Ahhh!" Lou said getting up and hugging me. With his arms still wrapped around me, he said, "This boy is going to devastate you, isn't he?"

"Probably."

"Don't worry, I'll be here to pick up the pieces, Lamb Chop. I'll always be."

"Unless you have a hot date?"

"Unless I have a hot date. But, other than that, I'll be right here," he said pulling away and giving me an irresistible smile.

Chapter 4

Cage

I can do this. I can spend a little time with Quin, not fall head over heels for him, and not blow up my entire life to be with him. I'm sure I can. Although, the closer our meeting time got, the clearer it became that I wasn't going to have a say in the matter.

How is it that every guy, or girl, or whoever he's interested in, didn't see everything I did in him and snap him up? I don't understand it. The guy is gorgeous and awkwardly adorable. I could push my fingers through his dark, wavy hair until I was lost in it.

Oh, and his eyes. Don't get me started on his eyes, those soulful, electric eyes. Just thinking about them makes me so hard. How is he able to do this to me?

It's like… what is that thing that animals release to attract a mate? Pheromones? It's like he's releasing pheromones and there is nothing I can do to resist it.

I really shouldn't have asked him to tutor me. He was probably the last person I should have asked. How will I be able to concentrate with him in arms reach of me? It was such a mistake. But, I can't wait. And time has never moved slower in my life.

I waited at The Common for our meeting time instead of driving home and driving back. Staying with Tasha might have also been an option considering she lived on the floor above his. But odds were that she was hanging out with Vi.

The two of them were inseparable. It was no wonder she suggested Vi join us for sex. They did everything else together. Why not that?

Once the painfully long wait for me to head over had passed, I hurried across the quad. Slipping into the building as someone exited, I ran up the stairs two at a time and knocked on his door. I heard some scrambling inside before an unfamiliar voice said, "I just want to see," and the door opened.

"Hello," I said to the puckish-looking guy standing in front of me.

"Lou, nice to meet you," he said neither offering me his hand nor inviting me in.

"Cage."

"The football star?" Lou said with a smile.

"I guess. Is Quin here?"

"He is. But first, two questions. What intentions do you have with my friend? And, would you consider yourself a dog or a cat person?"

"What?"

"Lou!" Quin yelled from behind him. Pushing past Lou and placing his body between the two of us, Quin said, "I'm sorry about that. He was just leaving."

Quin's body was so close to mine.

"That's Okay. Lou, I would invite you to stay and hang out, but we have two weeks of classwork to go over… Unless Quin thinks we could do both?"

"We can't do both and Lou was just leaving. Bye, Lou."

"Toodles," Lou said pushing past me allowing Quin to invite me in.

"I'm sorry about that. Lou means well."

"It's always good to have a friend who'll look out for you."

"It is. So, welcome to my room."

I looked around. "Is this how the other half live?"

"What do you mean?"

"The Plaza dorms are pretty fancy."

"Doesn't your girlfriend live in here, too?"

"Yeah, but that doesn't make it any less impressive. Besides, she has two roommates and has to share a bedroom. Your place is better decorated than my house."

"You live at the fraternity?"

"No. I'm not a member. I know, a football player who doesn't belong to Sigma Chi, unthinkable. But, fraternity life was a little outside my price range."

"Where do you live?" Quin asked ushering me to the couch in their living room.

"At home with my dad."

"Not your mom?" Quin asked gathering books and sitting next to me.

"My mom died when I was born."

Quin froze. "I'm sorry to hear that."

"No need to be sorry. It happened a long time ago."

"So, it's always just been you and your dad."

"Yep. And sometimes just me."

"What do you mean?"

"Nothin'. We should get to studying. I have a feeling there's a lot we have to cover," I said changing the topic.

Although I never knew my mother, the topic was still a sore spot for me. Mostly because of my dad. He would never say it, but I think her loss hit him hard. At least, that was my guess.

Quin started by showing me the most organized flow chart I had ever seen in my life.

"Here's what we're going to have to cover by Thursday," he said getting right to business.

His assertiveness was almost enough to distract me from his knee hovering inches from mine as it supported the textbook. Or, the whiff I got when he leaned over to point out something on an opposite page.

His sweet musk kept making my dick hard. Bending forward was all I could do to hide it.

"You keep leaning forward, is your back okay?"

"My back? Yes. That's why I keep bending over, because of my back. I need to keep it stretched. You know because of practice."

"If you want, we can move to the dining room table? The chairs have a little more support," Quin suggested sweetly.

"Yeah, maybe that would be best."

I was about to get up when I realized I was still massively hard.

"Um, maybe in a second."

"Your back's really hurting, huh?"

"Yeah, it's hurting really bad."

"I'm so sorry. I wish you would have said something sooner. This might sound weird, but I can give you a massage if you'd like. I taught myself a few years back. I haven't had many opportunities to practice, but I think I'm still pretty good."

"Umm..."

"I'm sorry, is that weird? Offering to give you a massage is weird, isn't it?" Quin said wilting before my eyes.

"No, it's not weird at all. I'd love to have one. It would really help... my back."

"You sure?"

"You don't know how much," I said with a smile.

"Okay. Then…"

Quin looked around. "My bed would probably be more comfortable."

There was no way I was going to be able to get up now.

"I think the couch will be fine."

"Okay."

Quin got up and began stretching his fingers.

"Undress to your level of comfort and lie down."

Heat flashed across my cheeks. Did he just tell me to undress to my level of comfort? The idea of getting naked for him made me so hard my cock started twitching. Only God knew what would happen if I were to take off my pants. There was no way I could do that. But, I could take off my shirt.

Slowly pulling it off, I peeked up at Quin. The way he stared did all sorts of things to me. I was going to have to think of a lot of baseball if I wasn't going to cum in my shorts as soon as he touched me. It was worth the risk, though. I needed his hands on me. And when I lied down and he got on top of me, I was in heaven.

With him pulling and kneading my muscles, I lost myself. Jesus, did this feel good. It was better than sex, at least, any sex I had ever had. And it didn't take long before, I felt a familiar gnawing start at my balls and slowly climb.

Oh god, I was cumming.

"I need to go to the bathroom," I said tossing the smaller guy onto the couch.

Luckily I knew where it was and it was open. Throwing the door closed behind me, I could barely get my pants down fast enough before I exploded into orgasm.

I groaned fighting myself from screaming with pleasure. I managed to catch most of it in my palm instead of spraying it onto the ceiling. But with it came lightheadedness that tossed me to my ass. I hit the ground with a thud.

Chapter 5

Quin

"Are you alright in there?" I asked hearing what sounded like the towel rack break and then someone falling to the floor.

"I'm fine," Cage shouted back. "But, I think something broke. Sorry about that."

"Don't worry about it, whatever it is. Are you sure you're alright?"

"Yeah. I just need a second."

What the hell was I doing? This wasn't me. I didn't offer to give guys massages. I didn't ask them to undress for me. It was just that there was a smell coming from him I could barely resist. I couldn't tell what it was, but it made me think of sex.

But, sitting on top of him had clearly freaked him out. I know it did. That's why he threw me off of him and sprinted to the bathroom like his hair was on fire.

It had to be my wolf who was doing this to me. It was taking over again. But, at least that was better than shifting and ripping Cage's throat out. I was making progress. And, it wasn't that weird to offer a massage if someone said their back was hurting, was it?

Agh! I don't know. I don't know anything. Why am I so bad at this? Maybe it would be better if I let my wolf do whatever was on his mind. It couldn't end in a disaster worse than the one I had already created.

"Are you sure you don't need any help in there?"

"I have everything in hand," Cage said before turning on the faucet and eventually coming out.

Damn, did he look good standing there with his shirt off. His muscular, bulging shoulders, his thick pecs, his abs. How did he have abs without flexing? He was just standing there. How?

Staring at me with the most heart-melting puppy dog eyes, he said, "Sorry about that?"

"No, I'm sorry," I told him feeling bad for crossing the line.

"Why should you feel sorry," he asked me as if he didn't know.

"You know, because…"

"…Because you were willing to tutor me in a subject I need to pass to have any sort of life, and I made things weird?"

"You made things weird? I'm the king of making things weird."

"You might be the king of something, but this is on me. Look, why don't we get back to studying."

"How's your back?"

"It's much better now, thank you," he said grabbing his shirt and putting it on. "That helped a lot. I can focus now. I'm also a little sleepy but, I can definitely focus."

Continuing from where we left off, I did my best to quiet the impulses coming from my very happy wolf. He loved being around Cage. I couldn't blame him. I did too.

But thankfully, even though we had a lot of material to cover, we covered a healthy chunk of it by the time Lou came back.

"Still at it? You two are like a dog with a bone, aren't you?" Lou said playfully.

Cage stared at Lou uncomfortably. "Yeah, I should go."

"Don't let me stop you," Lou said. "You won't even know I'm here."

"Or, we could just go to my room," I suggested.

"No!" he said abruptly. "I mean, maybe we can pick it back up tomorrow. There are a lot of things swirling around up here and I need to process it all," he said circling his hands around his head.

"Oh, yeah. Sleeping helps you retain information. Tomorrow, then. If you want to start earlier, my last class ends at four."

"That sounds great. How about we meet at the study hall next time? That way we don't disturb Lou."

"Oh, you don't have to worry about me. You two can do it wherever you'd like," Lou added as he stood watching the two of us.

"Yes, we could study here," I confirmed not sure I was ready to sit in public where anyone walking by could recognize me.

Cage fumbled his words. "I think study hall would be better. I mean, if it's okay with you."

I was disappointed that I had screwed things up so badly that he didn't want to come back to my room, but I understood. I had done this and now I was going to have to deal with the repercussions.

"No, that's fine. We'll be covering the rest of the material, so you might want to bring some snacks."

Lou added, "Knowing Quin, it will be a long, hard session. Very long… if you know what I mea…"

"…Alright, I'm gonna go. Text me," Cage said before escaping, glancing at Lou as he did.

"What was that all about? Okay, I get the dog and the bone thing. Very funny. Haha. But saying, "It's going to be a long, hard session?"" I asked Lou pissed.

"Very long," he said with a smirk.

"What were you doing?"

"You said he has a girlfriend?"

"Yes. He has a girlfriend!"

"Very interesting," he said smirking at me like he knew everything and I knew nothing. "Very…

interesting," he continued before slipping into his bedroom and not returning.

I didn't get much sleep that night. If I wasn't trying to figure out what Lou was seeing that I wasn't, I was thinking about how I had made things weird with Cage, or what it would be like to see his naked body again.

I was a complete mess. That man did things to me. And after only the third time seeing him, I couldn't get him out of my mind.

Why did he have to have a girlfriend? Why did he have to be so perfect? And, why did he have to smell so good? Someone explain to me why his scent made me want to shift into my wolf and chase him down like a gazelle. Why?

God does it suck being the only one in existence like me!

The next day at study hall was less weird than the night before. For the most part, we stuck to the course material and only veered away when we took our dinner break.

"I brought an extra sandwich if you want one?" I told him pulling it from my bag.

"You brought an extra sandwich?" He asked more surprised than I could have guessed.

"Yes. Do you want it? I figured you would have a lot swirling around up there and might not remember to bring something."

"Wow! I'm not used to people being so thoughtful."

"What? Come on. You're a famous football player. You must have people doing things for you all of the time."

"It's not the same," he said taking the sandwich. "Thank you, by the way. Yeah, there's a difference between someone doing something for you because they're getting something from you, and someone doing something just to be nice."

"I get that. There are a lot of people who can see you as a stepping stone on their path to getting what they want. You're just an object to them. They forget that you have feelings too. And, maybe your desires don't line up with everyone's expectations for you."

"Wow! Exactly," he said staring at me and once again turning me into a heaping pile of boy-crush.

"What?" I asked when his gaze became too much.

"How would you know that feeling so perfectly?"

What was I supposed to say to that? I liked Cage. I liked him a lot, maybe more than I should. So, I didn't want to freak him out. At least not yet.

Besides, I chose a school in the middle of nowhere for a reason. Coming here was the best shot I had of fading into the background. I just wanted someone to see me as a normal guy for once. Was that wrong of me? I couldn't tell.

"My uncles played in the NFL. They told me."

"Oh. Yeah, they got it right," Cage confirmed leaning back and relaxing his gaze.

Finishing our sandwiches, we got back to work. By midnight, we had covered everything.

"So, that's all of it?" Cage asked.

"All that's going to be covered in the quiz tomorrow. Do you think you have it?"

"You're a very good tutor. If I've missed anything, it wouldn't be your fault. By the way, I spoke to my coach. He told me you have to contact his office to get paid."

"Oh. Don't worry about it," I told him.

"You put so much work into helping me. No one could have made everything clearer than you have. Not even the professor. You deserve to get paid for your hard work."

"Okay," I said relenting.

Cage looked at me strangely and I couldn't figure out why.

"Since you're not excited about getting paid, how about the other thing I promised you?"

"Oh right, 'How Not to be so Awkward' classes."

Cage laughed. "I don't know about all of that. I was just thinking that we could play some flag football at the park."

"On your time off from football, you play more football? You must really love playing."

Cage gave me a muted smile. "You would think."

"So tell me, Mr. Expert, how is playing flag football in the park supposed to help me not feel like a freak at a party?"

Cage became pensive. "I've been thinking about this. The reason why I feel so comfortable in social situations is because I know that, no matter what happens, I'll be able to handle it. Also, I know that if I do say something stupid, which I do… often, everything will be fine. The world's not going to implode. I'm not going to be sent into the desert to live alone. My life will most likely go on unchanged.

"And, the only way I got to that realization is because I have been put in many comfortable and uncomfortable social situations and have worked my way through them. You need to be in those situations. You need your own opportunities to work your way through it.

"Then, when you've gotten familiar with all of the most common situations that come up, and you've figured out what to do and say when they do," he held up his hands, "I'm done."

I stared at Cage with my mind blown.

"That's kind of genius. You're absolutely right. Social comfort is experientially based. Familiarity breeds comfort. So, the answer is being willing to be uncomfortable. I'm not sure I could have thought of that."

"I guess I'm good for something after all," Cage said proudly.

"Although, I'm not exactly a football player. So, I'm not sure being stampeded by jocks will fill me with the confidence you think it will."

"I guess you'll have to trust me on that," Cage said with a wink.

Why did he have to wink? Didn't he realize I was doing my best to see him as a friend? Why did he have to remind me how sexy he was?

Offering him a lingering goodbye which turned into an awkward hug, I headed back to my room and bed. Tucked away, I heard Lou enter the apartment and approach my door.

"I know you're not asleep," he said without knocking. "I know you're hiding in there because you don't want to tell me how it went. Or, is he in there with you. Are you guys doing it? Oh my god, you two are doing it!"

"Goodnight, Lou!" I told him needing the teasing to end.

"Night, Lamb Chop," he replied smiling as he left.

The idea of Cage and me naked together ran through my, and my wolf's mind for the next three hours. I blame Lou for that. By the time I woke up, I was already late for class. Sprinting across campus and bursting through the auditorium doors, I learned how Cage had felt.

As everyone turned to look at me, the only one I cared about was Cage. Was he there? Had he made it?

When I saw him my heart fluttered. He was smiling at me. It was five cups of coffee all at once.

Professor Nakamura held up a handout and pointed me to an open spot. It was on the other side of the room from Cage. Maybe that was for the best. I wasn't sure I could look him in the eyes considering all of the things I made him do in my fantasies the night before.

With my brain moving slower due to the lack of sleep, I wasn't close to being done by the time the class ended. I figured I would keep answering questions until I was told to stop. Keeping one eye on the professor I didn't miss when Cage handed in his paper and said something to her. She looked at me immediately after and then Cage winked at me again as he headed out.

When I was the only one left, Professor Nakamura said, "Cage told me you were up late tutoring him, so I'll give you an additional 20 minutes."

"Thank you, Professor," I said gratefully.

The 20 minutes were barely enough. I did get it done, though, and it was thanks to Cage. The guy was doing something to me that I wasn't going to be able to come back from. I could barely wait for our flag football date to roll around so I could see him again. He was all I could think of until I did.

When I saw him park his truck and approach me at the entrance of the park, I couldn't help but smile. He was smiling too. God, did I love the way he smiled. It almost made up for the stress I felt about what was going to happen next. Not only was I going to be stampeded by a bunch of jocks, the odds of someone recognizing me was through the roof.

"You ready for this?" Cage asked looking confident and gorgeous.

"No."

"Nervous?"

"Petrified might be more accurate."

"There's nothing to worry about. Be yourself. If you say something that feels awkward just push through it. Remember the world isn't going to end, and no one here will be any less awkward than you."

"I highly doubt that. And your teammates are going to demolish me. I don't know if you know this but I'm not a big guy."

"Everything's relative," Cage said with a smile.

"What do you mean?"

"Cage!" A voice said grabbing my attention. I turned and looked. It was a kid who said it. He was about ten years old and he was one of 15 kids the same age.

"You guys ready to play some football?" Cage yelled enthusiastically.

"Yeeeaaahhh!" They shouted back.

"We're playing with kids?" I asked him confused.

"I organize this event with the kids in the local peewee league. When neither of us has games, I spend some time with them sharpening their skills. Iron sharpens iron," he said with a smile.

"So, I'm supposed to practice being social with kids?" I asked confused.

"I didn't start too difficult for you, did I?"

I laughed. "No, I think I can handle this."

"There's the confidence I was hoping for," he said before jogging over to the group.

Cage was a natural with kids. He treated them like adults without forgetting their age.

"Whose team is the big guy on?" One of the kids asked referring to me.

"I don't know," Cage replied and looked at me. "Tell me, Quin, what team do you play for?"

"Do you mean, which team am I playing on?" I corrected unsure if he was asking what I thought he was.

"Isn't that what I asked?" Cage said with a knowing look on his face.

"No," a kid corrected. "You said, what team do you play for."

"Oh. My bad. Quin, which team are you going to play on?"

"Which team usually wins?" I asked.

Cage looked at the kids who were split up into red and blue shirts.

"Usually the red team."

"That's not true," a kid on the blue team protested. "We won the last time."

"But, was it luck?"

"No!" he protested.

"Then let's see if you can do it again. You have the big guy."

"Yes!" He said pumping his fist.

It was just a kid, but it felt good to be wanted for a team sport.

Thinking the whole thing would be a cinch, I was wrong. My being so much bigger than everyone else turned out to be a disadvantage. The object of the game was to pull the flag from the belt of the person with the ball. However, the waist of a ten-year-old is surprisingly close to the ground. The most I could do was block them from running while one of the players grabbed their flag.

Cage's role in the game was as the designated quarterback. No matter which team was receiving, he was the one throwing the ball. Not only was his throws pinpoint accurate, but the kids could catch.

"I see a few NFL stars in the making out there," Cage told me as the kids ate orange slices at halftime.

"You enjoy this, don't you?"

"I really do," he said with a smile.

"Hence taking 'Intro to Childhood Education'?"

He tightened his lips and nodded his head.

"You ever thought about teaching instead of going to the draft?"

"All of the time. But I can't. There are too many people counting on me. And, it's hard to fight people's expectations for you. Especially when you know the whole world is watching.'"

"I understand that."

"Do you?"

"I do," I told him thinking of the world I left behind.

It was getting harder to think of him as just a guy I was crushing on or who I was tutoring. Cage was beginning to feel like a friend. I was sure he was someone I could share things with if they needed sharing. And, the things I was keeping from him about my life were starting to weigh on me.

"I get the feeling you're not much for revealing stuff about yourself," Cage said picking up on my hesitation.

"I don't know what I am."

"I know the feeling," he said with a sad smile.

"I know what you are."

"And, what's that?"

"You're a hot football player with a girlfriend, who is preparing to go pro."

"You think I'm hot?"

"Shit, did I say that?"

"You did," Cage said amused.

"I meant that you're popular. Like, you're trending. You're hot right now."

"I'm not sure that's what you meant," he said cockily.

The truth was that I wasn't sure either. The man was sexy as hell and there was no denying that.

"Well, it wouldn't matter even if it was what I meant. The other thing I said was that you had a girlfriend. I definitely said that."

Cage's smile dropped. "Yeah, there is that."

"And, how is Tasha, by the way," I asked not wanting to know but wanting him to keep her in mind before he flashed another of his irresistible smiles.

"She's good," he said soberly. "She's hanging out with her best friend this weekend. I think they're hiking trails or something."

"You didn't go with them?"

"No. I just feel like a third wheel when those two get together. Hey, maybe the four of us could all hang out together?"

"That sounds like the worst idea I have ever heard," I told him honestly.

"Yeah, it probably is," he said searching his thoughts. "Did you want to, maybe, grab something to eat after we're done here?"

I looked at Cage settling in his kind, light eyes. I wanted to spend every moment of the rest of my life with him. Of course, I wanted to grab something to eat with him after this.

"I can't," I told him meaning that I shouldn't.

"Oh, okay. Are you doing something with Lou, later?"

"With Lou?"

"Yeah, you two seem close. It was almost like he was a little jealous when I came over."

"Jealous? Lou? No, he's just a little protective of me, I guess."

"Are you sure because it felt like a little more than that? And, I mean, he's a good-looking guy. I don't know if you're into guys are not, but…"

"I am," I told him wanting it to be clear.

He smiled before catching himself.

"Well then, I'm pretty sure he is too. Why wouldn't you…," he slowed choosing his words carefully. "Why wouldn't you try to make things happen with him?"

"Are you saying I should?"

"You're, like, an amazing guy. You deserve to be with someone who will make you happy. If Lou could do that, then why not?"

I looked at Cage as pain shot through my chest. He was trying to hand me off to someone else. I wanted him to want me. I wanted him to feel jealous that someone else would want to be with me.

But, he didn't. I was a fool to entertain the thought of the two of us together. He didn't like me like that, and it hurt.

Chapter 6

Cage

What was I saying? I didn't want Quin to be with Lou. I didn't want Quin to be with anyone. Hell, I didn't know what I wanted, whether it had to do with Quin, or football, or anything. I was the last person who should give someone relationship advice. All you had to do was spend two minutes with Tasha and me to know that.

"We should get back to the game," Quin told me looking a lot sadder than when we sat down.

I was ruining things with him. I thought this would be something fun we could do together, but I was turning it all wrong.

"Yeah. We should probably get back," I repeated willing to do anything to stop myself from talking.

Returning to the game, I made sure that the kids had a great time even if the person I most wanted to didn't.

"Are we playing again next weekend?" One of the kids asked me with her mother standing behind her.

"I have a game next weekend. I think you do too, don't you?" I asked looking up at her mother.

She shook her head.

"Oh yeah, I forgot," the little girl said with a smile.

"I'll let your coach know. It should be in a few weeks."

"Okay, thanks, Cage," she said waving bye.

Her mother mouthed 'Thank you,' and the two walked off.

"Is there anyone who doesn't love you?" Quin asked turning me around.

"All I care about is one," I said without thinking.

"Who's that?"

I had meant it to be something casual and flirty. Of course, Quin would call me on it.

"Anyone."

"Just anyone?"

"I meant, I would be happy as long as I had someone to love me."

"And, you have that don't you?"

"Do I?" I asked wondering who he was talking about.

"Yes. Tasha."

This had to stop. Every time Quin brought up Tasha, he made me say something about our relationship which wasn't necessarily the case. Yes, she and I were together and we were trying to make it work. But, trying to make it work, and succeeding at it, weren't the same thing.

"Tasha and I aren't what everyone sees us as."

"Oh," Quin said suddenly giving me his full attention.

"Yeah. I mean, we've been dating for a while and we've talked about our future together. But sometimes it feels like there's something missing. Actually, it feels like that a lot."

"What do you think is missing?"

"Her presence, for one. She's never around. And, that's fine when I'm in the heart of football season with twice-a-day practices. That might even work if I were to get drafted and spend a third of the year on the road. But, shouldn't she want to spend time with me more than she does? Shouldn't I want to spend more time with her?"

"You don't want to spend time with her?"

"It's not that don't want to spend time with her. It's that I don't care whether I do or not. It's harsh to say out loud, but it's true."

"If you don't want to spend time with her, then why are you with her?"

"It's not that I don't want to spend time with her."

"I get it. I get it. But, it would seem to me that if you two are talking about, um, spending a long time together, you should look forward to it."

"I can't argue with that," I told him.

"Then, why don't you?"

I stared at Quin not sure what to say. I wanted to say that it was because she wasn't him. But that felt unfair.

"Because she doesn't give me the tingles," I said meaning the same thing.

"That's important," Quin said suddenly in a better mood than moments before. "Have you ever felt the tingles from someone?"

"From one person," I told him hoping he wouldn't ask anymore.

"Who's that?" Quin asked hesitantly.

Staring into his beautiful eyes was too much. I couldn't do this, not to him, not to myself.

"Someone I shouldn't feel them for."

"Oh," Quin said deflating.

"So, change your mind about grabbing something to eat? I could always grab a bite. And Tasha wouldn't be back from hiking with Vi for a few hours."

"No. I should go," Quin said resigned.

"Okay. That's fair. Did you have fun?"

"It had its moments," he said with a smile.

"You still trust me to teach you how to be the life of the party?"

"First of all, I never trusted you to be a miracle worker."

I laughed.

"But, I'm willing to see what you have to offer," Quin said with a smile.

Man, did I love his smile.

"Fair enough. I think I passed the quiz, by the way."

"Good! I guess I'm not that bad of a tutor after all. Though, I would have hoped you did more than just pass."

"I'm sure I did. And you are a hell of a tutor. I can't wait to see what you have in store for me next."

"I guess you'll find out," Quin said with a devious smile.

Wait, was Quin flirting with me? However he meant it, it shot a tingle through my body and shook me to my core. When that guy did something, he did it right.

"I can't wait to find out," I told him before walking him back to campus and awkwardly returning to my truck.

I had never wanted to kiss someone so much in my life. I knew I couldn't and I wasn't even sure if Quin was interested in anything like that. At least I was able to establish that he was into guys. For the time being, that was enough. I could survive on that hope for a while.

When Tasha texted that there was traffic and that she wouldn't get back to campus until late, I drove home. It was probably for the best. After spending the day with Quin, my mind was elsewhere.

After a forty-minute drive, I turned onto the empty road that led to my house. My dad's truck was running in the driveway with its lights on.

"Oh no," I said knowing how the rest of the night would go.

Parking next to my father's truck, I got out and looked into its windows. He wasn't there. It was a worse sign that he had made it into the house. At least if he was passed out, his night would be over.

Opening the truck's door, I reached in and shut it off. With the keys in hand, I looked back at the cabin. The kitchen and living room lights poured onto the ground outside the windows. The TV was blasting. I took a long measured breath, gathered myself, and made the short walk to the front door.

Stepping inside, the place was a mess. This wasn't the way I had left it. The lamps shone from the floor where they had been tossed, the couch was overturned, the TV was sitting on its side, and things that used to be in the fridge were now scattered between the two rooms.

"I don't want to hear it," my father grumbled drawing my attention to the kitchen table.

The red-headed man looked his usual shade of ruddy pink. Like I suspected, he had a near-empty bottle of Lonehand Sour Mash Whiskey clutched in his grip. Tennessee's finest.

"Dad…"

"I don't wanna hear it. Do you know how much I sacrificed for you?"

"I know, Dad. You sacrificed everything," I recited from our script while looking around to see what I had to clean up first.

"That's right, everything! I God damn sacrificed everything. And for what?"

"So, I could become a big star," I said skipping a few pages ahead.

"Don't you fuckin' do it. Don't you talk to me like that," he bellowed. "I should just go. I should get in my fuckin' truck and never come back to this shit hole again."

This was always that part that hurt the most. You would think I would have gotten used to him talking about leaving, but I never could. Maybe it's because I knew his leaving was in my hands.

My father saw what I was capable of doing on the football field long before anyone else did. He saw that I would be a top NFL draft prospect and with it would come millions of dollars. He always made clear that he would stick around for that. There was no telling what he would do once he got his cut, but until then, I was pretty sure he wasn't going anywhere.

"This wouldn't be a shithole if you stopped wrecking the place."

"Fuck you!"

"Nice Dad. Way to talk to your son."

"You're not my son."

"Come on, Dad. Don't start this again."

This was a new subplot he had added to our script not too long ago. It went that I embarrassed him for not living up to my potential, so I couldn't be his son.

"You're not. You're just some baby I stole thinking I could make some money…"

"Enough, Dad! I can't take it anymore! You wanna leave so bad? Here!"

Pitching back my arm, I through his truck keys so hard it shattered the window and disappeared into the night.

"You wanna go? Take your fuckin' truck and go. If you wanna stick around and milk me of everything I got for eternity, then stay. I just don't give a shit anymore. You hear me? I can't take this anymore."

Bubbling with anger, I stormed to my room. The cabin shook as I slammed the door behind me. Staring back at it, I panted in fury. Tears rolled down my cheeks in rage. I wasn't crying because of the things he said, it was because I was trapped. My skin burned as his words danced in my mind.

I had no mother or family. He was all I had. Without him, I was alone. But the only way I would ever get his horrid voice out of my head was if I let him go.

Yet, being left by myself felt like a fate worse than death.

The thought of it made the blood vessels in my temple throb. It hurt. My pounding heart ached. It felt like my body was about to tear itself apart until I heard a terrifying sound and my swirling thoughts stopped.

"No," I said sprinting back into the living room and finding my dad gone.

As hateful as he was, I knew I wouldn't be in the position I was if not for him. When sober, he reminded me of it every day. And, he was right.

Yeah, it was me on the field for 6 am practices and 7 pm sprints. But all he did for sixteen years was drive me from place to place and stand on the sidelines watching me play.

I knew what he was doing. He was keeping an eye on his investment. And, when I was 10-years-old and I would beg him in tears to do anything else but throw another football, he forced me to continue.

I truly wouldn't have anything without him. Not my scholarship. Not my football-loving girlfriend. And not my chance to play in the NFL. I don't know who I would be without everything he did. But, was the price I paid too high.

All of my swirling thoughts stopped when I heard a terrifying sound.

"No," I said sprinting back into the living room and finding my dad gone.

It was him starting up his truck. He was doing it. He was leaving. I didn't want him to go.

Running outside I saw him sway as he ground his gears looking for reverse. As drunk as he was, he was going to kill himself. I had to stop him.

"Dad!" I shouted running to the door of his truck and throwing it open.

"Get the fuck off me!" He yelled as I reached across him and again took the keys.

He didn't put up much resistance after that. We were both out of breath and dazed.

"You were really gonna go, weren't you?" I asked him staring into his eyes for the truth.

"You're not my son," was the only thing he replied.

Hurting me was so easy for him that he didn't even look evil when he said it. He stated it as if it were a fact.

"Ya know, sometimes I wish I wasn't. But I am. And you're my dad," I said resigned. "Come, let me get you to bed."

"I don't want to go to bed," he mumbled.

"Then I'll put you in front of the TV. You want that?"

His mouth puckered like he was trying to remember how to pout. "Yeah."

"Okay. Let me help you inside."

He leaned towards me and the door and I took his weight into my arms.

That was the beginning of a few very hard weeks. I'm not sure how different it was for my father. But, for me, it was when I realized that, if I didn't watch him every chance I got, he could be gone.

I still went to practices, games, and classes, but not much else. The only thing that brought my life any joy was the few hours a week I would spend with Quin. I was barely keeping up my end of our deal, but I told him I was having a little trouble at home and he seemed to understand.

I think he saw how stressed I was. I definitely didn't feel like myself. The strange thing was that Tasha didn't even notice. She didn't notice that I wasn't around as much and that my life was crumbling around me. I was starting to wonder if this was what I should expect for the rest of our lives together.

With final exams and the end of the semester quickly approaching, Quin suggested that we increase our study time. Although I was on top of everything mentioned in class since I started attending, there were still a few weeks of material that Quin hadn't caught me up on.

"The final exam is going to cover all of that material," Quin said with the serious look he always got whenever we talked tutoring.

"As you keep reminding me," I said with a smile.

"You need to pass this class. It's not funny," he implored.

"I know."

"Then what are you laughing at?"

"You," I said teasingly.

"Oh, that's nice. Laugh at the guy trying to help you."

"Come on, it's not like that. It's just, you get this little crinkle in your forehead whenever you start worrying about me. And when you get it, I know I'm going to get a lecture about how important it is that I pass this class. At this point, I'm pretty sure you care more about it than I do and my entire future rests on it."

Quin looked at me for a second and then relaxed and laughed.

"Okay. I guess I've gotten a little intense about it," Quin admitted.

"A little?"

"Just a little," he insisted. "But it's that I want this for you. You've spent your life working towards this one thing. I can't be the one responsible for you not getting it."

I looked into Quin's worried eyes and stepped towards him. Gripping his shoulders in either hand, I squeezed.

"Quin, that is so sweet of you. I'm not sure anyone in my life cares about me more. But, you have to know, if I don't get what I've been working for, you won't be to blame. Everything I do and have done, has been my choice. You are simply the angel sitting on my shoulder whispering in my ear trying to get me to do the right thing. I thank you for that."

"I just want you to get everything you deserve. You're so close."

I let go of Quin and scanned the campus quad through the window of the study hall.

"I want it too, but I feel like I'm burning the candle on both ends. Between school and football, and watching over my dad, I can barely breathe."

"What's wrong with your dad?" Quin asked concerned.

"What's not wrong with him?" I said searching my mind for what I could tell him that could explain it. "He just needs me around a lot. That's all."

"If it helps, maybe we could meet at your place," Quin said hesitantly and with a hint of something else in his eyes.

When he looked at me like that, I usually lost all resistance. As much as I wanted to return our sessions to somewhere where we could be alone, I wasn't sure if I wanted to subject him to my life. He didn't talk much about it, but everything about him told me that he came from a stable home and money. My life was exactly the opposite.

I liked him thinking of me as the famous football player without a care in the world. I liked it when everyone did because the truth was so far from that fantasy. I didn't know if I was ready for Quin to see me for who I was.

"I'll think about it," I told him.

"Why not just say yes?" He asked softly.

It suddenly felt like this wasn't just a request to change our venue. This somehow felt like he was asking me to... I don't know, choose him, or something.

"I'll think about it. But, I'm here now. Maybe we should get to work?"

Quin's request haunted me for the rest of the night. Was I reading too much into it? I didn't think so. He had asked me why I didn't just say yes. It was a great question.

It was like two worlds were clawing at me. The first was the one I had known my whole life. It included my dad, Tasha, football fame, and a huge payday. The other included Quin, happiness, and a life I couldn't begin to imagine.

Would choosing a life with Quin mean I would have to give up playing in the NFL? It was hard to tell. I had heard of a few ex-players coming out as bisexual. But as far as I knew, there were no current players who had.

And, if I did come out, what was I supposed to come out as. At least gay was acceptable. Everyone cheers for the gay guy who pushes against societal pressure and overcomes. Who cheers when someone comes out as bisexual? No one. And, that's what I would be, wouldn't I?

I'm not foolish enough to believe that because Quin makes me tingle unlike anyone has before, that all of the feelings I had for girls growing up meant nothing. Sure, I've been drawn to guys before Quin, but that didn't change what I thought about Tasha when we first met.

The reason I'm questioning my future with her isn't because I'm questioning my interest in women. It's because I'm questioning if Tasha and I work together. She clearly wants to spend more time with her best friend than she does me. And, now that Quin has shown me how it feels to be cared about, I'm wondering if what Tasha is offering me is enough.

Who's going to champion that struggle. What organization is going to offer me an award for having the courage to acknowledge that? And, without society pushing back on the NFL, what team is going to invite a person like me into their showers?

So, choosing the world with Quin in it does feel like giving up on football which also means giving up on having a father. Because, I can't be sure how the NFL would react to an openly bisexual player. But I can be sure how my father would react to a son who doesn't make it to the NFL.

At the same time, though, I might be falling in love with Quin. I've never felt like this for anyone. I can't stop thinking about him. I fantasize about touching him. I can't wait to see him.

I thought I loved Tasha. I really did. But it was because I didn't know what love was or how it felt. This feeling is what people write songs about. I get it now. And, I get all of those movies that implied that love came at a cost.

My cost would be everything I have. I could have fame, family, and financial stability for the first time in my life. Or, I could have love. That was the choice I had to make.

Chapter 7

Quin

"You know you're eventually going to have to make a move on him, right?" Lou said with his elbows on the table and cut of stripped steak gangling from the end of his fork.

"I do not know that," I protested.

"You don't expect him to do it, do you?"

"I'm not expecting anyone to do it. I'm not expecting anything."

"Ahh, Lamb Chop, sometimes you make me so sad."

"There's nothing to feel sad about. Nothing's going on between us."

"That's what makes me so sad. On one side there's you, an obliviously scrumptious love nugget who can't seem to lose of his virginity…"

"You're a virgin, too," I quickly reminded him.

He put his hand on his chest and gave me a sad look.

"But for me, it's by choice. I'm saving myself for the right man. You? You want to get rid of yours like it's the plague. Yet you're hooked on a guy who is clearly in love with you but can't see past the sham relationship he's in. Tragic!"

When I didn't respond, Lou said, "Not going to say anything?"

"No. I think you said it all. And I am kinda sad."

"Wait, I didn't say you were sad. You're great. You're hot and smart, and you come from a good family…"

"What does my family have to do with this?"

"You're marriage material! Some guy needs to put a ring on that."

"Wow, that progressed quickly."

"That's my point. You're moving too slow. Get on that man, preferably with him on his back and you riding him like a cowboy. Or, are you a top? I can't tell with you. What is your preference? You like it Lone Ranger or side-saddle?"

"Which one's which?" I asked confused.

"Doesn't matter. You like it going or coming?"

"I don't know. Both, maybe."

"So, you're vers? I've seen you in the shower. That makes sense."

"When did you see me in the shower?"

"When haven't I seen you in the shower? That's not the point."

"Then what is the point?"

"The point is that you're vers and that man, Cage, is a definite top."

"You think so?"

"I know these things," he said confidently.

"But you've never had sex?"

"You don't have to have had sex to feel the energy. That boy has serious top energy. He's a quarterback for crying out loud. He's used to being in control... holding onto people's butts. It's quarterback stuff."

"I see."

"And, usually he would be the one to make the first move. But, in this case, you're going to have to find your big dick energy and sack up."

"Seriously, though, when did you see me in the shower?"

"This is you trying to change the topic so you don't have to think about moving things forward."

"No, this is me wondering if I need to start locking the bathroom door."

Lou put his hand on his chest. "I have so little. Do you really want to take that away from me, too?"

I stared at Lou wondering if this was him teasing me again. It wasn't that I was shy about my body. Clothes were considered optional in my household growing up.

But, there were times when I thought about Cage in the shower. The thought of bending over and hiking that quarterback the ball usually made me have to take things into my own hands... And then again once I was back in my room.

God, did that man make me feel things. Mostly, what he made me feel was thirsty — the human body only had so much fluid in it — and... sore.

My phone rang stopping me from exploring the shower situation with Lou any further. Pulling out my phone, I was surprised to see Cage's name.

I held up my finger asking Lou to give me a moment.

"Cage, what's going on? You never call me."

Lou reacted with childish delight. I ignored him.

"Do you think we could do our study session at my place tonight?" Cage asked sounding distressed. "If the final exam wasn't tomorrow, I wouldn't ask. But..."

"No. Of course. Is there something going on with your father?"

"Um, yeah. He's having one of his bad days and I don't think I should leave him alone."

"I'm sorry to hear that. Yeah, I can come by. Just tell me when."

The phone fell silent.

"Cage?"

"I'm here. Um, before you come, there's probably something you should know."

"Okay."

"We don't have much."

"What do you mean?"

"I mean, I attend school on a scholarship and my father isn't working right now. He hasn't worked in a while."

"Should I bring snacks, or… something?"

"I mean, if you want. But, that's not what I'm trying to say. I just don't think you should expect much. I'm not… Just don't expect much."

"Will you be there?" I asked clarifying.

"Yeah, of course."

"Then, your place will have everything I need."

Cage was again silent.

"Cage?"

"I'm here. I'll text you my address. I would offer to pick you up, but…"

"Don't worry about it. I'll do rideshare or something."

"It's kind of far. If you ever turn in your timecard for all of the tutoring you're doing, I'm sure the football program will reimburse you for it."

"Unless you're commuting every day from Florida, I'm sure I can handle it."

"Okay. I'll see you then."

"See you."

I ended the call and stared at my phone.

"Ouuuuu!" Lou said excitedly. "Quin and Cage sitting in a tree. K I S S I N G."

"Shut up."

Lou stuck out his tongue miming a French kiss.

"You're disgusting," I said with a smile.

"I'm just proud my Lamp Chop is gonna be gettin' some fixin's."

"You're ridiculous," I said still staring down at my phone.

"Okay, what's wrong?"

"Cage is embarrassed about me seeing his place."

"I get that."

I looked up at Lou surprised.

"Why should he be embarrassed? He shouldn't be embarrassed. Whatever he has has made him who he is and I like him… a lot."

"Says the guy whose father owns a billion dollar genetics company. And, have you shared that fact with him."

"I didn't want to make it an issue. Besides, that's not my money, it's my father's money."

"No. You just have access to as much of it as you want whenever you want."

Lou's words stung. He wasn't wrong. And, as much as I would like to believe that it didn't shape me, it did. Just like how Cage grew up had shaped him.

"More important than your family's ungodly amount of wealth, have you told Cage about the other thing? Because to me, that feels a slight bit more important than being able to charge an airplane to your credit card."

"It hasn't come up yet," I admitted knowing Lou was right.

"Then, maybe you should get on that. Because, he needs to know who he is getting involved with… you know, if he ever grows a pair and asks you out. Or, you ask him out. You know that's an option, right?"

"He has a girlfriend."

"From what you've told me, I need to ask, does he?"

"He does."

Lou leaned back and crossed his arms. "Okay."

"But, you're right. He might need to know."

"That's my Lamp Chop," Lou said with a sober smile. "And Quin, I know you think of it as a big deal…"

"It is a big deal. Do you know anyone else who has a wolf running around in their head and periodically changes into a room destroying animal?"

"I think he'll care more about if you're an animal where it counts… in the bedroom?" Lou said with a suggestive smile.

"Come on, Lou. I'm being serious. This is a big deal for me. I've been dealing with this my entire life and no one has ever stuck around after they found out."

"I'm still around," he said sincerely.

"And, why is that, by the way? You've seen what happens with me. Or, at least, you heard it. I'm… a monster. Why haven't you run for the hills by now? I'm serious, Lou. Why?"

I was expecting Lou to make another joke, but he didn't.

"It's because I've met you. Yes, it was a little unnerving when you told me about it during our roommate chat before we moved in together. I'll admit that I had my reservations. But then we continued talking… and we met. It didn't take me long to see who you are. You're a good person, Quin. I trust you. You'd never let anything happen to me."

"You don't know how difficult it is keeping that part of myself under control."

"But, you do. And, I know you'll continue to. If Cage is the guy you've been telling me he is, he'll see that to. I can only imagine how hard it is for you to trust people. But, haven't I shown you that you can?"

"You have. You've been the best friend I've ever had."

"That's because you let me in. If you give that boy a chance, he might do the same. But, you'll never know unless you put yourself out there. Quin, you have to try," Lou concluded with a thoughtful smile.

Cage wasn't exaggerating when he said he lived far away. For him to make a 7 am practice he would have to leave his house at 6 am and get up at 5:30 at the latest. The amount of devotion it would take to do that every day for years, if not his entire life, was impressive.

And, the closer I got to his place, the more nervous I got. Whatever it was that he was embarrassed about, I was sure I would be able to accept. But, what I had to tell him could easily be too much for him.

Telling him might be the end of what we have going on… whatever that is. Tonight could be the last night that he looked at me like I was the only person in the world. That would hurt.

By the time the car pulled up in front of Cage's place, I was nearing a panic attack. Everything surrounding me was too much to ask someone to be around. Cage had his whole life ahead of him. He was going to be a famous football player with millions of fans. I would be an anchor around his neck.

It wouldn't even be fair to ask him to deal with my stuff. He had his own stuff going on. Add that to whatever he was dealing with with his dad, and my stuff was starting to feel like something best kept to myself.

Cage stepped out the front door before I could call him letting him know I was here. Adding a healthy tip for the driver, I got out and approached him. He wore a plaid shirt, shorts, and he was barefoot. I had never seen his feet before.

I didn't have a foot fetish, but his were wide and strong looking. It made me think of other parts of him that I did have a thing for. But I quickly pushed aside the thought knowing that I didn't want to meet his father for the first time with my wolf humping Cage's leg.

"You made it," my host said uncomfortably. "Did you have any problems finding the place?"

"No, it was pretty easy."

"It was far, right?"

"You don't live close to campus."

I looked around at the thick woods surrounding the cabin and imagined what it would be like to let my wolf roam free out here. I could tell he was thinking it too. His excitement for it made my heart race.

"Did you grow up out here?" I asked pushing the thoughts aside.

"From as early as I remember. You said you grew up in New York, right?"

"Manhattan, mostly," I clarified. "But, I did spend some time upstate. It wasn't like this, though. This is…"

"Where Bigfoot lives?" Cage joked.

I laughed. "Pretty much."

Cage seemed to relax for the first time.

"Well, Bigfoot actually lives a few miles from here, so… Great guy, by the way. You don't even notice the fur once you've talked to him for a while."

I chuckled, but I hadn't missed his fur reference. I also wondered if he was being serious. If wolf shifters existed, what else could be out there?

"Let's go inside. We have a lot of stuff to cover," Cage said leading me in.

With the door closed, I looked around at the space. I didn't know what to expect after Cage's warning. It was certainly nicer than I was picturing.

As a kid, not only did we live in upstate New York, but we spent a lot of time in the Bahamas. My dad bought a private island where I could learn how to control my shifts without anyone getting hurt.

As part of his plan to domesticate me, my father would take me to eat in the homes of locals. They were on what were called the Out Islands and were usually very modest. Not only was Cage's cabin bigger than many of them, it was also nicer.

Of course, I couldn't explain any of this to Cage. So, instead, I said, "It must have been cool growing up here."

"It was okay. If not a little isolating."

"I know what you mean. My dad owns an island with only the house on it. So, replace the trees surrounding this place with water and the birds for sharks, and you have every one of my summers since I was three," I said with a smile.

"Did you say that your father owns an island?"

I froze realizing what I had said. Not only was Cage looking at me like I was a freak, someone on the couch in front of us turned around and stared at me. He captured my attention immediately. I didn't know why.

Was it his smell? He didn't smell like Cage did. His scent was totally different. It was unlike anything I had ever smelled before.

Cage followed my gaze and said, "Dad, this is Quin. He's my…"

I was whipped out of my fascination with his father to feel a rush wondering how he was going to describe me.

Cage paused making me more than anxious to hear how he was going to describe me.

"He's my good friend. He's helping me pass the class I was telling you about."

"It's good to meet you, Sir," I said to the red-headed man.

Cage's father looked me over, grunted, and then returned to watching TV.

"We should go to my room," Cage told me.

"It was good meeting you, Sir," I said getting nothing in reply.

Entering Cage's bedroom, he closed the door behind us.

"You have to excuse my Dad. He's having an off day."

"He seemed fine to me."

"Well, fine is relative. We can sit on the bed."

I took off my shoes, emptied the contents of my backpack into the center of the bed, and sat cross-legged. Cage joined me searching my eyes.

"What?"

"Are you expecting me to forget that you just said that your father owns an island?"

"Oh, that."

"Yeah, that."

"It's small. Everyone in the Bahamas owns an island."

"Everyone in the Bahamas owns an island?" Cage asked shocked.

"Okay, that's not true. I don't know why I said that. Actually, that's not true either. I do know why I said it, it was because I don't want you to think we're that different."

"We are that different," Cage said matter-of-factly. "But that's okay. I like your differences. I just hope you aren't too disappointed by mine."

"I literally don't know what you're talking about. You are the most normal person I know. Of course, the only other person I know here is Lou, so that's not saying much."

Cage laughed. "So it's a low bar."

"You just have to be able to deal with me and you've surpassed 99% of the population."

Cage laughed. "Come on you're not that bad. Maybe 95% of the population," he teased.

"You're right. Thinking about it now, it's 95%. I stand corrected."

Cage laughed again. God, did I love hearing him laugh.

"You know, you do that a lot," Cage said with a smile.

"What?"

"Put yourself down."

"Do I?"

"Yeah."

"I didn't realize I was doing it."

"You do. You should be nicer to my friend. He's a great guy," Cage said playfully.

"Great is a relative term."

"There you go again. Take the compliment."

"It's easier said than done. What if I said you were the most amazing guy I've ever met and that every time I was with you I wished the time would never end?"

Cage froze.

"Not so easy to take a compliment now, is it?"

"Do you really feel like that?"

"Oh, that was kind of a lot wasn't it?"

"No, seriously do you feel like that?"

"Does it matter? You have a girlfriend."

"What does it matter if I have a girlfriend?"

"It matters because if I did think that, it would be because I wanted more to happen between us than was possible."

"What if it was possible?"

"What do you mean?"

"I mean, what if I didn't have a girlfriend?"

I looked into Cage's beautiful, soul-crackling eyes. He was serious. He was considering breaking up with his girlfriend for me.

"There are things about me you don't know," I said unable to stop myself.

"What? That you're more adorable than I already think you are?"

"No, stop. There are things I need to tell you before you do or say anything that we won't be able to come back from."

"Oh, you're serious."

"I am."

Cage shifted uncomfortably. "Okay. What's up?"

My heart pounded. I could feel my wolf perk up as if he was listening to our conversation.

"Where do I begin? Okay. I mentioned my father has an island."

"I remember something about that, yes."

"It was ten minutes ago. I hope you do."

Cage chuckled. "Yes, I remember."

"Well, he owns an island because he is very rich."

"Like how rich."

"Like, he owns an island, rich."

Cage laughed. "Got it. And you grew up very rich?"

"Yes."

"I figured. Is that what you were scared to tell me? That you grew up with your own island?"

"Not even close."

Cage leaned back startled. "Okay."

I touched my brow wondering if I was sweating. I was starting to.

"Here's the thing. My dad is rich because he's Laine Toro."

Cage's brow furrowed. "Why do I know that name?"

"He became famous because he was the face of the last pandemic. But that was before we were born. Now he owns a genetics company," I offered.

"Oh, I think I learned about him in history class. That's your father?"

"That's my father," I conceded wondering if Cage knew about the part of my father's life that included me.

"Wow! Okay. That's a little intense but not really that big of a deal… I guess," he said slowly coming to grips with it. "I thought it was going to be something serious. Is that it?" he said beginning to brush it aside.

"Not even close," I told him.

"Oh!"

"Yeah, there's another reason why my father's famous."

"Why is that?"

"Because of me," I said sheepishly.

"Because of you?"

"Yeah."

"Why is he famous because you?"

I took a long, deep breath. My heart was beating so hard it hurt the inside of my chest.

"Have you ever heard of a... wolf shifter?"

"I guess. I think my Bigfoot neighbor is married to one. They make a cute couple," he said with a smile.

I stared at Cage confused. "I can't tell if you being serious."

"What do you mean, you can't tell? Have you ever met a Bigfoot or a wolf shifter? They're myths, aren't they?"

"They used to be," I said hesitantly.

Cage looked at me skeptically.

"What are you talking about?"

I took another deep breathe. This was it. I was going to do it.

"My father is really famous because he and my mother couldn't have a baby. Being a geneticist, he thought he could figure out a way. And, he did. But there were side effects."

"What kind of side effects?"

"Like I said, have you ever heard of a wolf shifter?"

Cage stared at me not knowing what to say... and then laughed.

"Okay, you had me going for a second there. How gullible am I?"

"Cage, I'm a wolf shifter."

"No you're not."

"Why not?"

"Because there's no such thing."

"Do you have the internet?"

"On my phone. Why?"

"Type in my name."

Cage looked at me confused. "Okaaaay," he said hesitantly reaching for his phone. "What's your last name?"

"Toro," I said, my voice cracking. "Quin Toro."

Cage's confidence disappeared as he refocused on his screen and typed in my name. I didn't have to see his phone to know the moment the search results appeared. He stared down stunned.

"Didn't you ever hear about any of this?" I asked hoping I hadn't lost him.

"I did, but you hear a lot of things living out here. I never believed any of it."

"Well, this one happens to be true. Are you freaking out?"

Cage looked up at me for the first time. I couldn't tell what he was thinking. Was he scared, or angry? When I had told Lou about it last summer, it had been over the phone and from thousands of miles away. The only thing I knew was that it made him stop talking as much. I didn't know how much until after we met and he relaxed around me.

But, this was the first time in a long time I was doing it face to face. The one benefit of being as famous as I was was that most of the people I met already knew.

"I'm not freaking out. I'm just tryin' to wrap my head around it. So, you're like a werewolf?"

"No. First of all, werewolves are made up... I think. And, they turn into a half human, half wolf creature. I have full control over when I shift, at least most of the time. And, when I do, I change into a wolf."

"How?"

"How what?"

"How anything? How do you do it? How did this happen? How does it feel?"

I paused and took a breath. In spite of what he said, Cage seemed pretty freaked out. But, he wasn't freaked out in the way that would result in him shooting me with a silver bullet or something. He just needed time and explanations, the latter of which I didn't have.

"I don't know how I do it. It just happens. It always just happens. As to how it happened, I don't know. The only person who knows for sure is my dad and after I shifted for the first time, and after what happened to my mother, he swore he would take the procedure to his grave..."

"What happened to your mother?" Cage asked cutting me off.

Prickly heat washed through me hearing his question. Darkness quickly enveloped me and I knew that the only way to stop it from consuming me completely was to just say it.

"I killed her."

"What?"

"It was my wolf. When I was too young to speak, I used to shift without warning. My parents thought they had a handle on it, but they underestimated the response of, at two years old, was an adolescent wolf.

"I was told my mother was trying to discipline my wolf for something I had done and my wolf snapped. It's a wild animal. The only way to control it is to lock it away."

Even as I said it, I wondered if what I was saying was true. Yes, at one point it was a wild animal. But the wolf I met in my dorm room, wasn't that at all. And the presence I felt in my head even now, wasn't savage.

"I wanna see it," Cage said suddenly looking at me intrigued.

"I just said that I can't control it," I told him a little offended that he would ask. How would he feel if I asked him to drop his pants and show me his dick?

"I think you can," he said confidently.

"And you think that because of your vast knowledge on the topic you just learned about two seconds ago?"

"No. I just feel it. You have more control over it than you think."

What was Cage talking about? Why did he think he knew anything about me or this?

Certainly I might have misrepresented how wild my wolf was given my interaction with it in my room. But, he didn't know that. And, although I was sure I couldn't control it, perhaps I could reason with it. But, again, Cage had no way of knowing any of this. So, why would he say what he had?

"Well, putting your life in danger to test that theory wasn't why I came over tonight. We have an exam tomorrow and there is still a lot of material we have to go over."

"I don't know how I'm gonna concentrate on any of that after what you just told me."

"Figure out a way. Your future will be determined by what happens tomorrow. Please don't make me regret telling you."

That seemed to snap Cage out of his bug-eyed fascination with me.

"You're right. We have work to do. But, thank you for telling me. I feel so much closer to you now," Cage said turning his attention to the books in the bed between us.

That made my wolf's ears perk up. He felt about it the same way I did. It aroused us. For so long I had wanted to find someone who could accept this part of me. I had found him, and he looked like he was chiseled out of marble. Why did he have to have a girlfriend?

Filling him in on the last of what he missed before he joined the class, I found it hard to stay focused. Every so often he would look up at me. When he did, he would give me a smile that would melt my heart.

I pushed through because Cage needed to understand the material for the exam. But, it was hard not to melt in his gaze. Neither me nor my wolf wanted to be apart from him again. Knowing I couldn't have that ripped my heart out.

"That's all of it. I think you have it," I told him when he repeated the last of it back to me without having to refer to the textbook.

"I think I do," he said proudly. "That took a while."

"Did it?" I asked pulling out my phone. "It's 1:30?"

"Time flies when you're having fun," he said looking as charming as sin.

"Do rideshares still run at this hour?"

"They do in the city. But, you're not going to be able to get one to come out here."

"A taxi maybe."

"You could stay over. I have practice before class tomorrow. I could get you back early."

"Stay over?" I said feeling my wolf run wild. "I guess I could sleep on the couch."

"You're not gonna sleep on the couch. Besides, my dad probably fell asleep out there."

"Then, the floor?"

"I'm not letting you sleep on the floor! You're only here this late because you were helping me pass my class. If anything, that's where I'm sleeping."

"I can't let you sleep on the floor. It wouldn't be good for your back. How is your back, by the way?" I asked remembering him having an issue with it the night I started tutoring him.

"My back?"

"Yeah. Remember at my room?"

"Oh, yeah! No, it's, um, a little stiff but not as bad as it was. It was probably just all of the tension that night."

"You were nervous about not being able to play next season?"

"Something like that."

"So, if neither of us is going to sleep on the floor, where are we going to sleep?" I asked hoping I knew what he was going to say.

"We could share the bed."

"Are you sure that's a good idea? You're not afraid I'll shift in the middle of the night and eat you or something?"

"No, Quin, I'm not afraid of that. I'm not afraid of you. And, we're just gonna be sleeping."

Or, not sleeping considering how hard my heart was beating just thinking about it.

"I guess. Okay."

"Okay," he said confidently.

We cleared off the bed and stared at each other.

"Would you like something to change into? You probably don't want to sleep in your jeans."

"I'm fine," I told him nervous as all hell.

"You sure, because I'm gonna get comfortable," he said before taking off his shirt. "See."

I definitely saw. The man was a god. His muscular arms, his rippling chest, everything about him sent tingles through me that landed between my legs.

"Come on. You can get comfortable," he said with a smile.

I badly wanted to get naked with him. It was the beginning of every one of my fantasies. I didn't know if I should, but I couldn't resist anymore.

"Okay," I said slowly pulling off my shirt.

"Woah!" Cage said once my shirt was in my hand.

"What?"

"You are in surprisingly good shape."

"Genetics," I admitted.

Sorry. Am I making you uncomfortable?

"No." I quickly replied. "When you grow up constantly shifting into a wolf, you become very comfortable with the way your body looks when naked."

"Nice. So, are you going to sleep in your jeans?"

"Are you?"

"No," he said not making a move to take his pants off.

I stared at him waiting. Was he actually going to do it? If he did, maybe I would too. What was he waiting for?

When he finally reached for the button on his pants, my dick grew hard. Without a shirt, there was nothing to hide my bulge. What was I supposed to do?

He wasn't looking at me as he pulled down his pants. As he stepped out of them and pushed them aside, he didn't look up. I wondered why until I saw the outline of his large dick stretched across his boxer briefs. Cage was hard. Very hard. At least I hoped he was because he was already humongous.

I couldn't believe what was happening. Were we just getting comfortable for bed, or was something else going on? I drank in all of him making my hard cock flinch. My wolf went wild. When he finally met my gaze without looking down, he said,

"What about you?"

My cock flinched again. There was no way I was going to be able to hide my arousal even if I wanted to. Did I want to hide it?

I don't think I did. I wanted him to see all of me. I wanted to see all of him. And with his eyes still locked on mine, I lowered my pants standing in front of him in just my underwear.

Cage did nothing but stare into my eyes until for a brief moment, he blinked down to see me. It made him smile.

"Should we get into bed?" He asked me.

"Okay," I told him unsure what was going to happen next.

The two of us climbed into bed and under the sheets. We both laid on our backs staring at the ceiling.

"I should get the lights," Cage said to me.

"I guess," I told him barely able to hear him over the sound of my heartbeats.

Cage got out of bed again, flicked the light switch next to the door, and returned to bed in the dark.

It took a while for my eyes to adjust to the darkness, but it was a moonlit night. Still not sure what was happening, I stayed on my back not looking at him. At no point did he move. Had he already fallen asleep? Could anyone fall asleep so quickly?

With the deafening silence enveloping us, I couldn't take it anymore. Cage was so close that it was torture not to touch him. I had to at least see the beautiful body whose heat consumed me. So, moving like it was the most natural thing in the world, I rolled over settling on my side.

Buried in the shadows, I opened my eyes. He was on his side facing me. His eyes were closed. Maybe he was asleep. If he was, it meant that I could look at him unhindered. I could examine every contour of his angular, masculine face.

Cage was the most gorgeous man I had ever seen. His wavy hair that lay gently across his forehead, his broad shoulders that sat uncovered, his lightly hairy chest, I desperately wanted to touch him. To feel the heat of his skin next to mine would be enough to live the rest of my life on.

Needing to be closer to him, I moved my hand onto the bed between us. I was less than a foot away from his sleeping body and didn't dare to get any closer. I wanted to. God did I want to, but I knew I couldn't… until, as if sensing me there, Cage moved his hand between us an inch away from mine.

I could feel the heat of him on me. I could barely breathe. Parting my lips as my heart thumped, I couldn't stand it. I needed to be closer. Being apart from him hurt too much.

Moving my fingers slowly, I stretched them out. They weren't long enough. He was right there. I could practically feel them. I would need to move my entire hand if I wanted his touch. Could I do that, though? Should I do it?

My debate didn't matter because as if he needed it too, his strong hand crossed to mine and moved on top of it. It was him who had done it. It could have been the reflex actions of someone asleep, but I didn't think it was. He wanted to hold my hand and I wanted to hold his.

So, shifting my fingers delicately, I allowed his fingers to fall between mine. When they did, I moved mine so that they touched his. It was everything I had hoped it would be. I tried to breathe without making a sound but it was the most erotic moment of my life. His touch was a swirling wind that encircled my warm, naked body.

I was in love with Cage. I could no longer deny it. And, touching him in the moonlight, there was nowhere else in the world I would rather be. I wanted this moment to last forever. It lasted for hours, but eventually, my exhausted heart slowed down and I fell asleep.

Chapter 8

Cage

I'm falling in love with Quin. I can't deny it.
Even as I lie in the morning light not getting nearly
enough sleep, all I could think about was how I could
touch him like I did last night.

When I heard him place his hand on the bed
between us, I sent out my hand in search of his. I didn't
know if I should or if he would want me to, but I
couldn't stop myself.

I need Quin. I ache to be with him. I feel like I
would go crazy without him. And to be so close without
being able to wrap my arms around him was torture.

I was about to relieve myself of the painful agony
when I moved and something buzzed. When it did, I
realized I was still half asleep because it woke me up. I
knew the sound. It was my alarm clock. I had forgotten
to turn it off.

It was probably more accurate to say that I wasn't
foolish enough to turn it off. Ever since I had met Quin,

getting eight hours were impossible. Even if I was in bed in time to do it, alone in the darkness was when I thought about him the most. So to have him here now was like a dream come true.

The alarm buzzed again. Oh right, the alarm. I didn't want it to wake up Quin.

Instead of letting it ring like I usually had to, I popped open my eyes and figured out where I was. I was on the right side of the bed. The alarm clock was on the left. I had to reach over Quin to get it.

Not thinking about it, I straddled the guy beneath me and hit the switch. With it off, I realized where I was. Although our bodies weren't touching, I was hovering above him. I froze and looked down. He was on his back facing up.

My God, did I want to bend down and kiss him. I was right there. He was so close. And then he opened his eyes.

I stared at him, caught. He smiled, or was it a blush?

"Good morning," he said in a raspy morning voice.

Looking at him, I relaxed.

"Morning," I said getting one more good look at him and then rolling back to my side of the bed. "Sorry about that," I told him.

"No, I liked it," he said smiling ear to ear.

"You liked the alarm?"

"Oh, I thought you meant…" He blushed again. "It was fine. Does that mean we have to get up? It's so early."

"I have to get to practice. It's a long drive."

"Okay," he said squirming his body adorably.

Watching him settle, I was about to get up when I noticed something. I had a serious morning wood situation going on. Sure, I was only too happy to show him my hard dick last night. But, I was so turned on by being with him that I had lost all inhibition.

After a night's sleep, as short as it was, I wasn't so bold. Yeah, I was still as turned on as all get out. But, we weren't getting into bed. We were leaving it. That made a difference.

"We could sleep a little while longer, right?" Quin asked facing me, his gorgeous eyes begging for me to hold him.

"You can, but I have to get up. The bowl game's on Saturday. This is our last full practice before it. I can't be late."

"Fine," Quin said disappointed.

Staring into his eyes I tried to think of the next time I could get him back here.

"Do you want to come to the game? Have you ever been?"

"You want me to come to your game?" He asked with a smile.

"Yeah. Why wouldn't I?"

"I don't know. I thought it might be your manly space or something."

"Manly space?"

"You know, a place for your girlfriend and all of your football friends to meet and do football things."

"First of all, the stadium seats 20,000 people. There's room for everyone. Second of all, Tasha hasn't been to one of my games in I don't know how long. You should come. That way you can see what all the fuss is about."

"I can see what all of the fuss is about from here," he said making my heart melt.

"I mean, why it's so important for me to pass the class we stayed up all night studying for."

"Oh, yeah. Okay."

"I can get you a couple of tickets. You can bring Lou."

"I don't know how much he's into football."

"Is he into football players?" I asked with a smile.

"He's into anyone with a dick."

"Then tell him that everyone on the field is guaranteed to have a dick," I said with a smile.

Quin chuckled. I loved hearing him laugh.

"I'll see."

"Cool."

"Will you win?"

"For you? Anything. I wouldn't have been able to pass the class without you."

"You haven't passed it yet," he reminded me.

"But I will. I'm confident. You're a good teacher. Thank you."

"Does that mean my tutoring time with you is done?"

I looked at Quin realizing it for the first time.

"I guess it does."

The thought of not having an excuse to be with him broke my heart.

"You definitely have to come to the game. I mean it. Promise me you will even if Lou doesn't."

Quin looked me in the eyes and smiled.

"I will. I promise."

"Good. Now, I guess I have to get up."

I flinched my dick finding that it was now only partially hard. That meant that I could look impressive for Quin without making things incredibly awkward for our 40-minute drive back to campus.

Getting out of bed, I was sure to stand profile for him as I readjusted my shorts. I gave it enough time for him to get a good look at me, before turning and heading for the bathroom. There was only one in the house and it was outside my door. Leaving Quin, I closed the bedroom door behind me and I did what I had to to prepare for the day.

When I got back to the room, Quin was dressed and ready to go. As he took care of morning business, I made a breakfast smoothie and packed my bag getting ready to go.

Our ride back to town consisted mostly of him drilling me on what we had gone over the night before. What I really wanted to talk about was the bomb he dropped on me about being a wolf shifter. That was crazy. Yet, I don't know… Hearing it made me want to be around him even more. I couldn't tell why. I just did.

I also wanted to pepper him with a bunch of questions about what it was like. But, the way he had changed the topic told me that I was going to have to wait. I didn't want to scare him off — if wolf shifters even got scared.

Did they? Why would they if they did? I could only imagine being something so… cool. The strength and confidence that came with it had to be incredible.

I liked to think of myself as confident and strong. But, I knew I wasn't. I had my moments. On the football field I felt unstoppable. That was another reason I wanted Quin to see me play. I wanted him to see that part of me.

When I had floated the idea of breaking up with Tasha, he hadn't responded how I had hoped. Now I understood why. Who was I in comparison to Quin Toro, the famous wolf shifting heir to a billion dollar fortune?

I was going to need a little more enthusiasm from Quin before dismantling my world to be with him. My life was nothing compared to his. But coming from the back woods of Tennessee, what I had was a lot to give up, even for the chance to be with someone as incredible as he was.

I was going to have to think hard about this. But, before I got there, I had practice, an exam, and what was probably the biggest game of my life.

If you are a legitimate NFL prospect, NFL teams might request film on you at the beginning of the school year. After sifting through the hundreds of hours they get from around the country, teams select where they will send their scouts.

Bowl games were where scouts came to see you in person. College bowl games were highly attended, televised games during winter break. They allowed scouts to see how we played under pressure. At the end of bowl season, most teams knew who to put on their draft board. Bowl games were what allowed players to go pro.

As a senior, it would be the last bowl game of my life. It had to go well or else everything everyone sacrificed to get me here would have been for nothing. But, it wasn't like my relationship with my father hung in the balance and the weight of it was an elephant on my chest. Nope, it wasn't like that at all.

"Good luck at practice!" Quin wished me when I dropped him off at his dorm.

"Thanks."

"See you in class. And don't worry, you won't need luck for that one. You got it," he said with a smile.

"Thanks… for everything," I said hopelessly taken by him.

I watched him walk away. God, did his ass look good. He looked back a final time before disappearing into his building.

As I sat there, what I wanted became clear. I could no longer imagine a future without Quin in it. He had quickly become everything to me. What the hell was I supposed to do now?

Fortunately, I didn't have time to think about it. If I didn't get my ass to practice immediately, I was going to be late. Whatever I decided to do, it would probably affect my NFL prospects and I was going to need Coach's help. So, the last thing I wanted was to be on his bad side.

"You're late!"

"I'm sorry, Coach. I was up all night studying," I said as I ran past him on my way to the locker to change.

He followed a step behind.

"Studying, huh? It's funny how you're doing it without a tutor. You better not be bullshitting me, Rucker. If you don't pass that class, you'll be suspended from the team. There won't be anything I'll be able to do about it."

"I promise, I have a tutor. I keep telling him to register with you guys, but I don't think he needs the money. I'll pass the class, though. He's pretty incredible. He has me ready."

"You better be ready."

"Coach. I'm ready."

"Huh," he huffed looking at me suspiciously.

I couldn't tell what Coach was thinking or what it would mean, so I put it out of my mind by giving it all I had in practice. I was on the verge of puking by the end.

"I gotta go, Coach. I gotta take my exam," I told him staring at the giant clock at the far end of the stadium.

"Take it and get back here! We have more plays to go over."

"Got it, Coach."

I took off my helmet and upper pads before running across campus. Unlike the first time I did it, I was there at the beginning of class. There were no open seats left near Quin so I took one up front.

"Good luck, Mr. Rucker," the professor said as she handed me the exam.

"Thanks," I said before looking back for the only encouragement I cared about.

Quin smiled at me and mouthed, "You have this."

I mouthed, "Thanks," back.

It turned out that Quin had been right. I had never taken an easier exam in my life. I didn't pretend it had to do with anything other than Quin's preparation. It was like he knew what was going to be on the exam. The guy was incredible.

It did worry me a little that I was the first person to turn in my paper. I handed mine in before Quin did. There was no way that could be right. I probably hadn't gone over my answers enough times. But that couldn't be helped. I had to get back to practice.

Handing it in, the professor gave me a surprised look. I wasn't about to do anything that would indicate that I found it easy. I knew that would be tempting fate.

But I did make eye contact with Quin on the way out. I gave him a cocky look telling him it had been a breeze. He stopped himself from chuckling and then returned to his exam.

Leaving the room, I considered waiting for him. He couldn't be too far behind me. But, I had told Coach that I would head back as soon as I was done. Also, I didn't want to be the douchebag hanging out in the hallway in his football gear and cleats.

Running back across campus I got there in time for the film section. There was a lot to go over. From there, the team had another walk-through of plays. Coach was preparing us like Quin had prepared me for the exam. So, by the time I got back to the locker room, I was exhausted. All I wanted to do was go home.

Turning on my phone, I found a message from Quin.

'How was it?'

'So easy,' I wrote back. 'It's a good thing you stole the exam. I could never have passed without it.'

I thought it was funny, but Quin didn't reply.

'You'll be there on Saturday, right?'

'Wouldn't miss it,' he immediately wrote back.

'I'll put the tickets at 'Will Call'.'

'Okay. Thanks.'

'No. Thank you!' I said not knowing how else to express how grateful I was to him.

I knew that I didn't deserve to have someone like Quin in my life. My life was a mess. I had a girlfriend I didn't love. I didn't want to leave my house in fear that when I returned my father would be gone. And my career was set to take me away from him.

Quin was an incredibly amazing guy who deserved so much more than someone like me. He was someone who would literally go down in history. On top of that, he was sweet, and thoughtful, and brilliant. Who was I compared to all of that?

"You'll be at the game on Saturday, right Dad?" I asked him when I found him drinking in front of the TV.

"Yea," he said without looking at me.

I didn't stop staring at him. As much as I tried to put it out of my mind, I kept thinking about what he said about me not being his son. There had always been things that had made me wonder.

For example, my father was a real redhead who went from pale to freckled pink, while I had dark hair. He was left-handed while I was right-handed. He liked foods I found disgusting. He was super hairy while at 22, I still struggled to grow facial hair. And, I was pretty sure he was colorblind. Either that or he severely rejected societal pressure to match his socks.

None of those things meant anything on their own. But add them all together? It had always made me think. Now add that to my dad's rants and I couldn't ignore it anymore.

"What?" My father said having felt me stare.

Did I ask him about it while he was still somewhat sober? Would my asking him be the thing that finally made him leave? I couldn't deal with this. Not now, at least.

"What?" He asked again, this time a little pissed off.

"Your ticket will be at 'Will Call'," I told him looking away and heading to my room.

He grunted in reply.

"Boy?"

"You know I don't like it when you call me that," I told him.

"You know scouts will be there on Saturday, right?"

"I know."

"You prepared?"

"Coach has us ready."

"Good. Who was that boy you brought around last night?"

I stopped my exit as soon as he brought up Quin. If I was going to have a life with Quin, at some point I was going to have to talk to him about it.

"I told you. He's my tutor."

"He didn't leave last night."

"We were up late preparing for the exam I took today."

He grunted not taking his eyes off of me.

"By the way, I know you like her, but I don't think it's working out between Tasha and me."

"Make it work. She's good for you. Teams will like her."

"I can't be with someone because some team might like the way we look together. There's more to life than that."

"Do you know how much I sacrificed to get you where you are? You couldn't even begin to guess."

"And I appreciate that, Dad. But I don't see what that has to do with who I date."

"Don't you go ruining this now, Boy."

"I'm not ruining anything. I'm just telling you that she might not be the one."

"And, who is?"

"I don't know. But there are a lot of people out there."

"And none of them would do what she can do for you."

"You mean stand beside me on draft day and look pretty? I can't base my life on one moment that will have more to do with how I play on Saturday than who I stick my dick in."

"Don't you ruin this, Boy."

"I told you, don't call me that."

"I'll call you whatever I God damn want, Boy."

"Okay, I'm done," I told him seeing where the conversation was headed.

"Don't you walk away from me," he said after I exited to my room and shut the door behind me.

"Don't you fuck this up. Don't you go fuckin' this up, Boy. This is the best thing that will ever happen to you. Don't you give it all up for some piece of ass."

He had heard me. He knew what I was hinting at with Quin and it was clear that he didn't approve. But, it didn't matter. I was falling in love with him and there was nothing my dad could do to change that.

If Quin let me, I was going to make him mine. To others, it might seem like a choice, but it wasn't. I didn't think I could stand to be away from him if I tried. He had me and nothing that happened was going to change that. Not my father. Not what some scout would say. Nothing.

'Did you get the tickets?' I texted Quin as I sat in the locker room waiting to go out for the game.

"Put your phone away, Rucker. Get your head in the game," Coach said forcing me to return it to my bag before I got a reply from Quin.

Holding out as long as I could, I stared at the screen until the phone was out of sight. Still nothing. I had texted him yesterday and he had told me he and Lou would be here. I told him that I would make sure to win the game so that he enjoyed himself. He had just told me that he was looking forward to it, but nothing else.

I was expecting more from him. The truth was that I was having a hard time interacting with him since our class ended. Our class had been our excuse to spend time together. Without it, the only thing remaining was my intense feelings for him. But I didn't feel right expressing how I felt as long as I was still in a relationship with Tasha.

Tasha, on the other hand, was nowhere to be seen. I had put tickets for her at 'Will Call' like I always did, but I hadn't spoken to her in days. I would say our relationship was over except even when she disappeared like this, she would reappear and remind me of the dream we had had where I traveled the country playing for the NFL and she got involved with some charity.

I don't know what it was about that dream that always got me to excuse the shittiness of our relationship, but it did. It had to stop, though. I wasn't sure what I wanted my life to be, but I was feeling more confident that it wasn't that.

How did I break that to her? How did I break that to my dad?

Taking the field, I looked around at the stands. The place was jammed packed. I knew where Quin's seats were but there was no way to see them from here. Past the row closest to the field, the stadium became a blur of cheering, colorful dots. Usually, that was how I preferred it. Today, there was one person I wished I could pick out.

Was Quin here or not? Whatever the case, I was going to play like I was only playing for him. I wanted him to be proud of me. I wanted him to think that I was worthy of someone as great as him.

Our offensive team took the field to start the game. As quarterback, I surveyed the defensive line looking for all of the weaknesses Coach had been training us to spot. I didn't see anything until my tight end shifted indicating that he thought he could make a hole for our running back.

We had run this play in dozens of games. The other team knew that. That meant that the opposition would be looking to adjust to it as soon as we committed to the play. So, if I called the play and waited for the defense to commit…

"Orange, 52, summer, hike," I said telling my guys my plan.

As expected, our tight end opened a hole in their defensive line. As soon as he did, our running back charged from behind me looking for a hand-off. Wrapping his arms around nothing, he charged the line causing the defense to collapse on his position. The right safety moved into place to stop our running back if he got through. And the man who was defending our wide receiver favored his right to back up the charging safety.

That was when our wide receiver broke loose and sprinted down the field. This was it. He was open. I just had to stay on my feet long enough for him to reach the ten-yard line.

The grunts of 300-pound men echoed in my ears. They were coming. My heart pounded.

'Stay calm. Wait for it,' I told myself.

When our guys couldn't hold back their line any longer, their linebacker cut through like a bullet through metal. He was going to get me. I had to throw. Whipping my arm back, I let go. The second the ball left my fingertips, a freight train hit me leaving me on the ground for dead.

Lying there, I heard the collective awe of the crowd. They were watching something. It was my pass. I had gotten it off in time. It was spiraling forty yards through the air. It took a while to get there. When it did, the screams of the crowd were deafening.

"Touch down!" The announcer yelled.

20,000 people shot to their feet. Celebration. Agony. The rush of it all was amazing. Dan ran over to me and helped me up.

"Fuck yeah!" He yelled slapping me on my back.

Jogging off the field watching everyone go wild, there was only one person who I hoped had seen it. I looked toward his section again. There were too many people and it was too far away. I didn't see him. It broke my heart to think he might not have been there.

I played like a man on fire for the rest of the first half. I had never thrown a more perfect game in my life. I had my offensive line to thank for it, of course. And, it didn't matter how well I threw if my receivers didn't catch it. But, there was one name the crowd chatted as we jogged off the field for halftime, mine.

Hurrying back to the locker, the only thing I cared about was checking my messages. I would have given anything to see Quin's name pop up. Ripping my glove off to unlock the phone, I tossed it aside and illuminated the screen.

There were two messages from him. One said, 'Got the tickets. Heading up now!' And the other one said, 'WOW!!!!' That was it and it was enough.

I was so happy I felt drunk. He had seen me do what I did best. I couldn't feel better if I tried.

I entered the field for the second half beside myself. I felt like I was glowing. I felt intoxicated. It was a good thing we started the second half playing defense. It gave me a few extra minutes to pull myself together.

As much as I tried to focus, I couldn't help but search the crowd for him. He was out there somewhere. I could now feel his gaze on me. I wanted to show off for him. So with my helmet in hand headed back onto the field, I called a series of plays that would guarantee we would win the game.

It started with a few passes that got us closer to the end zone. I just needed to be within thirty yards. That was it.

When my final pass got us there, I gathered the guys into a huddle and called the big one. They looked at me questioningly but I was their quarterback. They listened.

In the line, I called for the hike. With the ball in hand, I pulled back my arm ready to launch it. After a continuous parade of passes, the defensive line stepped back. That's when I lowered the ball tucking it under my arm and charged.

Caught by surprise, the other team was late to react. It opened a gap down the sideline. Ahead of me, I could see the end zone. I wanted this touchdown. I wanted Quin to see me do this.

Rifling towards me was the free safety. He was going to get to me before I got to the goal. I had two options. I could run out of bounds, or I could risk my life and charge through.

I wanted this. I wanted it bad. Picking up speed I made my decision. Nothing was going to stop me.

An arm's length away, the safety lunged. That was when I leaped into the air. I was going to jump over him. I had seen it in movies and the most spectacular games. I could do it.

Leaving the ground, I watched as the safety cut under me. I wasn't high enough. I would have to step on him to clear him. But when my foot reached down for his body, I felt his hand.

It was hard to tell what happened after that. What I know is that I heard a crack. It was as my body hit the ground.

There was nothing, and then there was a roar of fire. The pain consuming me was unlike anything I had ever felt. It was my left leg. Something in it had shattered.

I was told that athletes know the moment a career-ending injury has occurred. I used to wonder what that felt like. I didn't have to wonder anymore. Because in that moment, I knew this was the end.

Chapter 9

Quin

"Oh my God! What just happened? Why isn't he getting up? Lou, what's going on? Lou?" I asked turning to him.

With his face painted in the school colors, Lou stared at the field with his mouth hanging open. Like everyone else, he was speechless.

I turned back to see medics running onto the field. Cage flopped around in so much pain they could barely get to him. I couldn't believe what I was seeing. This was a nightmare.

In a few moments a paramedic was pushing a stretcher to Cage. It took two men to get him onto it. Tears rolled down my cheeks watching it. I was in shock. I didn't know what I could do to help, but I had to do something.

"I need to go to him," I told Lou.

"Yeah. Of course. Where do we go?"

"I don't know. The locker room?"

"Lead the way," he said ushering me on.

As I headed to the stairs I realized there was one problem, I had no idea where I was going. Not only was this my first time at the university's stadium, this was the first stadium I had ever visited. I could barely navigate us to the bathroom.

Despite that, we descended the stairs from the upper deck and wandered around the concession stands.

"Excuse me, how do I get to the locker rooms," I asked one of the security guards.

"It's off-limits to visitors," the burly man replied.

"But, my friend's injured. I need to go see him."

"Off limits," he repeated before looking away.

It took almost an hour to circle the stadium and realize where the entrance to the lower levels was. We got there in time to see an ambulance pull away with its lights flashing. My wolf and I were beside ourselves.

"You think that was Cage?" I asked Lou.

"I would guess," he said sympathetically.

"They're probably taking him to the closest hospital, right?"

"That would make sense."

"We need to get a ride to the hospital."

"I'm on it," Lou said whipping out his phone and arranging a ride.

Between the congestion around the stadium and the traffic, it took another hour before we got to the emergency room. I was going insane with worry by then.

Dropped off at the main doors, I rushed in with Lou in tow.

"I'm looking for Cage Rucker's room. He was just brought in. He was probably wearing football clothes," I told the stout woman behind the desk.

"I saw him come in. I think they took him for an MRI."

"Great. Where do I find that?"

"It's going to take a while before he's assigned a room."

"So, where do I wait for that?"

The woman held out her hand gesturing towards the seats in front of her desk.

"Okay. When do I check back?"

"Give it an hour."

I was disappointed everything was going to take so long. I liked to think of myself as patient but my wolf wasn't and he was starting to take control. I had to stop myself from snapping at everyone.

I had to keep reminding myself that the only thing I could do was get in the way. And that the most important thing was that Cage was being taken care of. I was willing to wait here all night as long as that was happening.

Lou and I took a seat and waited as I was told. In an hour we checked back. Cage had been moved into a room on the third floor. She wasn't sure I would be able to see him yet, but she allowed us to go up and check.

Getting off the elevator I saw a few familiar faces. Hovering in the hallway was Tasha and Cage's father. Both turned and saw us. I wasn't sure what I was supposed to do, but I continued towards them anyway.

As I got closer, Cage's father looked back at Tasha. When he turned back toward me, he had darkness in his eyes.

It was darker than anything I had ever seen. Not only did it scare me, it made my fearless wolf retreat. So, when he suddenly charged toward me, my heart clenched.

"You're Cage's friend, right? The tutor?" He said with his eyes locked on me.

"Yes, sir," I told him getting a chill down my spine.

"Come here," he told me gesturing for me to leave Lou.

I swallowed not liking where this was going. The ruddy, grizzly man was terrifying to look at. And when I finally approached him, he put his arms around my shoulder, gripped it like a vice, and pushed me into an empty room.

Before I knew what was happening, the man's hefty body had pinned me against the wall. He was manhandling me. I couldn't get away. With his hot, alcohol-laden breath flooding my ear, he said,

"I know what you are."

As soon as he said it, something changed. The black of his pupils swallowed his eyes. What stared back was empty and soulless. He wasn't human. He was something... evil.

"If you contact my boy again..." he continued before sticking something sharp into my stomach. Was it a knife or a claw? "...I'll gut you like a hog. You hear me? You contact him, you text him, you reach out to him in any way, I'll kill you, then I'll kill your friend out there. Then I'll find your family and kill them too. You hear what I'm tellin' you?"

I was in shock. I couldn't move. When I didn't respond, he pushed the blade harder. It was cutting into me.

"I hear you," I said terrified out of my mind.

"Good. Don't let me see your face again. Get the fuck out of here," he ordered before letting me go.

As soon as his grip loosened, I escaped his grasp and the room.

"What?" Lou said seeing me approach him with terror in my eyes.

"Let's go!" I demanded grabbing his arm and pulling him to the elevator.

"What are you doing? We just got here."

"Let's go!" I insisted not daring to look back.

As soon as the elevator doors opened, I was on it. Lou followed confused. I hit the lobby button continuously until the doors closed. Still not feeling safe,

I leaned against the wall watching the floor's numbers descend. It was like I could still hearing him in my head.

"Quin, you're bleeding," Lou said grabbing my attention.

He was pointing at a growing red spot on my shirt where Cage's father had stabbed me. It didn't hurt until I pulled up my shirt and saw it.

"It's nothing. I'm alright."

"What did he do to you?" Lou asked horrified.

"He didn't do anything. Let's just go."

"Quin?"

"Let's just go!" I yelled before something took over me.

It was happening. I was shifting. And we were in a confined space. No!

As much as I tried to resist, there was no stopping my wolf from coming out. Lou looked on with horror.

"I'm sorry," I said before losing myself to the pain and darkness.

When I was conscious again, I was closer to the ground and standing on a pile of clothes. I was looking through my wolf's eyes. He was staring at Lou intensely.

"Please don't!" I begged him. "He's a friend. My best friend. You can't hurt him."

To my surprise, he listened. Hearing the deafening sound as the elevator dinged, my wolf turned his attention and watched the doors open. As soon as the crack was big enough, he shot out.

It took a moment for everyone to realize what was sprinting off of the elevator. Initially everyone thought it was a dog. When it dawned on them, there were screams. The high-pitched wails only angered my wolf.

Imagining the lobby would turn into a blood bath, I quickly learned I was wrong. He hadn't come out to hurt anyone. He had emerged to take me to safety.

Slipping through the automatic doors, we emerged in the parking lot. Racing past that, we crossed the street and entered the woods. He seemed willing to run forever. Who knows where I would be once he stopped.

But, with him in control, that left me free to think. Whatever Cage's father was, I didn't doubt that he would kill me. It was screamed at me as I stared in his terrifying eyes.

Cage's father wasn't like me. He was something I couldn't imagine. Something darker. I might have been falling in love with Cage, but was I willing to die to be with him?

Chapter 10

Cage

"The good news, Mr. Rucker, is that you're young. With time to heal and rehab, you'll be able to play football again," the doctor said in a soothing tone.

"That's good," my father said happier than I was.

"The bad news is, the recovery time will be long. You are certainly out for the season."

"This is his senior year. He wouldn't have any more time before a draft to prove himself. No, he has to come back before the end of this season. I don't care what you have to do."

"Healing doesn't work like that," the doctor explained to my father. "It takes time. He couldn't come back before the end of the season if he wanted to."

"He can play. He'll just be in a little pain, right? My boy has played through pain before. He's tough."

The doctor looked at my father with sympathy.

"I understand your passion for your son's career. But, if he were to play before he's ready, his return would be short and he could do damage that wouldn't only threaten his long-term prospects, but could hamper his mobility for the rest of his life."

"I don't care. Fix him. Get him on that field."

"Dad!"

"You need to get to that draft. I've sacrificed too much to have you not make it now."

"He's talking about me not being able to walk," I clarified.

"I knew you should have entered the draft last year," he said looking at me with hate. "I told you. You didn't listen. Now, look at you. Crippled. Useless. A big sack of nothing."

"Mr. Rucker, I would like to remind you that your son should be able to play football again. He can make a full recovery."

"And, who's gonna care?" My father spit back.

The doctor was getting a taste of what I had been dealing with my whole life. It was comforting to see the horror on the doctor's face. It told me I had been justified in hating my father in the moments that I did.

"Don't worry, Boy. You're a fast healer. You've always been. You'll play before the end of the season. Trust me."

"I'm not," I said before I realized what I was saying.

"Yeah, you are."

"I'm telling you that I'm not. I don't care if there's no pain. I don't care if I can dance for hours on it. I'm not playing again this year. I might never play again."

"You will play again," my father insisted.

"Have you ever asked me if I wanted to play football?"

"It doesn't matter because you're good at it."

"It does matter, Dad. It matters what I think of it."

"I saw you throwing those passes today. No quarterback leaves the pocket to run the ball for a touchdown if they don't love what they do."

"Well, I guess you're wrong because there's a part of me that's relieved that I'll never have to play again."

"You'll play again. I'll guarantee you that," my father said with his eyes narrowing on me.

"No, Dad. I won't," I said taking the first stand of my life. "I'm done. You forced me to do it my whole life, but you heard the doctor. I'm done."

"That man doesn't know who you are. I do."

"You don't, Dad. You've never known. I'm not doing it again. It's over."

After twenty-two years, I wasn't sure what had given me the courage to say that to him. Maybe it was meeting Quin and realizing I could have a life outside of football. Before him, all of my friends and everyone I dated was there for Cage Rucker, the football star and NFL prospect.

Quin was the most thoughtful, wonderful guy I had ever met and he couldn't care less about who I was. Besides that, he was a wolf shifter. Why should I spend my life living other people's dreams when he was proof that anything was possible? Maybe if I let it, life could be more amazing than any dream.

As painful as it was, maybe my injury was a blessing. It was my way out. The doctor was very clear, I was out for the rest of the season. Coach and my teammates would understand that. The media will think it's tragic and they'll quickly forget about me. And, I could have the freedom to do what I really want to do. I wasn't sure what that was yet. But what I was sure about was that it included Quin.

My father left my hospital room without another word. There was no question that he was leaving to get drunk. He would be back, though. I knew my father. He wouldn't give up on his cash cow just like that. I might have made my decision about it, but what I wanted never mattered to him. He wouldn't give up on getting what he wanted.

"I'm sorry about that," the doctor said sympathetically.

"Injuries happen," I told him hiding the relief I felt that my football career might finally be over.

"I meant, about your father."

"Oh. Yeah," I said finally numb to his constant heartbreak. "Thanks."

"Do you have any other questions?"

"Yeah. Has anyone else come to see me? Maybe there was a guy, 5'9", shaggy dark hair, cute as all get out?"

"I can check. But your visitations haven't been restricted. So, if he came, you would have seen him."

"Okay. Thanks," I said disappointed.

I understood, though. Yes, something was developing between us. But we weren't at the 'rush to the other's hospital bed' level yet.

There was no question that I wanted to see him. He was the only person I cared about coming. Everyone else was great and I appreciated them for it. But staring into his beautiful eyes always made my day. Doing that now would make me feel like everything was going to be alright.

When the game was over, there was an endless parade of teammates and coaches in and out of my room. They all looked at me like I was dying. It was obvious that I was out for the season. They could figure out what that did to my NFL prospects.

I played along as if I was devastated. But each time someone knocked on my door, I had to hide my excitement that it would be Quin and the two of us would begin our new life together.

After I didn't hear from Quin the first day, I was sure that I would the day after. I didn't. In fact, I didn't hear from a lot of the people I thought I would. I knew that part of the reason was that winter break had begun and the majority of the school had headed home.

Dan couldn't afford to fly home for winter break so he visited a couple of times. So did Tasha who grew up an hour away. My father never came back after that first day. And confusingly, Quin never showed up.

I tried not to feel heartbroken. He was a good guy. If he didn't come to visit, there had to be a good reason.

For the life of me, I couldn't figure out what it was. The best I could come up with was that he had booked a flight home for immediately after the game. If that was the case, he wouldn't have had the time. But, why wouldn't he have at least texted?

When I realized that he wasn't going to, I decided to text him.

'Didn't I promise you a helluva game?' I wrote.

I stared at my phone waiting for a response. A day passed and nothing came. I was about to text something else when Tasha arrived to drive me home.

I would have asked my father to do it but he wasn't texting me back either. I didn't want to think about what that meant. He couldn't be that pissed at me, could he?

He had to have heard what the doctor had said. If I tried to come back this season it could cause permanent damage. If not for that, I probably would have played in the NFL for ten years, not because I wanted to, but because he wanted me to.

I was a good son. That had to be enough. How could that not be enough for him?

"You ready?" Tasha asked in a somber tone.

It felt like something was up with her.

"Yeah. Thanks for doing this. I don't know what's up with my dad."

"Of course," she said grabbing my bag as I maneuvered my way onto my crutches.

The drive back to my place was a long, quiet one. I wasn't sure what I was supposed to say to her. My playing football was at the heart of the dream that held us together.

She hadn't been in my room when I told my dad what I had. She did know that my season was over, though. And, she was smart enough to guess it meant that my easy path to the NFL was gone.

What did we have left together? I had to bring our relationship to an end. I couldn't do it now because she was in the middle of doing me a favor. But, I was going to have to do it whether or not I heard from Quin again.

Pulling into my driveway, I saw my father's truck. He was home. Relief washed over me. Things were going to be alright. I was about to get out of the car when Tasha stopped me.

"Can we talk?"

"Sure. What's up?"

"I feel like it's kind of shitty to do this now, but whatever. I think we should break up."

I didn't know if I was more relieved or rattled. Certainly, our relationship was going to end and her saying it meant that I didn't have to. But, with everything in my life changing and Quin being M.I.A., I was hoping we could have waited at least a few more days to have this talk.

"I agree," I told her.

"You agree?" She asked like she had said it as a test.

"Of course. You were with me because you wanted to be a football wife. You didn't care about me. If you did you didn't act like it."

"You think I didn't care about you?"

"If you had to choose between me and Vi, who would you choose?"

"Vi is my best friend."

"Exactly. I feel like I should have been your best friend. Or, let me rephrase that. I feel like the person I spend the rest of my life with should be my best friend. And, I should be theirs. You have your best friend and it's not me."

"So, you're blaming me for this?"

"I'm not blaming anyone. There were probably things I could have done to be a better boyfriend."

"Yes, there were. So many things!"

"That's fair. And, I don't know how much of a difference doing those things would have made. I think you've just found someone you love more than me, and... I've found someone I love more than you."

"You're interested in someone else?"

"Yeah, I am. But, so are you."

"You think I want to date Vi?"

"I think you're in love with her. And, I'm happy for you. I think you two might be really happy together."

"Are you saying I'm a lesbian? Fuck you, Cage!" she said refusing to entertain the idea.

I shifted to get out and then stopped.

"Look. I know how hard it is to escape the box that we put our lives in. When we're kids we think we know what we want and we keep going after it even when we realize that it's not. But there is a liberation that comes when you don't allow everyone else's dreams define you... even when the other person won't text you back," I said solemnly.

"Goodbye, Cage," Tasha said not giving me an inch.

"Goodbye, Tasha. Thank you for the ride," I said throwing my bag across my shoulder and exiting on my crutches.

Tasha didn't wait for me to reach the door to pull off. I didn't blame her. She probably wasn't ready to accept how she felt about her best friend and I had forced her to look at it. If the situation was reversed and she was saying that about Quin, I would probably be pissed too.

But, there was no doubt that she was in love with Vi. I hadn't realized it until I said it, but it all made perfect sense.

The girl was practically heartbroken when I said that I didn't want to have a threesome with her. I didn't know if she was lesbian, or bisexual, but Tasha had unresolved feelings and she needed us to break up as much as I did.

The only problem was that the person I was in love with might not feel the same way about me. It had been days since the game and Quin was gone. Why? I didn't understand. What had changed?

The only thing I could think of was that he was no longer my tutor. Could that be it? Was everything I thought that was happening between us just in my head? Was I just a stray puppy to him, and once he found me a home he was done?

I didn't want to think about that now. I had more pressing things to deal with like how I was going to smooth things over with my father. I was sure he'd be pissed. The man hadn't checked up on his only son as I lay in the hospital. I would have been upset if I hadn't come to accept it. The bar for him was so low that all he had to do was come home and that would be enough.

Balancing on my good foot, I retrieved my keys and let myself in.

What I found sent a wave of terror through me that rattled me to my core.

There was something sprawled across the kitchen and living room floor. It was huge. I didn't know what it was.

It had featherless wings that extended twenty feet as it stretched from the kitchen window to the far end of the living room. Its rounded body laid where the dinner table used to be and its limbs ended in six-inch claws.

Laying on its back, its long neck pressed against the wall displaying an elaborate design of scales. And its head, which was three and a half feet long, looked like that of an ancient reptile.

I only knew what this was because of what Quin had told me about him. This was a dragon. And the way it laid limp with its eyes closed told me that this horrifying creature was asleep.

"Ahhh!" I screamed falling back onto my ass.

Losing my crutches I frantically rolled over retrieving them. Rushing back to my feet I left my bag behind and raced to my father's truck. I half expected to find him in there passed out or worse. Instead I found the truck empty and locked.

"Oh no! He's still in there!" I said turning back to the cabin. "Dad! Dad, can you hear me?"

If he was in there, I had to save him.

"Dad?" I shouted a final time before returning to the door and again staring at the beast.

It was still and haunting. Was it asleep or was it dead? I couldn't tell. All I knew was that unless my father was crushed under its mammoth-sized body, he wasn't in the kitchen or living room. That only left the bathroom or the two bedrooms.

Moving as quietly as I could, I stepped over its python-sized tail. My crutches clicked like cheap aluminum sending waves of panic through me. Snapping my eyes up to the fearsome monster, it didn't move. I hadn't awoken it.

Feeling freer to search without immediately being eaten, I worked my way to the bathroom. The door was unlocked and the dark space was empty. I then moved to my bedroom next to it. It was exactly how I had left it days before.

I retreated within and quietly closed the door. My heart was thumping like I had just sprinted a mile. Whatever was going on was insane. I still needed to find my father and get out of here, though. So using my moment of familiarity to focus, I pulled myself together.

When my heartbeat returned to something approaching normal, I came up with a plan. The last place my father could be was the obvious one. If he was here when this massive creature somehow got it, he would have retreated to his room like I had. I needed to figure out a way past the beast's five-foot wide wing to get to my father's bedroom door.

I was really hoping my father was there to let me in after that. Unlike my room, my father kept his bedroom securely locked. I would hate to be banging on the door just to have the creature wake up and... what? Eat me? Burn me to a crisp with its breath?

What did dragons actually do? The fact that I was asking myself this was nuts. How did this happen?

None of that mattered right now. What mattered was rescuing my father and getting the hell out of here. Taking a final deep breath, I readied myself and went to work.

Although my shattered leg hurt, it didn't hurt enough to confine me to my crutches. I could get by without them. Quietly opening my bedroom door I did just that. And when I got to the leathery wing which I couldn't jump across, I looked for another way around it.

I could climb under it where the tip of it propped up against the living room wall. God, was this thing big. It was as if the largest elephant you'd ever seen grew wings large enough to keep it in the air. How could things like this exist? What did they eat?

Easing my way under and around the dinosaur-like wing, I climbed over the couch and to my father's bedroom door. Trying the knob out of habit, I was stunned to learn that it wasn't locked. How? Why? My father didn't even leave it unlocked when he got something from his truck.

When I was 10, I had climbed under his bed and had discovered a loose plank. Removing it I found a metal box containing a gun and more cash than someone without a job should have had. He must have realized I had found it because the next day he locked his room tighter than Fort Knox. Why was his door unlocked now?

Slowly opening it and slipping in, I was shocked to find what was in there. My dad wasn't a tidy man. But the amount of stuff squeezed into the tiny space was overwhelming. Most of it was household décor. Lamps, jewelry boxes, electronics, it was all piled on top of one another. And more important than that, my father wasn't there. Where was he?

I guess it was possible that he had escaped as the beast had entered. Maybe his room was open because he hadn't had enough time to lock the door behind him. But, if he did get out, why hadn't he taken the truck?

I stood within the mountain of junk until I relented and sat on the bed. My mind swirled considering everything. Nothing made sense.

What was I going to do next? I couldn't leave without the keys to my father's truck. And I hadn't seen them on the counter where he usually left it. Maybe he took them with him when he left. But, if he did, why hadn't he driven away?

Without the keys, the only thing I could think to do was the only thing I ever thought of doing. I had to contact Quin. Maybe he could explain what this was, or how something like this could exist. Maybe he could tell me what happened to my father.

My father could still be here somewhere. Hell, that could be him lying out there. That was the obvious conclusion, right? If anything was possible, than why not that my father was some type of dragon shifter? And, if that was what he was, what was I?

I pulled out my phone and stared at it.

'I'm not sure why I haven't heard from you, but I really need to talk to you,' I texted hoping beyond hope that Quin would finally text me back.

He didn't. Not that day or the next.

With nowhere else to go that first night, I spent it barricaded in my room sleeping on the furthest corner of the floor. Though, "sleeping" wouldn't describe what I did. It was mostly tossing and turning while I thought about Quin and the monster laying on the other side of the door.

When I left my room the next morning, I found that the dragon hadn't moved an inch. It was either dead or slept in a comatose state. Either way, I needed to get something to eat and it was lying in between me and the fridge.

On that first day, I snuck around the place as if it could rouse at any moment. When it didn't, I slowly began thinking of it as an oversized piece of furniture.

Eventually I went hunting for my father's truck's keys. What I found disturbed me more than I could image. Under its hefty torso, I discovered the edge of my father's favorite shirt. Either he was dead underneath the beast or I was looking at my father. How? I didn't understand.

Between my heartbreak over Quin's disappearance and the mystery in front of me, I spiraled into darkness. Days earlier I had everything and a girl I loved. I had lost it all and now staring at something that shouldn't exist, I was barely holding onto my sanity.

I probably would have wallowed in despair forever if it wasn't for one thing, hunger. I had no money to buy anything so the only thing I could eat was what was in the cupboards. That lasted me a week and a half before it ran out.

Luckily spring semester was about to start. I couldn't lose my scholarship in the middle of a school year even with an injury. And with my scholarship came meal stipends.

As crazy as it was that I still had this thing petrified in my living room, I had to think about survival. I would be fine as long as I attended classes and found a job. Both things meant that I would need to reengage in life. I wasn't ready to do that, but what I was ready for didn't matter. I needed to eat.

"Dan, could you give me a ride? I need to get back to campus to pick up my truck," I said calling him instead of sending a text.

"Of course, man. Anything you need. Just let me know."

It was good to hear someone else's voice. I was going crazy living with that thing. I had been hesitant to do it, but talking to Dan reminded me that there was still a world where things were normal.

"Did you register for class yet?" He asked me on the long ride to campus.

"Not yet."

"You gotta get on that."

"I know. Which reminds me, do you know of any campus jobs I could get? I'm a little short on cash."

"Of course. There's an opening where I work. I could get you a job there no problem. And you don't even have to stand up to do it."

As hesitant as I was to call Dan, I left his car with a new lease on life. Transferring over to my truck, I reminded myself how lucky I was that I had broken my left leg instead of my right. Driving wouldn't be fun, but at least it was possible.

From the stadium parking lot, I followed Dan to the student activity center. There we met with his boss. There was an opening for a job behind the front desk like

Dan had said. Being a fan of football, the manager gave me the job on the spot.

"When would you like to start?" He asked me.

"Is tomorrow too soon?"

"No. That would be perfect."

"How quickly can I get paid? I'm going to need gas money to get here."

"I'll rush the first paycheck through. It will be every two weeks after that."

"Thank you!" I said overwhelmed with relief. "You don't know how much this means to me."

I was there the next day for training and the job was even easier than Dan had said. All I had to do was watch as people slid their student I.D.s into the scanner and then compare the picture on my monitor to the person entering. It was a mind-numbing job, but I didn't know where I would be without it.

With not everyone back from break yet, barely anyone came in. Once the semester started, it was a different story. School began for me too bringing a little normalcy to my life. I had signed up for more education classes. It was too late for me to switch my major from athletics to education, but taking the requirements would open up a few more doors.

Entering the classrooms for the first time, I desperately looked around for Quin. In spite of being a genetics major, he had taken a class on childhood education. He might have taken another. If he did, it wasn't any that I had signed up for. And with a campus of 30,000 students, the odds were slim that I would randomly run into him.

Knowing that, I considered going to his dorm to see if he was there. There had to be a reason he hadn't contacted me back, though. Maybe the darkness I had fallen under was causing me not to think straight. But if he had wanted to see me again, he would have replied to any of my dozen texts, wouldn't he?

It was hard for me to believe that it had ended how it had, but it did. Quin was the one person I thought wouldn't care that I couldn't play football. Yet, he had vanished the same moment everyone else had.

Doing what I could to regain my sanity, I focused on class instead of everything else going on. But every time I did, I would remember that Quin had helped me overhaul the way I took notes and studied. I would remember how into it he was and how it would make me laugh. I would then spiral off into a million other things about him that I missed.

After that I would think about all of the things he could tell me about the creature whose wing hogged my couch. The only thing that would snap me out of it would be hunger or the beep of the scanner at work.

Lost in a spiral of thoughts about Quin, it was a beep that brought me out of it this time. Remembering where I was, I looked at the monitor doing my job. The image that came up was for someone named Louis Armoury. It made me think of Quin's friend Lou.

Not bothering to look, a second name quickly appeared, Quinton Toro. My heart stopped. My face immediately got hot and my eyes flicked up.

It was him. I couldn't breathe. He and Lou were ten feet in front of me and neither of them was looking my way.

I froze not knowing what to do. He hadn't died or dropped out of school. There he was. Even if he had lost his phone, he could have found a way to contact me. I had been injured. It was his job as a friend to reach out.

Do I speak to him now?

As they passed, Lou seemed his usual energetic self. As he spoke, his arms bounced around wildly. Quin, on the other hand, looked like he had the weight of the world on his shoulders. He looked achingly sad. My chest clenched feeling his pain. Why was my Quin so sad?

"Quin!" I said unable to stop myself.

Both guys turned and stared at me. Quin had a look of shock that melted into elation that quickly dissolved into distress and then finally panic. He backed away as if he had seen a ghost and then ran. What was going on with him?

"Stay away from him!" Lou told me as if I had ruined his life.

I was in shock. What was I supposed to say to that?

"Wait! I don't understand. What did I do?"

"Just stay away," Lou said before retreating down the hallway and into the facility.

I sat frozen and dumbfounded. What could I have done that would elicit that reaction from Quin? Was he traumatized by watching me break my leg? That was ridiculous, but it was the only thing I could think of.

With everything that had happened between us, I knew I couldn't let things end with him running away from me like that. I at least needed an explanation. If I had done something, I needed to know what it was.

Leaving the desk unattended, I grabbed my crutches and rushed after them. The hallway spilled out into the multi-purpose room. There was a juice bar on the right, an area with weights in the middle, and a rock-climbing wall on the left. I couldn't be away from my desk for long so I chose a direction and took a shot.

Heading to the rock climbing wall, my gaze bounced onto everyone in the area. I thought I had chosen wrong until I saw my guy sitting on the mat with his face in his hands and Lou comforting him. I needed to know what was making Quin so upset. I needed to save him from it.

"Quin!"

Quin looked up in a panic about to flee.

"Please don't go. I can't move that fast and I can't stay that long. But, I need to know. What did I do? Why do you hate me so much?

"I thought we had a good thing going. But then I got hurt and you disappeared. Now you're running from me like you're scared for your life?

"None of it makes sense. You used to be the one thing in my life that made sense. Help me understand what changed. You owe me that much. Please!"

Both Quin and Lou stared at me as if I had three heads. Why wasn't anyone saying anything?

"It's your father," Quin spat.

I jolted shocked. Of all the things he could have said, that was the last thing I would have guessed.

"What about my father?" I asked hesitantly.

Quin didn't reply.

"He threatened to gut Quin like a pig if he contacted you again. He said he would kill Quin, then he would kill me, and then he would go after Quin's family."

The words hit me like a punch in the face. I had to force myself to speak.

"He what? When?"

"At the hospital," Quin said gathering himself and standing up.

"You came to the hospital. I didn't think you did."

"Of course I came."

Lou added, "We waited in the waiting room for two hours to see you."

"So, what happened?" I said looking between the two.

"Your father pulled me into a room, stuck something sharp against my stomach, and said that he knew what I was and would kill me if I contacted you again."

"I can't believe this!" I said with my mind swirling.

"You can't tell him we spoke to you," Quin pleaded.

"My father's gone."

Quin stared at me confused. "What do you mean "gone"?"

"I mean, when I came home from the hospital, his truck was there but he wasn't."

I paused and considered what I could say in front of Lou. I didn't know how much he knew about Quin being a shifter.

"He had been threatening to leave me for years. I think he did it. I don't think he's coming back. I don't think you have to worry about him anymore."

"Cage!" A voice called from behind me.

I turned. It was my boss.

"You can't leave the desk unattended."

"I'm sorry. I'll be right there."

I turned back to Quin.

"I don't know what to say about what happened to you, to both of you. All I can tell you is that I'm sorry. I never meant to put you in a spot like that. If you don't want to ever speak to me again, I get it. But, I wish you would. Maybe we could just get together and talk? Crazy things have been going on."

"Cage!"

"Coming! Please, Quin. Please," I said not wanting to leave his soft, vulnerable eyes but knowing I had to.

Chapter 11

Quin

"You know that if you go talk to him and his father finds out, you're putting everyone you know at risk, right? Including me," Lou asked.

Lou was right and that was the reason I never replied to any of Cage's texts. I wanted to. When they appeared on my phone it would tear me apart. I wanted to be with him. I wanted to take care of him and relax in his arms. But I couldn't.

Cage's father was something ungodly. Even my wolf feared him. When I had finally shifted back, I was naked miles away from school. Walking back to civilization took more than a day. Once there I told the first person I met that I had been robbed and borrowed their phone.

Lou, bringing clothes, got a rideshare and picked me up. I didn't tell him about what I saw in Cage's father's eyes because I was still figuring it out. He was already dealing with enough having seen me shift for the first time. He didn't need to know that the thing that had threatened his life was evil incarnate.

"He said his father was gone," I reminded Lou.

"But, what does that mean? Gone for the weekend? Gone for a vacation? Will he be back in a week or a month?"

"If you don't want me to talk to him, I won't. I'm not going to put you in danger. Tell me not to and we'll leave through the back door right now."

I tried not to look desperate to get his approval but I couldn't help it. Everything in me pleaded for him to say it was okay. I needed to talk to Cage. The pain of being away from him kept me from eating and sleeping. Lou had suggested coming to the activity center because all I had the strength to do was lie in bed and he was worried about me.

"Lamb Chop, you can't not see him because of me. You know I can't do that to you."

"How about this? I could talk to him and find out if his father is really gone. If I get the sense that he could be back at any minute, or if he's coming back at all, I'll walk away. In that case, it wouldn't be because of you. It will be because I can't trust him. And, if I can't trust him, then what would be the point of being with him?"

Lou smiled. "Well, there's a little more to being with someone than that. But I appreciate what you're saying."

He closed his eyes and sighed with resignation.

"I trust you, Lamb Chop. Go talk to him. I know you wouldn't put me or anyone you cared about in danger. And, for what it's worth, I don't think Cage would put you in that situation either."

"You sure, Lou. Because I don't have to."

Lou chuckled. "You have to. Don't pretend that you don't. Go. I'll just be here climbing this wall on my own."

Lou looked around and spotted a cute, dark-skinned guy putting on climbing shoes.

"Unless I can get that scrumptious bit of man meat to tie me up."

"Isn't the phrase, 'Tie you in'?"

"You heard what I said. Go. I have some rope work to do."

I watched as Lou walked over to the guy and struck up a conversation with him. That was immediately followed by Lou stretching in front of him. The guy was interested.

It amazed me how easy it was for Lou to talk to guys. He didn't know if they would be into other guys or not. He just did what he wanted to do and somehow it always worked out. It was like he had some sort of device that could tell him which guys were open to being with guys. It was like a built-in radar or something.

As smart as I was supposed to be, I could never tell what anyone else was thinking. That's what made parties so uncomfortable for me. If I could predict peoples' behaviors, I could relax.

But, for me, people were a series of random events. They rarely did what they said they wanted to do making it hard for me to tell when they were joking. Why couldn't they just say what they were thinking and do the things they say they want to do?

As smart as I was supposed to be, I could never tell what anyone else was thinking. That was one of the reasons I liked being around Cage. Yeah, he was the hottest guy ever. But, more than that, he was easy. He did what he said he was going to do.

Cage shared things about himself that told me who he was. He was exactly the man he presented himself as. He was the type of guy I could shut off my brain and relax with. I always felt safe when I was around him. So, why would I question whether he would keep me safe now?

Realizing that there wasn't a reason, I turned to the hallway to the front desk and headed back to Cage. As he came into view, our eyes met. He made me melt. The tingles were back.

"You came," Cage said telling me how much he wanted me here.

"Before you say anything, I need to know for certain. Will your father be coming back."

Cage opened his mouth to speak and then lowered his head instead.

"I don't know."

"I thought you said he was gone?"

"I did. And, he is. But, he's my father. I don't want him to be."

"Do you know where he went?"

"No. And, there's something else. Something you might know about."

"What?" I asked concerned by the look in his eyes.

Cage's eyes darted around looking for anyone listening. When he didn't find anyone, he opened his mouth struggling for words.

"I know you said you were that thing you are."

I rocked back onto my heels. I hadn't expected this to be what he was asking about, but of course it was. I settled myself and prepared for whatever he might say next.

"It's called a wolf shifter. What about it?"

"The articles I read said that you were the only one. Is that true?"

"There's only me," I said stoically.

"Do you know if dragons exist?"

Of all of the things I had prepared myself to hear, that was not one of them.

"Dragons? No. They're made up," I explained insulted that he would have made such a leap. Wolves were real things that existed, dragons were not. The next thing he would ask me about were fairies.

"Are you sure? Because I think there's one dead in my living room. And I think it could be my father."

"What?"

"Yeah.

Dragons are real. What the hell is going on, Quin?"

Cage looked at me with such desperation that I knew he wasn't making this up. Dragons? Dragon shifters? It couldn't be. Of course...

"Your father's eyes..."

"What?"

"When he threatened me, his eyes shifted. They became inky black and they felt like they were swallowing me."

"Then it's true. That thing is my father. I didn't want it to be but somehow I knew it was."

"You say it's dead in your cabin?"

"I think it is. It's been laying there since I got back from the hospital. I've kicked and punched it and it hasn't moved. At the same time, it's not decaying. I don't know what's going on with it."

"Can I see?" I asked knowing I was taking a risk. If it wasn't dead and it was Cage's father, it could come after me like it promised.

"Yeah, of course. And maybe when you see it, you could tell me what I am," Cage said vulnerably.

Oh right! If Cage's father is a dragon shifter, what did that make him? Could that be why I'm so drawn to him? Maybe I've been sensing his difference.

As much as I wanted to rush there right then, we made arrangements to meet at his place the next morning, a Saturday. It was good because it gave me time to process everything. Dragon shifters? What had my father done to create me? Could I have as easily ended up with scales and wings?

I needed to talk to my father about this, but not yet. I needed more information. First I needed to make sure that what Cage was saying was true. After that, I had to figure out where it came from. Could I be from there to? Was everything my father told me about myself a lie?

Maybe I wasn't the only wolf shifter to exist. What would that mean if it were true? And if Cage were a dragon shifter like his dad, what did that mean about us… if there was an "us".

Didn't he still have a girlfriend? He hadn't mentioned her, but he never did unless I brought her up. I needed to know where I stood with him before risking the lives of everyone around me. I also needed a way to show him why he should be with me if he was still with her.

"I brought ice cream," I told him when I arrived at his place the next day.

"You brought ice cream?" he asked me standing in front of his closed front door.

"And a few other things. Milk, juice, a couple of frozen pizzas, a couple of TV dinners... and ice cream."

"So, you brought groceries?"

"You said your father was gone. I didn't know who did the shopping. And I was already at the grocery store..."

"Getting ice cream..."

"Yeah. So, I figured why not pick up a few things. You could always just stick them in your freezer if you don't want them."

Cage chuckled. "Thank you. You're gonna make it really hard for me to stop dreaming about you."

"Who says I want you to?" I asked feeling my cheeks flush.

"Good point," he said looking at me like he wanted to kiss me.

I didn't know what to do. I wanted to kiss him too. But...

"Before we go any further or before I see whatever it is you want to show me, I need to know, what am I to you?"

"What do you mean?"

"Am I just a friend or a wolf shifter who might have answers? I could be putting my life in danger by doing this. I mean, I'll probably still help you no matter what you say. But, I need to know."

I stared at Cage feeling more naked than I had ever felt after a shift. I wanted to run and hide, but I wasn't going to back off. Not this time. Even standing a foot from him, my heart ached to be closer. So, before whatever was about to happen next, I needed to know if he could ever love me.

Cage stared at me unflinching.

"That's right. You don't know."

"Know what?" I asked practically shaking.

"Tasha and I broke up. Or, I guess it would be more accurate to say that she broke up with me."

"She did. Why?"

"For the same reason I would have broken up with her if she hadn't beat me to it. We're both in love with someone else."

I froze. Did he just say what I thought he did?

"Who's that?"

Cage laughed. "Well, for Tasha, I'm pretty sure it's Vi. For me, it's… you."

I stared at him. My wolf was going wild. I, on the other hand, didn't know what to say.

"Oh."

"Oh? You sure you don't want to say anything else?" Cage asked amused.

"Thank you?" I said at a true loss for words.

Cage stared at me stunned. "Okay, then. How about I just show you what you came to see?"

"Sure," I said proving once again why I was going to die alone.

Here he was telling me he loved me, the thing I had been hoping to hear since the moment I met him, and all I could say is "Thank you." What was wrong with me?

Cage, looking as confused as I felt, chuckled ironically and then opened the door revealing something beyond my imagination. Everything Cage had said was true. There was a dragon laying belly up between his kitchen and living room. It looked like it was sleeping if not dead. What the hell was going on?

"Can you take these?" I said handing the grocery bags to Cage without taking my eyes off of the beast in front of me.

"I'll put it in the freezer," he said before pushing past the creature as if it was a novelty bean bag.

Seeing him interact with it so casually, I relaxed and moved in for a closer look. Approaching it I smelled something familiar. It was the same scent that I smelled the night I came over and when his father pushed his body against mine in the hospital. It was possible that the smell was just lingering in the room. But I didn't think so.

"What do you think?"

Cage asked me nervously.

"I can't be sure. There's something I can do that will give me more information, but it might freak you out."

"More than having a dragon in my living room that might be my father?"

"Good point," I said realizing that he was way beyond being startled by anything I could do. "I could shift into my wolf and let it take a look."

"Shift into your wolf?"

"Yeah. You had said you wanted to see it, right?"

"I did." Cage paused looking down at the beast. "Does it hurt?"

"Shifting?"

"Yeah. But you get used to it. And afterwards there's a bit of a rush that makes you forget about it. I imagine it's like giving birth."

"So, it's like something else I can't relate to?"

"It's exactly like it," I said trying to lighten the mood.

Cage laughed. I had forgotten how much I liked the sound.

"Okay. So, do you need me to leave the room or something?"

"You can if you want. You don't have to, though. I think my wolf likes you. Let me rephrase that. I don't think, I know he does. On that, we agree," I said with a smile.

"Okay. Cool. Then, do I just stand here?"

"Wherever's fine. I've never really practiced shifting. Most of what my father taught me was how not to shift. But there's something about being around you that brings my wolf to the surface. I think if I just let it, it will come out."

Cage lifted his hands telling me to take the floor. I did. And closing my eyes to center myself, I shifted immediately. I wasn't ready for it. I was planning on undressing first. Instead, I lay on the ground floating behind my wolf's eyes tangled in cloth.

Scrambling to his feet, my wolf looked at Cage. I had understated how much he liked Cage. I was sure Cage would freak out from how much he was staring at him. He didn't. He stepped closer and offering my wolf his hand.

Doing what I wished I could, he sniffed his fingers and pushed his head into them. He wanted Cage to touch him. He wanted to be covered in his scent. Cage pet him like a long lost pet and it filled him with warmth.

The sensation overwhelmed the both of us until something else snatched his attention. I had been right, the smells were the same. This was unquestionably Cage's father. Now the question was whether he was still alive.

With my wolf standing still, the room's sounds encircled us. He was like a guide through all of them. He was listening for a heartbeat that never appeared. There was something coming from it, but it was hard to say what it was.

Was it the sound of flowing blood or a slowly decaying carcass? It was too faint to know for sure. But what I could be sure of was that the dragon had left a scent trail that led somewhere outside.

My wolf trotted to the door and looked back at Cage to be let out. Cage obliged and I thought it would result in him taking me on another ride to who knows where. It didn't. He instead moved to a few feet past the door and stuck his nose in the air.

I could smell it too. The dragon had flown here and its path from where it came from was laid out before me like a colorful ribbon. Cage needed to know this. So, without having to negotiate it with him, I shifted back into myself ending on my hands and knees.

"Oh!" Cage said quickly looking away.

That's right, I was completely naked. It didn't embarrass me as much as it titillated me. I didn't have to see myself to know that I was turning red.

"I'll get your clothes," he volunteered.

"Thanks," I said before getting dressed and returning to the cabin.

"What's the verdict?" he asked me.

"It's your father."

Cage looked at me hesitant to ask what came next. "Is he... alive?"

"I don't know. I don't hear a heartbeat. But, do dragons even have hearts?"

"My father didn't. But that could be more psychological than biological," Cage said with a painful smile.

I didn't know how to reply to that.

"I do have some good news, though."

"You do? What?"

"I might be able to lead you to wherever it was before it arrived here and ended up like this," I told him.

Cage looked at me stunned.

Chapter 12

Cage

"How? It's been here like this for at least two weeks."

"It has a very distinct scent. There's still a trail."

"What would he have to do to follow it?" I said referring to the wolf as Quin had.

"He would just have to come out and do what he does. We could either pack some supplies and hike through the woods for a couple of days to find it. Or, we could hop in your truck and I could stick my nose out of the window in my wolf form."

"And you're sure your wolf likes me, right?" I asked knowing that we would be trapped in a small space together.

"I'm positive," Quin said with a blush.

"Okay, then let's do the truck thing but we should eat something before leaving. I'll warm up one of the pizzas for lunch. Are you hungry?"

"There are things I wouldn't mind getting into my mouth, but I don't know if it's pizza," Quin immediately regretted what he said. "I'm sorry, I'm not very good at flirting. I guess I like you so much that I forget how to use words sometimes."

"Did you just say you liked me?" I said feeling it swirl around my insides like warm caramel.

"Of course I like you. I've liked you from the moment I saw you at the party. The night we met I was hoping you were going to take me home and do things to me. I could barely breathe the weeks I was away from you. I…"

And that was when I kissed him.

His lips were a soft peach pressed against mine. Tense at first, they slowly loosened. As they did, I slid my hand around the nape of his neck pushing my fingers through his curly dark hair. His head fell into my grasp.

Gently parting my lips, he followed. Tilting my head, my tongue entered his mouth in search of his. They touched with a spark.

Curving the tip of my tongue inviting his, our tongues danced with one another. Tingles raced up and down my body holding him. My cock grew hard as I lost myself.

Not knowing if Quin wanted this, I loosened my grip about to let go. That was when Quin pushed his hands up my side and onto my back. He pulled my chest onto his removing the space between us. When he did, my hard cock pressed onto him.

The blood that rushed to my head made me lightheaded. I wanted to be with him so badly that I ached for him. And when I felt his hard cock push against my thigh, I nearly lost it.

I pulled my lips away from his burying my cheek into his mess of hair.

"Don't stop," he whispered making it even harder for me to let him go.

"I shouldn't distract you. This is important to me," I told him not sure if it was more important than kissing him.

Quin didn't reply, nor did he move. We both kept holding each other with our hard dicks pressed against one another. With him in my arms, I wondered what his soft lips would feel like around my cock. I flinched thinking about it. Quin felt it and his cock flinched in reply.

Jesus, I wanted him. I wanted everything about him. But, I wanted the first time we were together to be somewhere special and meaningful. I didn't want it to be an intermission from tracking down whatever did this to my dragon shifter dad.

"I really care about you," I whispered, my lips right above his ear.

"I care about you too," Quin told me before slowly loosening his grip.

Our release was gradual and painful. It took everything in me to peel off of him.

After eating one of the frozen pizzas Quin had brought, he shifted, I collected his clothes, and we both got into my truck. I wasn't sure how this was going to work. But when he looked at me and then stared at the road leading left, I understood.

We drove for over an hour like this. It was weird how natural it all felt. I was in the truck with someone who had shifted into a wolf and it was telling me where to drive. I should have been freaked out. Yet, there was something inside of me that was energized.

Nothing changed until we had spent 20 minutes on a small county road and the wolf suddenly got restless. Frantic, it looked at me and growled. The hairs on the back of my neck prickled.

What was I supposed to do? I was locked in a box with a creature that could tear me to shreds if it wanted to. The only thing I could think of was to stop the truck. When I did, it stopped growling and paced back and forth on the bench seat. It was acting like it needed to get out.

Risking my life, I leaned past it and opened the passenger door. As soon as I did, the wolf sprinted out. It was heading back up the road. I pulled the truck over and slowly got out. Having entered the mountains, the temperature had dropped tremendously. I stuck my hands in my pockets and tensed to stay warm.

I was expecting the wolf to keep running forever, but it didn't. It ran for a hundred feet and then sniffed frantically. It circled a particular area and ran into the woods. It was gone for less than a minute before crossing the street and disappearing on the other side.

I didn't know what to do as I stood chilled to my bones waiting for him. Looking around, I did my best to figure out what was going on and then noticed the remnants of a stone wall. I was about to take a closer look when the wolf returned and shifted.

In moments, Quin was standing naked in front of me. I couldn't help but sneak a peek at his body. God was he gorgeous. And the way he approached told me that he didn't feel the freezing temperature at all and that he felt no self-consciousness about being undressed.

"There's something here," he said.

"Something like what?"

"I don't know. But, the trail just stops. And when we drove into it, he lost his sense of smell. Whatever it is continues for as far as he went on either side," Quin told me suddenly contracting. "It's cold here."

That was my signal. I took off my shirt and put it on him. I then wrapped my arms around him and hurried him back to my truck. When we got there, he climbed in and got dressed. Even though he had been standing in front of me naked moment before, I gave him privacy. When he was clothed and settled, I joined him.

"Do you know where we are?" Quin asked me shivering.

I turned on the truck and the heat.

"I've had the map on my phone on, but according to it, there's nothing out here."

"There's something here. I don't know what. But, it makes him uneasy. It was like he couldn't breathe even though he could. I guess it felt like if you suddenly went blind."

"And you've never experienced anything like that before?"

"Nothing."

"I saw what might have once been a wall back there."

"I saw that too. My guess is that none of this is a coincidence."

"Do you think we should keep going?" I asked hesitantly.

"Shouldn't we? Don't you want answers? I know I do."

"I do too."

"Then, let's keep going," he said with a smile.

Driving for another half-mile, we entered what looked like a functioning town. Although it couldn't have much of a population, there was a gas station, a restaurant, and a mom-and-pop grocery shop.

"What do we do?" I asked as Quin scanned our surroundings intensely.

"Let's go say hi?"

"I had to force you to go to a party back on campus, yet this is where you're choosing to be social?" I asked teasingly.

"Somewhere here could be answers. And not just to where the dragon came from or who he was... or, who you are. There could be something here that will tell me what I am.

"I'm thinking that whatever is dampening my sense of smell was designed to keep people like me out. But, why would they be keeping my kind out if I'm the only one like me who exists?"

Pain gripped my chest hearing Quin's words. I understood what this meant for him. But, what it meant for me was just as important. The thing lying dead or comatose in my kitchen was my father. Did that mean that I am what he is? At some point, was I going to sprout wings and fly away?

We both needed answers. Here was where we were most likely to get them.

"Where do we go?" I asked.

"Should we see if the general store has jackets?"

I parked the truck in front of the quaint wooden building and took a breath.

"Are you okay?" Quin asked watching me stare at the building.

"It's a little overwhelming."

"It is for me too. You would think that shifting into a wolf would prepare me for dragons and magical barriers. But, nope. It's all nuts."

His admission made me feel better. I had thought that I was the only one having a hard time with all of this. It was good to know that I wasn't alone.

The two of us left the comfort of our heated truck and were hit by the biting cold evening air. I had a bit of bulk to me to keep me warm, but I could see the cold air cut through Quin like a knife. It was only a few feet to the door, but I quickly wrapped my arms around him. Holding him like I was, aroused me immediately.

Scrambling into the general store, I wasn't quick to let him go. A bell sounded when we entered. Still holding Quin, a portly, dark-skinned man with a friendly face approached.

"Can I help you two?" He said in a way that told us he was surprised to see us here.

"Yes. Do you sell jackets?" I said forgetting that Quin was still in my arms and that there was anything unusual about it.

"We sell a few. They're right over here," he said leading us to the far side of the small store. "You two here to check out the falls?" He asked confused.

"The falls?" Quin replied holding onto my waist not allowing me to let go.

"That's how most people end up here. They make for incredible viewing this time of year."

"Are they frozen over?" I replied.

"They are. You should go see them on your way out of town."

Was he trying to get rid of us or being practical?

"Thanks for the tip. But that's not what brought us here," Quin volunteered.

"No? Then what did?"

"We were looking for someone. We thought he might have passed through here."

"You were looking for someone. And you think they might have come here?"

"Yes. Is that strange?" Quin asked narrowing his eyes on the portly man.

"No. Not at all. We don't get a lot of visitors but we get a few."

"Because of the falls?" I asked.

"Yeah," he said offering us his first smile. "Who did you say you were looking for?"

"He's about 5'10". Red hair, red face. Maybe a little rough around the edges. It would have been about three weeks," Quin explained.

"I can't say that I've seen anyone like that around here. But, you know who might have? Sonya. She runs the bed and breakfast. It's close by. You should stay the night and check out the falls in the morning. It's also an interesting town with a bit of a history. It was established in the 1920s by a couple of moonshine runners."

"Really?" I asked hiding my confusion by his sudden change of tone. Minutes earlier it felt like he was trying to get us to leave. Now he seemed to be trying to get us to stay.

"Yes, it's all very interesting. But the person who could tell you more about it is Sonya. She's also the town's unofficial historian. My husband also knows quite a bit, but Sonya is the one who enjoys talking about it. Tom can be a bit of a grump sometimes. You two married?"

It was only then that I let go of Quin. I don't know why I did. It wasn't like the idea of marriage scared me. And, it wasn't like I wouldn't consider spending my life with Quin. I guess I wasn't ready to be asked something like that considering Quin and I were still just figuring things out.

"No," I volunteered so Quin wouldn't have to. "Just friends."

"Good friends," Quin added making me feel tingly.

"How did you two meet?"

"We attend East Tennessee University. He was a brilliant tutor. I was the dumb jock," I said with a chuckle.

"Yep, my Tom is the brilliant one between us. He's a doctor. I think it's important to find someone out of your league," he said giving me a wink.

I laughed. "Well, Quin here is definitely out of my league."

"That's not true," Quin objected. "You're out of my league. The star quarterback?"

"Not anymore," I told our new friend as I pointed at my cast.

"Oh!" He said looking down at it. "I think we also have some crutches around here somewhere. If you need to use them, I'll get them for you. You can just return them before you leave."

"Wow! Thanks. I guess it is starting to hurt a little."

"I'll go get them," he said quickly heading to the back of the store.

"He's so friendly," I told Quin.

"He really is. Do you think we should stay over?"

"I thought you were saying that we should get back."

"I was just seeing what information he would volunteer. He is clearly trying to get us to stay."

"Isn't it cool that he thought we were together and he was still being so friendly?" I asked.

"I noticed that too. I didn't expect to feel so welcomed in Tennessee."

"Hold on there. There are a lot of welcoming people in Tennessee. You met me in Tennessee."

"You know what I mean. East Tennessee isn't exactly New York City."

"You mean because the whiskey is so much better?"

"Yes, that was exactly what I meant."

I looked at Quin surprised. "Is that sarcasm I detect?"

Quin looked at me as if I had caught him doing something wrong.

"No. Sarcasm works on you. It gives you a bit of an edge," I said with a smile.

"So, you like bad boys?"

"I like whatever you are," I told him meaning it.

Quin stared into my eyes melting my heart.

"Sorry about that. It took me a while to find them back there," the man said returning to us.

"No problem," I said tearing myself away from the guy I could look at for hours.

"We'll take these jackets," Quin said handing them to our friend.

"Oh! I don't think I can…"

Quin cut me off. "I got it."

"You sure?"

"Of course. Don't worry about it. Maybe you can think of some way of paying me back for it," he said with a smile.

"Maybe," I replied.

Yeah, he was getting good at flirting. I had to stick my hand in my pockets to hide how good he was getting at it.

"I'm sorry, what was your name?" Quin asked as he approached the cash register.

"Glen."

"Glen from the general store. Got it."

"And you are?" Glen asked.

"I'm Quin and this is Cage."

"Nice to meet you two."

"Nice to meet you two. Did you want directions to the bed and breakfast?"

Quin looked back at me as if he was still thinking about it. I knew it wasn't up to me. I couldn't afford to pay for it if I wanted to.

"Sure, why not," Quin said with a smile.

"Excellent. The place is run by Sonya. She likes it when you call her Dr. Sonya probably because Tom hates it. "She's not a medical doctor," he says. I keep telling him, you don't have to be a medical doctor to be called a doctor. But he's just a grump," Glen said with a smile.

Slipping on our jackets, we returned to the truck feeling really good about the town. Glen made a great first impression.

The bed and breakfast was a half-mile away. It was easy to imagine the walk into town being a relaxing experience. It was now dark, but even in shadows, the place looked like a postcard.

The bed and breakfast had to be the highlight. It was a converted farmhouse and looked expensive. There was a large veranda surrounding the mocha, shingled, exterior, and a short flight of stairs that led up to it.

Standing outside the main door was a petite woman in her early 60s who wasn't wearing a jacket. She had to be freezing as she hugged herself for warmth.

"Welcome!" The woman said with an engaging smile.

"Hello," I said waiting for Quin and putting my arm around him as we approached. If people were going to mistake us for a couple and Quin was going to play along, I was going to make the most of it.

"Glen told me you would be heading over. Come in, come in. It's cold out here."

Stepping inside, the interior didn't disappoint. It was quaint but clean and very well put together. The floors throughout and the walls of the entrance were dark honey wood. The living room furniture was beige with floral print and comfortable looking. And the small tables that lined the room were dark wood and elegant.

"We can't afford to stay here," I whispered to Quin before remembering that he summered on a private island. "I mean, I can't afford to stay here."

"Don't worry about it," Quin said sincerely. "Affording places like this is the upside to my crazy life. Let me share it with you," he said with a smile.

I felt uneasy watching him pay for our room without me being able to help. But I knew the only alternatives would be driving the two hours back or sleeping in my truck. I wasn't about to make Quin suffer to satisfy my pride.

"Okay," I told him knowing the only issues were in my head.

"Glen said you're in town to see the falls," the energetic woman said in a faint Jamaican accent.

"Quin?" I said not sure what he was going to say.

"We're actually in town looking for somebody. Glen said you might have seen him."

"You're looking for someone? What does he look like?" She said focusing a suddenly intense gaze on Quin.

Quin described my father again.

"I haven't seen anyone who looks like that. Why are you looking for him?"

I looked at Quin unsure what he wanted to say.

"He's Cage's father. He's missing and we think he passed through here."

"Why would you think that?"

"Just a hunch," Quin replied.

The woman's green eyes narrowed on Quin. "Do you get hunches often?"

I turned to Quin wondering how he would respond to the unusual question.

"Not more than anyone else," Quin said brushing the question aside.

The woman relaxed. "Me neither. But, you know who might be able to help you, Titus? He gives tours of the falls. I could have him give you a tour in the morning if you want."

"Titus?" Quin asked.

"He's someone about your age. He's a great guy. You'll love him. I'll let him know."

It was then that someone descended the stairs. He had Dr. Sonya's shiny dark hair and smaller build. He looked about 17 but could have been younger. And he didn't have anywhere near Dr. Sonya's rapid-fire energy.

"Mom, do you know where my sneakers are? I can't find them," he said intently staring at the two of us.

"If you put it back in the same place when you take them off, you wouldn't have to go searching for them every other day," Sonya said with the exhaustion of a mother.

"Mom!" He said embarrassed.

"I'll help you look for them later. Why don't you prepare room two for our guests. I'm sorry, what're your names?"

"I'm Cage and this is Quin."

"You know me. And this is my son Cali."

"Hi," he said with a shy smile. The kid stared at us fascinated. I didn't think he meant it to be rude. But, considering I was new to showing affection for another guy, it made me self-conscious.

"Cali? Now," his mother said sending him back upstairs.

Sonya rolled her eyes as if to say, "Kids."

"Everyone's so friendly here," I told her finally letting go of Quin.

"It's a very friendly town. And you two will find yourselves very comfortable here. Glen and Tom are our resident gay couple but don't think they are the only ones. I used to teach at the school. Believe me, I know," she said with a smile.

"Have you lived here long?" Quin asked again turning into the detective.

"I moved here three years before Cali was born. I was just fascinated by the history.

"So, about 20 years?"

"This June," Sonya said with a smile. "Time flies doesn't it?"

"You wouldn't happen to know of any mothers dying during childbirth or any babies going missing about 21 or 22 years ago, would you?"

"Oh, goodness no. That was before my time but it's a small town. Gossip lingers. I haven't heard anything like that, though. Is that why you're looking for your father?"

Quin looked at me surprised. I hadn't shared with him what my father had told me about my mother.

"Maybe. But it could be unrelated," I explained.

"If you want, I could ask around about both," Sonya volunteered.

"We'd appreciate that," Quin offered.

"It's ready," Cali said reappearing on the stairs.

"Cali will show you to your room. I don't know if you two have eaten yet, but the diner next to Glen's place is open until 9."

"Thank you. We'll check it out," I told her feeling very at home.

Approaching the foot of the stairs, I paused.

"I just realized I forgot the crutches in the truck."

"Do you want me to go get them?" Quin offered.

"I think I'm good," I said offering one hand to Quin while holding the railing with the other.

Cali waited for us at the top of the stairs. As soon as we got there he asked,

"Where are you guys from?"

"East Tennessee University," I told him.

"I was considering applying."

"You should. Are you a junior? Senior?"

"Junior," he said looking back at us puckishly.

"It's a good school," I told him trying to shake his gaze that had locked onto us. "Is this the room?"

"Yeah. If you need anything let me know," he said awkwardly.

"I think Titus is going to give us a tour tomorrow," I told him.

"Oh," he said immediately looking disappointed.

"Is there anything in particular that we should see?"

"The falls are cool," he said smiling again.

"We'll check them out."

Cali didn't leave.

"Anyway. Thanks for showing us to our room."

"Yeah. I'm down the hall if you need anything."

"Got it," I said with a smile.

When he walked away, we entered and closed the door behind us.

"I think someone has a crush," I said to Quin who looked at me amused.

"Yeah, he couldn't stop looking at you."

"Jealous?"

"Should I be?" Quin asked with a smile.

"You never have to worry about me wanting to be with anyone other than you," I told him.

Quin smiled.

"Besides, I meant, I think he had a crush on you."

"What?" Quin asked caught off guard.

"You didn't see that? He was looking at me because every time he looked at you, he would blush."

"Seriously?"

"Quin, how could you not see it? You're the most observant person I've ever met."

"I guess I don't pick up on stuff like that," he said as if realizing it for the first time.

"So, what do you think about this place? I can't tell if they're friendly or not."

"They seem to be. But there's something about how we ended up here that unnerves them. That would make sense if they know about the bubble around the town."

"And, what was up with that question about hunches? Is that something that wolf shifters have," I asked him hesitantly.

"I'm still the only wolf shifter I know of and I've never had them."

"Okay."

"But, what I'm more curious about is what you asked her. Is that how your mother died? During child birth?" he asked empathetically.

"That's what my father said... or, whoever he was. He didn't like talking about her, though. Every time I brought her up, he would act pissed off and change the topic. I always assumed it was because he was so broken up about losing her. But, I'm starting to realize that I didn't know him at all."

"So, you're thinking it's possible she could be from here. You think that's why he was here?"

"She had to be from somewhere. So did he. And there had to be a reason he came here after finding out my football career was over, right?"

Falling into silence, we both turned our attention to the one queen-sized bed. "We should get something to eat first," said Quin to break the tension and silence. Leaving our bedroom, we headed to the truck and drove to the diner.

Parking in front of it, we stared into the large windows as we approached. It was like any other in a small town. The space was aging, yet clean. The décor hinted that it had been around since the sixties. And there were no other customers inside.

"Sit anywhere. I'll be out in a second," a stout man yelled from the kitchen when we entered.

"I guess we can sit anywhere," I repeated taking Quin's hand and leading him to a booth against the wall perpendicular to the windows.

"I never asked, do you eat everything? It feels like something a boyfriend should know," I said loving the sound of it.

"I try to eat healthily, but I did stock your freezer with frozen pizzas and ice cream. And, most of that was really for me. So…"

I laughed. "Got it."

Quin had his arms relaxed on the table in front of us as he leaned towards me. I leaned forward wrapping my hands around his. I loved holding his soft hands. They were quite a bit smaller than mine.

My mind flashed on what of his I might hold later. I was about to tell him what I was thinking when the stout man from the kitchen appeared in front of us and handed us menus. I let go of Quin's hands and took the laminated sheet of paper from him.

"We're out of everything but the fried chicken, burgers, and sandwiches. We might be out of sliced ham, but I'd have to check," he said sticking around for questions.

"Well, I know what I want if you do. I'm starved."

"Burger and fries, please," Quin said handing the menu back to the stout man with the four-day stubble.

"The same," I told him handing back the menu and looking to pick up where I left off. "So, have you ever had a boyfriend?"

"No. What about you? Anyone before Tasha?'

"A few. There was a girl I dated my freshman year. That didn't last long. There were a couple of girls in high school, but none of those were very serious."

"Have you ever been in love?" Quin asked pulling out the big guns.

"I thought I was in love with Tasha. I mean, we could have been at one point. It's hard to tell now. I certainly had feelings for her. But, in the light of new experiences, I'm wondering if what I felt for her qualifies."

"Qualifies as love?"

"Yeah. I mean, it was definitely something, just not… Let's just say I've been given reasons to rethink things."

"I see," Quin said not asking any more.

"What about you? Have you ever been in love?"

"I thought I was."

"Really?" I asked surprised.

"He was a real prince."

"He was a nice guy, huh?"

"No. I mean he was an actual prince. I don't think he saw me that way, though. And he was a lot older than me."

"How much older?" I asked not expecting to hear that.

"I don't know."

"No, tell me. Was he like, ten years older or something?"

"Probably closer to 15. But, he was a great guy. I thought we had a lot in common."

"You thought you had a lot in common with a prince?"

"Not the shifter stuff, of course. But yeah. A few things."

"And you thought you were in love with him?"

"Yeah. I don't know if I would call it that any more. I mean, it was definitely something, just not... Let's just say I've been given reasons to rethink things."

I chuckled.

"I see. So, have you done anything with a guy before?" I asked feeling my hard cock pulse at the thought.

"Nothing," Quin replied glowing.

"At all?"

"No. Are you disappointed?"

"Why would I be disappointed?"

"I don't know. Because things might be easier if I had."

"Well, I haven't done anything with a guy either if that makes you feel better."

"I don't know if it does."

"I've thought about it, though. And I've thought about doing it with you."

"What have you thought about?"

I took his hands again.

"Let me see. I've thought about kissing you."

"I've thought about that," he said with a smile."

"I've thought about slowly undressing you and kissing you… there," I said suggestively.

"Where?"

"You know where. I've thought about sliding my hand down your body and taking hold of you," I said leaning in. "I've thought about taking you into my mouth. I've thought about running my tongue along the rim of your cock and seeing if I could make you squirm."

"Me too."

I stared into Quin's eyes. I never wanted to look anywhere else again. When I couldn't resist him any longer, I leaned further across the table and kissed him. Our lips lingered on one another's sending a chill down my spine. The kiss continued until the sound of someone grunting in disgust ruined the mood.

Hearing it, I lowered to my seat unsure how to feel. Still staring at Quin, he knew what I was thinking before I said anything.

"Let it go," Quin pleaded. "You know nowhere can be perfect."

Sure, I knew Quin was right. But I didn't like him having to experience that. And as long as I was around him, no one would ever disrespect Quin or our relationship.

I slowly turned searching the room for who had made the sound. Our waiter was back in the kitchen making our burgers. We probably wouldn't have been able to hear him over the sizzling if it had been him. And the only other person in the place was a young guy dressed as a busboy.

I eyed the busboy wondering how long it would take me to beat the crap out of him. The kid couldn't be more than 20 and clearly had a chip on his shoulder. His tussled, dark blonde hair highlighted his incredibly squared jaw. His angular features spoke to how lean and muscular he was. And, more than anything, he seemed like he was looking for a fight. Looks like he found one.

"You have a problem with something," I said getting him to lift his head and look at me.

"What?" He said using it as an excuse to bring his tray a little closer.

"I said, you got a problem with something?" I repeated sliding out of the booth and showing him who he was talking to.

By any comparison, I was a big guy. The only guys bigger were the 300-pound ones who hurled themselves at me on the field. This kid couldn't be more than 170 soaking wet. Yet, he kept coming like he had something to prove.

"Yeah, I got a problem with something. I got a problem with you two. Are you going to do something about that?"

"Cage, don't."

"Yeah, Cage, don't," he mocked sending my blood boiling. "You two come in here thinking you could do whatever? This ain't that type of town. We don't accept your type here."

This was it. I just needed to hear him say it and I was going to make it the worse day of his life.

"And what type are we?" I asked slowly readying to pounce.

"What type? The fa…"

"Nero!" The cook shouted cutting him off. "Come here!"

The guy shut up but didn't look away.

"I said get your ass back here. Now!"

I was ready to kick the snot out of him. But instead of him taking that final step, he looked to the ground and slithered back to the kitchen. I remained standing as I watched.

"What are you doing talking to my customers like that? I said what are you doing talking to people like that? Speak!"

"I don't know," he said avoiding the cook's eyes.

"You don't know, huh? Then get your ass out of here and don't come back until you figure it out. Go! And I'm docking you a day's pay for what you said."

"I didn't say anything!" The guy pleaded.

"You said enough. Now go before I change my mind and fire you instead."

The guy slithered out of the restaurant staring me down as he left. I was willing to finish my meal with Quin and meet him outside if he was going to wait. He didn't, though. And, it wasn't long before he disappeared into the dark of the night.

"I'm so sorry about that. The kid, he's got some problems. His mother's all messed up. I only keep him around for her.

"But, let me assure you that we welcome all types here. In fact, you know what, your dinners are on the house. Sorry about him again. Really," the cook said before returning his attention to our meals.

Calming down, I returned to the booth and found Quin's eyes.

"Have you ever experienced anything like that before?" I asked him knowing that I hadn't.

"Not like that. But, it's never too long before someone reminds me that I'm not like everyone else."

"You mean that you're hotter? Is that the difference you're talking about?" I asked with a smile trying to rescue the mood.

"No. But I can imagine that's an everyday problem for you," he said smiling at me.

I chuckled. "Maybe. But the only one I care who thinks that is you," I told him meaning it.

"I think it," he said allowing his soul to settle in my eyes.

"Good," I told him barely able to keep my eyes off of him.

It didn't take long after that for the cook to bring over our food and apologize again. The burger hit the spot and it was good. With dinner out of the way, all I could think of was what we were going to do next.

"Have a good night, now. I hope to see you again," the cook said as we got up to go.

"What are you doing?" I whispered as Quin retrieved a twenty from his wallet and left it on the table. "He said the burgers were on the house."

"I know but, we were the only customers there. It's a slow night for him. It's fine, Cage. Let's just go," he said leaving the money and ushering me out.

Back in the truck, I turned to him.

"You really are a great guy, aren't you?"

Quin gave me an adorably bashful smile and I immediately started thinking about all of the things I was going to do to him. I couldn't get back to the B&B fast enough. Luckily the town didn't have any traffic lights or stop signs. And when we were out of the truck and behind the closed door of our room, I stared at the drop-dead gorgeous guy in front of me and finally let myself go.

Staring into his eyes, I sprung across the room to him. With bubbling fury, I wrapped my arms around him gripping the back of his head. Meeting his lips, I became lightheaded. I wanted to kiss him forever and when he parted his lips and our tongues danced, my body sizzled needing his.

Quickly relieving him of his shirt, my lips returned to meet his earlobe. With my tongue tracing the ridges in his ear, he moaned. When it dipped in touching the outside of his canal, he giggled.

Again nibbling his earlobe, I licked the dent where his chin met his neck. I wanted to have all of him. Kissing down his alabaster skin, I had that. I wanted to know every inch of him. And, stopping on his protruding collar bone, I used my crouch to whip him into my arms and carry him to the bed.

I loved holding him. This was the way I would carry him over the threshold when the time came. I never wanted to be apart from him again. So, when I lowered him onto the center of the bed, I climbed on top of him.

With my thighs bridging his legs, he reached up and pulled off my shirt.

"Wow!" Quin moaned staring up at me.

His appreciation of my body drove me wild. Gathering his wrists, I pinned them above his head. Leaning forward, I kissed him. It was electric. It made every part of me tingle. I would have stayed there kissing him for the rest of the night if his smooth, lean chest didn't flood my mind.

I wanted to hold every part of him. I wanted to know what it felt like to caress his body with my fingertips. So, ending our knee-wobbling kiss, I sat up and wrapped my large hands around his narrow frame.

Gripping his sides, my thumbs were just inches apart. The feeling made me want to protect him. It made me want to circle my tongue around his areola. He groaned as I did, so I took it further by pulling his protruding nipple with my teeth.

It drove him wild. Teasing him, his chest rose. And, switching to the other nipple, his body danced with pleasure.

Easing my knees further down the side of his legs, I had to extend my chin to kiss the dip that fell beneath his rib cage. My hands were on either side of his hips. Tightening my grip, his jeans pressed against his flesh.

Although I was slowly kissing down Quin's stomach, my thoughts were entirely on my hands. They rounded his curves slowly heading for his zipper. I froze when my left hand touched something poking out past his hip. It was his hard cock. I hadn't been prepared for how big he was. My breath hitched.

Pushing my hand onto him, I explored him unable to do anything else. He was long and thick. I squeezed him. When I did, his cock flinched. He was very hard. That made my cock flinch in unison.

I had to touch his warm flesh. I needed to see him. So, moving my hands to his button, I unsnapped it, unzipped him, and pulled his jeans down and off of him.

Kneeling at the end of the bed, I looked down at the beautiful guy lying in front of me in his boxer briefs. He looked up yearning for my touch. His chest rose and fell waiting for my return. When he saw me shift my gaze to his underwear, his cock twitched again. That was where he wanted me and I gave him what he wanted.

Pushing my hand over his protruding cock one last time, I grabbed the band of his shorts and pulled them down. His dick was so big that I had to help it out. But when it was free, it sprung erect. It was an impressive sight. And he was large. His length and girth rivaled mine.

With him completely naked, I lost control. Pushing my hands up his thighs, both of my hands wrapped around his cock. There was more than enough of him still exposed to touch the tip of my tongue to the ridge of his head. When they connected, he inhaled.

I didn't give him a chance to relax. Teasing the ridge of his cock, his hands whipped down and grabbed the sheets. As he pulled at them, I flicked my tongue tickling him. He could barely breathe.

When he was ready to climb the walls, I did what I had wanted to do from the first time I pictured his hot body naked. Parting my lips I pushed his head into my mouth. I could taste the tang of his pre-cum. It turned me on as much as it did him. I had Quin's cock in my mouth. It was his most sensitive, secretive part and it was inside of me making us one.

Pushing him as far into my throat as I could, I released one of my hands to push further. To my surprise, my throat swallowed him. My tight muscles gripped the head of his cock squeezing the life out of it. Quin slapped the bed with pleasure. I was willing to stay like that for as long as I could, but he pulled my hair wanting to be released. Pulling him from out of my throat, he gasped panting for air.

He couldn't take being in my throat anymore, but I wasn't ready to stop increasing his pleasure. I wanted to see my boyfriend cum. So, wetting my mouth as much as I could, I stroked him with one hand while washing the ridges of his head with my mouth.

It didn't take long before his grip on my hair again tightened. He wasn't pulling me off of him. This time he was encouraging me to go deeper. Fucking him with my mouth, I jacked my hand faster. His body shifted lifting his chest. His leg muscles tightened. Then with the force of a firehose, the hottest guy I had ever seen shot his cum in my mouth.

It was like he would never stop cumming. I drank it all. Even when his fluids ceased, his cock continued flinching. Any movement I made sent his body into spasm. I couldn't move and he couldn't lift his arms.

When it felt safe to pull away from him, I released him and crawled up his body. I wanted to hold him. I wanted to cradle him in my arms and feel his warmth against my bare chest. It was incredible to have his naked body in my grasp.

I held him until he helplessly fell asleep. I loved this guy so much. Staring down at him, I couldn't figure out what I had done to be this lucky.

Quin was the love of my life. I was sure of it. And I didn't want to be apart from him again.

Chapter 13

Quin

I had really good dreams after falling asleep in Cage's arms. I hadn't meant to fall asleep. As he was giving me the most incredible sexual experience of my life, I was thinking about how much I wanted to see my boyfriend naked. I wanted to touch another man's penis for the first time. But, more than that, I wanted to feel that closeness with Cage.

That didn't happen, of course, because his blow job was too good. That's unfair to say. The truth was everything he had done was too good.

I had never been kissed like that or in any of those places. I was ready to explode so many times as his large hands moved over me. And I considered it the achievement of my life that I hadn't shifted as he did it and then howled at the moon.

I knew what I wanted next, though. I wanted to give him a fraction of the pleasure he had given me. I wanted him inside of me. I wanted the two of us to become one. I didn't care how. But if getting a blow job could feel that good, the best thing I could do would probably be to give him one back.

The thought of it sent a warm feeling rushing through me. What would it be like to hold his most intimate part in my hands? I wanted to find out.

Feeling more awake by the moment, I made my plan. Maybe I would wake him by wrapping my lips around his morning wood. That was a thing that non-virgins did, right? It had to be.

No longer feeling his arms around me, I was about to open my eyes and go in search of his body when a knock on the door snapped me awake. Remembering where I was, my eyes popped open. I looked left and then found Cage on my right. He had popped his head up as well.

Oh well, so much for waking him with a blow job. And as I thought of a new plan, I heard rustling paper. I looked at the door. The sound was coming from a note being slipped underneath it.

Feeling me move around, Cage looked over at me.

"Morning," I told him with a smile.

His tired eyes crinkled as it formed a smile in reply. "Morning. How did you sleep?"

"Like a rock. How about you?"

"I was a little restless."

"It was because I didn't give you any relief, right? I fell asleep so hard. I was going to give you a blow job to wake you up. I had this whole plan."

Cage chuckled. "That's okay. We have plenty of time for that."

"We have right now," I said with a devilish smile.

"We do. But, aren't you a little curious to find out what someone slipped under our door?"

He wasn't wrong. The intrigue of it screamed from the back of my mind. Never before had I felt more alive than I did unraveling the mystery behind Cage's past. Not only could it reveal something about what I was, but it might do the same for Cage. And doing it for him made it ten times more engaging.

I was figuring out something that would change Cage's life forever, something that he had been wondering about for a lifetime. If I could do this for him, it would be the best way to show how much I cared about him. So that meant, yes, I was far beyond "a little curious" about the note that was just slipped under our door.

"I guess," I told him not wanting him to think that I didn't want to put my hands all over him.

"Me too. I would get it but I'm a little limited," he said with a smile.

"Right! I keep forgetting that you broke your leg."

"So do I," he said with a chuckle.

"Doesn't it hurt?" I said about to get the note and then realizing I was naked and still hard as a rock.

"I wasn't kidding when I said that it hurts less when I'm around you."

"Do you think you're doing any more damage to it by walking on it?"

"That's a good question. But, I think my body would tell me if I needed to ease up. Last night when I was kneeling looking at you, I didn't feel it at all. And this morning, it doesn't feel perfect, but I wouldn't say that it hurts."

"Maybe you're running on adrenaline? It can reduce pain," I suggested.

"Maybe. But until my body tells me to pull back, why not keep going?"

"Because you know you should rest?"

"I'll rest on Monday when we get back to school."

"Hopefully we'll be able to figure out something today," I told him.

"Hopefully. Which makes me wonder what's on the note."

"Um, I would get out of bed and get it but I'm naked and really hard," I admitted.

"Is that supposed to be a bad thing?" Cage said with a smile. "I'm looking forward to the show."

Cage knew how to make me feel comfortable with anything. So, pulling off the covers, I scooted out of bed and stopped to give him a good look at my body.

"God damn, you're sexy," he said making me even harder.

When I turned, I bent over giving him a full view of my butt and hole.

"Are you trying to give me ideas?"

I stood up and faced him.

"I was hoping you had the ideas already."

"I can barely think of anything else."

It was good to hear. Without thinking if I should return to bed and collect my prize for the show, I unfolded the note and read it.

"What does it say?"

"It says that Titus is downstairs whenever we're ready for the tour."

"Titus?"

"Dr. Sonya had suggested she get someone named Titus to give us a tour of the town. I guess he's here waiting for us. What time is it?"

We both looked around for a clock. When neither of us found one, I retrieved my phone from my jeans that lay crumpled at the foot of the bed.

"My phone's dead," Cage said looking at his.

"I have a little juice left and it is 11:05 a.m.," I said shocked.

"Damn! I wonder how long he's been waiting?"

"I don't know. But did we confirm with Dr. Sonya that we wanted the tour?"

"Don't we want one, though? Didn't she say that he would be a good person to ask about my father?"

"I think so."

"Then, shouldn't we get down there?"

"Probably," I conceded.

"Could you come here for a second, though?"

I walked to his side of the bed.

"A little closer."

I got close enough for him to take my hand. He didn't.

"Closer," he said with a devilish smile.

I got as close to his head as I could get. That was when he took hold of my hard cock and wrapped his lips around it again. The sensation was coma-inducing.

He wasted no time in working his tongue around my head and stroking me off. I was able to hold back last night but I didn't have the strength this morning. I came in record speed. As I did, I placed my hand on his head to prevent myself from falling over.

"That's all," Cage said rolling off of me with a big smile on his face.

It took a moment for me to regain my bearings.

"I could have done that to you," I told him seeing my wasted opportunity.

"But, I did it to you," he said with a smile. "Staring at you all naked and hot, how was I not supposed to? Anyway, time for our tour," he said rolling out of bed knowing he had won.

I watched him thinking about how unfair it was that he had gotten to blow me twice while I still hadn't gotten to touch him. I had to figure out how to get my hands on him. And as he found his shirt and got dressed, he covered the humongous outline stretched across the front of his sweatpants. It looked like he was even bigger than I was.

"Wow!" I said letting him know what I was thinking.

"See something you like?"

"Yes, very much so."

"Maybe I'll give it to you later."

My erection which was finally shrinking after being sucked off, suddenly changed direction. I never became as hard as I was before he blew me, but I was getting close.

"Are you really getting hard again? Don't make me come over there," he said teasingly.

"Is that supposed to be a threat? Because I... um,"

I really wasn't good at this flirting thing.

"Nevermind. We should go."

Cage chuckled. "Yeah, we should."

After we both got dressed, we took turns in the bathroom and then headed down. A guy was sitting on the couch in the living room. He was tall with shaggy brown hair, a welcoming face, and a big beautiful smile. He looked like he could be twenty-one or twenty-two. Whatever he was, he looked older than I was and like he could have been in Cage's year.

"Hi," he said getting up and approaching us at the bottom of the stairs. His smile was beaming. "Dr. Sonya called me up yesterday saying you two were looking to get a tour of our fair town."

"She mentioned that you might be a good person to talk to," I told him taking the lead.

"I suppose you want to check out the falls."

"That and other things," I said looking back at Cage.

"Are you guys ready to go, or do you need some time? Dr. Sonya packed us a little brunch since you missed breakfast. I imagine you two were a little busy this morning?" Titus said suggestively. "I'm just kidding. No need to guess what two good-looking guys like yourselves were up to," he said with a knowing laugh. "Anyway, did you two want to head out?"

After all of that, I was stunned speechless. He had basically said that he knew we were having sex. As bad as I was with social things, I really didn't know how I was supposed to respond to that.

"We're ready," Cage replied jumping in.

"The falls are beautiful. They are snow-tipped if you pardon the expression. I assume they're what brought you here?"

"No. We came because we were looking for someone. Or, at least, information on them."

"Well, the population isn't that big. Who are you looking for? Maybe I've seen them."

"He has red hair, probably a stubbled beard. It would have been two or three weeks ago. His name was Joe Rucker."

"No, that doesn't sound familiar," Titus replied genuinely.

"Dr. Sonya said she'd ask around."

"She's pretty good at that. What do you think, should we go? I have the fixin's right here," he said bending down and picking up a wicker picnic basket.

"Yeah, let's go."

Titus turned and led us outside.

"I hope you don't mind if we take my truck. It seats three pretty comfortably."

"No that's fine."

"What about you... was it Cage or Quin? Which one's which?"

"I'm Cage, and this is Quin."

"What about you, Quin? Do you mind sitting in the back seat? I would suggest that you sit up front with us. It's a bench seat after all. But I figure you'll be more comfortable in the back."

"The back is fine," I said finding my voice.

"Alright then. Let's head on out."

Titus drove us back into town repeating some of the things we had already heard. The school used to be a moonshine warehouse. Glen's general store used to be the chief moonshine runner's main office, and that there used to be a wall surrounding the town. From there he made a U-turn and took us past the bed and breakfast.

"Alcohol prohibition ended in the late 1920s, didn't it?" I asked not having learned about this time in American history at my high school.

"1933," Titus corrected. "Between 1920 and 1933, this town was the richest little town in Tennessee. The amount of concentrated wealth rivaled that of Beverly Hills or downtown New York City."

"Then what happened?" Cage asked.

"The same thing that happens to most ideas when their times have passed. People moved on and moved away. There were a few people who stayed. They kept the community going through the dry times. Not alcohol dry times. Those would probably be the wet times for that.

"But the people here did what they could. At one point someone thought they could turn this place into a processing facility for Tennessee whiskey. But that didn't stick."

"I don't know if anything has," Titus explained. "We've seen some growth in population thanks to people like Dr. Sonya. And, every so often we get someone like yourselves who wonder in to see the falls. But, for the most part we like to keep the community pretty tight.

"It's a safe place to live. The people who run the town do everything they can to keep it that way. So, if you're here, you don't have to worry about anything sneaking up on you, if you know what I mean.

"Some of us might think we've cut ourselves off too much, but for the most part we're a tight knit pack."

Titus's eyes immediately bounced up to the rearview mirror staring me in the eyes. It was like he was searching for a reaction.

I hadn't missed him using the word "pack." That was what a group of wolves were called. It wouldn't be the first time someone had made that reference after realizing who I was.

Was that why he had said it? Or, was he trying to tell us something that related to why my wolf's sense of smell was still M.I.A.?

"When we were driving in, we noticed that the town wasn't on the map. Is there a reason for that?" I asked wondering how much more he would volunteer.

"I'm told it has to do with our lack of incorporation or some such thing. No one in the town has been in a rush to get it included. Don't get me wrong. There are a lot of friendly people here and they're very welcoming to the right types. But it's not always easy to tell who's the right type," he said glancing back at me again.

Cage, who had been staring out of the window lost in thought, spoke up. "By any chance, have you ever heard of someone from the town who might have died giving birth? It would have been around the time you were born."

"My memories don't go that far back," Titus said with a quick smile.

"Of course. What about any babies going missing?"

"You mean, like, kidnapped? Or, baby napped I guess it would be in this case."

"Yeah."

"Naw. I've never heard of anything like that around these parts. Does that have to do with who you're looking for?"

"We don't know," I said jumping in. "It could be unrelated. We're just getting to know the town," I said having a feeling that that would make him happy.

We fell into silence until Titus said, "I noticed your bum leg there. What's that, a sporting injury? You look like you've played some ball?"

"Football injury."

"I used to play football back in high school. We have a pretty good football program here. We don't get much of an opportunity to travel for games. Funds in this town are always a little tight. But it has potential. Do you play at East Tennessee?"

"I did. My season's over."

"Sorry to hear that. I've always thought about going there."

"Why don't you?" I asked.

"Money. Time. Motivation. Take your pick. I was thinking I could study something that I could bring back here."

"That's a great idea," I said appreciating his loyalty to the town.

"It is, but then I get stuck on what that should be."

"That's what University is for, to help you figure out what you want to do."

"Yeah, you're right. I need to give it some more thought. Now that I have two friends who attend, it might be worth considering," Titus said with another welcoming smile.

Starting about twenty minutes out of town, we began our tour of the frozen waterfalls. No one had oversold them. They were amazing looking. They all looked like they were frozen mid-stream creating icicles that were as much as twenty feet long.

"My friends and I used to skinny-dip out here when we were kids," Titus said as we stared at one of the falls from our parked truck. "When it wasn't frozen over, of course. Yeah, as beautiful as it is in the winter, they are twice as beautiful in the summer. Maybe more. They're hidden gems."

"You're right. I've never seen anything like it," I said.

"Well, that's not saying much because you're from the city," Cage joked.

"Oh, which city?" Titus asked.

"The big apple," Cage volunteered for me.

"Wow! What was that like?"

"It's... different," I told him.

"I bet it is. Are cars the only thing you hear?"

"Depends on where you are."

"I can't even imagine that. Do you hear this? It's the sweet sound of nothing. You can't beat that."

"I grew up a mile away from our closest neighbor," Cage volunteered.

"So, you two are the extremes," Titus said with a smile.

"We definitely had different experiences growing up," Cage said.

"We're not that different," I corrected not liking the distance he was putting between us.

"Come on. I can't even imagine the world you grew up in. Or, what it feels like to be in your situation."

"What situation is that?" Titus asked innocently.

Cage and I looked at each other. It was good to know that he wasn't going to blurt out anything that might make me uncomfortable.

"I grew up with a lot of pressure to do something special," I summarized.

"You never told me that," Cage said searching his thoughts.

"I thought I did when we spoke about... stuff."

"No. I remember that conversation very well. You didn't mention that."

I sighed. "Well, I do. I can't just do anything I want with my life. I feel like everyone is expecting me to do something that changes the world."

"To change the world?" Titus said jovially. "Wow! That's a bit of pressure."

"More than a bit," I clarified.

"So, how are you going to do it? What are your plans to change the world?" Titus replied.

"I have no idea. I thought I could figure it out on my own. Then I thought that I could figure it out if I backpacked through Europe. Nope. I still don't know. My father has a genetics lab. Eventually I'll join it and maybe I'll spend the rest of my life doing research."

"Those are big plans," Titus said mystified. He turned to Cage. "I suppose you're gonna do something as impressive?"

"No. My dreams have never been that big."

"What are you talking about? What about playing for the NFL?" I reminded him.

"That was never my dream. It was what other people wanted for me."

"So, what is your dream," Titus asked.

"To get married... have a family... raise a couple of kids. Maybe I could teach football somewhere," Cage said looking at me.

As nice as his dream sounded, I had to admit that it didn't fit with what I knew I had to do. My father had cursed me and the world with whatever I was. I needed to get rid of it. Seeing the dragon in Cage's kitchen did bring up a whole lot more questions. But, it didn't change the fact that my wolf killed my mother. I could never forget that.

When I didn't respond, Titus broke the tension by mentioning the food Dr. Sonya had packed for us. She had made us fried egg sandwiches with melted cheese and ham between toasted English muffins. The flavor was enhanced with a tart jam that was mixed with honey.

"They're good," Titus said enjoying one of them. "She doesn't cook often, but whenever she would bring something to a fair or school function, hers would always be the first I would check out. She's from the Caribbean, ya know? Jamaica, I think. Her jerk chicken is to die for."

"She's from Jamaica? I'm from the Bahamas," I said happy to hear that someone was from nearby.

"I thought you said you were from New York City?" Titus asked.

"He spent his summers in the Bahamas," Cage explained.

Titus just stared at me in the rearview mirror after that. I couldn't tell what he was thinking, but I felt the road being paved for him to think I was the freak everyone saw me as.

"Have we seen all of the falls?" I said wanting to change the topic.

"Not even close. I've only been taking you to the ones that didn't require much walking."

"You don't have to worry about me. I could walk a bit," Cage clarified.

"You sure?" Titus asked doubtfully.

"I don't think I could do a two-mile hike, but we could go further than we have."

"Alright then. Let's get to it," Titus said restarting his truck.

Titus drove for another twenty minutes and then parked the truck by the side of the road.

"How far is the hike?" I asked him.

"About a half a mile. Maybe a little less."

"Are you sure you're up for this? We don't have to," I said checking in with Cage.

"I'm fine. Really."

I didn't want to tell Cage he couldn't or shouldn't do it if he said he was fine. I had a hard time believing that someone who had an injury like his could hike a half-mile on it. That seemed crazy. But I had to trust Cage. No one knew how he felt except him.

The hike to the river was a snowy wonderland. We got quite a bit of snow in New York and Central Park was always nice in the winter. But I had never seen anything like this.

The deeper we got into the woods, the more snow-covered the trees became. It was beautiful. I hadn't imagined that places like this existed in real life.

The only sound I heard was the crunch of the snow under our feet. Past that, there was a light whirring as the breeze cut through the trees. It had to be one of the most relaxing experiences ever. I could feel my wolf thinking about running through the snow. I wasn't about to let him out to do it, but it energized me as we hiked.

With Titus leading, I continuously looked back at Cage to see how he was doing. He seemed fine just as he said he would be. I wasn't sure how.

The only reason I would be able to do it was because I was a wolf shifter. It caused me to heal faster than other people did. Could Cage be a dragon shifter like his father? But, if he was, wouldn't he know it by now?

I shifted for the first time within a minute of being born. Were dragon shifters different? Or, was Cage just a bad ass human with an incredibly strong will?

"This is it," Titus said leading us into a clearing.

I looked at the sight ahead of us. Forty feet away was a frozen lake that was a hundred feet across. At the far end was a thirty-foot high rock face. Stretching from the top to the bottom of it were icicles. It looked like a curtain made of ice. It was incredible.

"Wow!" I said unable to wrap my mind around the beauty of it.

"This is amazing," Cage said as blown away by it as I was.

"Come on. Let me show you something," Titus said ushering us forward.

Titus approached the edge of the frozen lake with us in tow.

"Is this safe?" I asked never having walked on ice before.

"Sure is. This has been frozen for the season. What you have to look out for is grey ice. When it's blue it's solid. When it's snow-covered like this, you have to be careful, but for the most part, you're fine."

It reassured me that Titus knew so much about frozen lakes. It was probably something every kid growing up here knew. I couldn't imagine all of the ways his upbringing was different than mine. Was Cage's upbringing more similar to Titus's?

I looked back at Cage seeing if he disagreed with Titus's assessment of the ice. When he didn't react, I took what Titus said as fact. I followed Titus's footsteps onto the ice and within a few feet, he looked back and corrected me.

"You never want to walk in a line on ice. Spread out. It reduces risk," he said.

I didn't see the logic in that, but I listened and stepped out of his cleared path. To me, Titus having walked on it was proof that the spot was strong enough to hold us. But, he grew up here while I spent winters on a tropical island. What did I know?

The further we got across the lake, the more I realized that the ice curtain in front of us wasn't a wall. It was a group of staggered icicles that appeared from a distance to be one piece. More amazing than that was the cave that was hidden behind it.

"It's a different experience in the summer when all of the water's flowing. But when everything is frozen over like this, I think it's something special," Titus said leading us through a gap in the icicles into the cave.

Standing within and looking around its ten-foot depths, I was awestruck. The sight was hauntingly beautiful.

"It's like we're in one of those survival movies," I said trying to wrap my head around what I was seeing.

"I could see that," Titus agreed. "Could you imagine Hollywood coming here and shooting a movie? That would be something, wouldn't it? This town has so much potential. All it needs is someone to recognize it and give us a chance."

"Maybe marketing could be something you study at University," I told him. "You definitely have the personality for it. You're selling us on how great it is here."

"That's something worth considering," Titus said with a smile. "I've never thought about that."

"You should listen to Quin. He's pretty smart," Cage said grabbing my attention.

It felt amazing to have a boyfriend who said nice things about me. How lucky was I? Everything I knew about him told me he was a great guy. I mean, he spent his free time playing flag football in the park with 10-year-olds. Who did stuff like that?

I smiled at Cage and reached for his hand. He took it and smiled back at me. It wasn't a blushing smile. It was one that told me he was content. I liked seeing that. I always had so much running through my mind that it was hard to find peace.

We sat in the cave and enjoyed the scenery for over an hour. Half of it was Titus answering my question about what it was like growing up here. He was a talker. That was fine, though, because he was easy to listen to. But nothing he said made me think that there was anything unusual about this place or the people in it. It was just a typical small town.

"It's getting late. You guys must be pretty hungry," Titus said finally running out of things to say.

"We could head back," Cage said checking in with me.

While we were sitting, he had pulled me into his arms. I could have stayed there forever. But, the only thing we had to eat all day was Dr. Sonya's sandwiches.

I was okay with that, but Cage was a much bigger guy than I was.

"Yeah, let's head back," I agreed. "But, this was an incredible tour. The town is breathtaking."

"Thank you! I'm glad you liked it. Remember, tell people," Titus joked as he got up.

"Or, you can tell them yourself when you start at East Tennessee next semester," I reminded him.

Titus laughed. "Right. There's that."

With Titus again taking the lead, I kept hold of Cage's hand and followed the group. I kept wondering what it was like walking in Cage's shoes so I did the next best thing. Finding his footprints in the snow, I matched our steps.

Being nearly 6 inches taller than me, his steps were longer. I had to bounce a bit to keep up. Leaping forward to match his stride, I lost my footing and slid. Slipping out of Cage's hand, the ice came at me fast. I hit the ground with a crack.

I couldn't breathe. The water was too cold. My face was going under. It was all happening too fast.

Once I realized what was going on, I started to panic. As soon as I did, I shifted. My wolf was now tangled in my clothes. Trying to free itself we started to roll.

Losing its grasp on which way was up, my wolf paddled its paws until its snout hit something hard. It was the ice sheet. It had swum past where I had fallen in.

It was so cold. Its heart pounded uncontrollably. We were going to have to calm down. How could we, though? Everything in us screamed for us to take a breath.

Forcing him and myself to slow down, we heard something. People were yelling. I couldn't understand what they were saying, but looking up, we could see their blurred images. One of them was pointing away from us. He was trying to get us back to where I fell in. They were pointing us towards the opening.

Turning around, my wolf forced its quickly freezing limbs towards the hole in the ice. The shadows above got larger. Something entered the water in front of us. It was someone's hand. It latched onto my wolf's paw and dragged us towards the opening.

With her claws free to dig into the ice, it scratched itself out of the water and into the air. Clawing, he pulled us out. When he was lying on his belly next to Cage, he sprung to her feet. Quickly looking around, we locked our gaze on Titus who was staring at us with a lot less surprise than he should have had.

"Cage, crawl back. Quin, you have to walk very carefully away from the hole," Titus instructed calling my wolf, Quin.

After Cage reached back into the water and snagged my pants, which luckily still contained my phone and cards, we both did what we were told and were eventually on what felt like solid ice. Once there, I quickly shifted back into a human. Kneeling on the ice, it took a moment for the heat from my shift to leave me. Once it was gone, I was wet and naked while kneeling on ice.

"Are you okay? You hurt?" Cage asked taking off his jacket and wrapping it around me.

That was a good question. Was I hurt? The sound of the crack as I hit the ice flashed through my mind. There was an ache in the back of my head where it had made contact.

"I think so," I said touching my head where it hit.

"Let me see. Are you bleeding?"

I removed my hand and looked at it. Cage moved around me to see for himself.

"I don't think so. I think I'm good."

"Jesus, Quin," he said again looking me in the eyes and throwing his arms around me.

"I'm okay," I assured him not convinced that I was.

"You're a wolf shifter. We didn't guess that," Titus said drawing our attention.

Cage turned to Titus angrily. "What do you mean, "We didn't guess that?" And my boyfriend just turned into a wolf. Why aren't you more surprised?"

"And, who's "we"?" I said through my chattering teeth.

"I need to take you to see Dr. Tom," Titus said calmly.

"I'm fine. I don't need to see a doctor," I told him.

"You might be. But, he's going to need to talk to you about a few things."

"Like what?" Cage barked defensively.

"Like why I'm not more surprised to find out you're a wolf shifter."

"We're not going anywhere until you tell us what's going on," Cage insisted.

"Don't do that. Quin is cold and wet. Let's at least get him to my truck. You can decide what you wannna do after that," Titus said soberly.

Cage looked at me. I was in no condition to refuse the offer.

"Okay. But we're gonna need answers."

"Dr. Tom will give them to you. And Quin, considering you're naked and barefoot, you might wanna consider shifting into your wolf for the hike back. I mean, unless Cage is planning on carrying you on a broken leg for half a mile."

I had to admit that it wasn't a bad idea. I looked at Cage for confirmation. He nodded. So, taking off his jacket, I fell onto my hands and knees and allowed my wolf to take over.

"Fuck, Titus, what the hell were you doing taking us on thin ice?" Cage yelled turning to him.

"I'm sorry. I didn't think it was thin. It's been frozen all winter. Didn't I tell him not to walk in a line?"

"Don't blame Quin for this."

"I'm just sayin', if he would have followed my instructions, nothing would have happened."

Cage stared at him angrily. "Your Dr. Tom better have some answers. That's all I'm saying."

"I promise you, he will," Titus assured us and then led us back to his truck.

Along with my wolf's body running hotter, the excretion of my fur had pushed most of the moisture away from my skin. Titus's suggestion had been even better than I had first thought. How did he know so much about being a wolf shifter?

Arriving back at the truck I was hesitant to shift back into human form. I was going to miss the warmth of my fur. It was the first time I wasn't counting the seconds before I could return.

But, when Cage opened the passenger door and took off his jacket, I did. It was clear that he wanted me back. And since I wanted nothing more than to return to his arms, I shifted.

After Cage put my wet pants on the heater vent in the back seat, he joined me up front. I cuddled against Cage's warm body.

"You're shivering," Cage told me.

"I'm alright," I assured him.

The truth was that I wasn't sure it was from the cold. I had just shifted in front of someone who had acted like he saw shifts every day. Then I hiked back to the truck not wanting to return to human form. Now we were driving to someone who might have more answers about who and what I am than I've gotten in a lifetime. A lot was going on. It was overwhelming.

By the time we were making a right turn past Glen's general store, I was, for the most part, feeling better. Lying in Cage's arms helped.

The place we pulled up to was two-stories with white siding. If I were to picture the home of a small-town doctor, it would have been this. His office was a similarly looking detached building to the left of the main house but set further back.

Putting my pants back on, the chill from the water quickly returned. Still wearing Cage's jacket, and having been blasted by the hot air in the truck, it didn't affect me quite as much. Even with there being a slight breeze, I made it to the office without my fun bits freezing off. I was happy about that. I had barely started using them for their intended purpose. I didn't want to lose them now.

"Dr. Tom?" Titus called bringing an older Latino man into the waiting room.

He was more serious-looking than his husband. He was also shaped differently. Whereas Glen was built like a teddy bear, Dr. Tom was more barrel-chested. Both looked like they enjoyed a good meal, though. This had to be what years of marital bliss in a small town looked like.

"Titus, what's going on?" The man said in a slight Spanish accent.

"He's a wolf shifter," he said casually.

"And him?" Dr. Tom said pointing at Cage.

"Nothing as far as I can tell."

Dr. Tom nodded and turned to me. "Quin, is it?"

"Yes," I confirmed.

"Why don't you join me in my office," he said leading me back.

"He's not going anywhere without me," Cage said approaching the older man threateningly.

"I'll be fine, Cage," I assured him. "I think if they were out to hurt either of us, they would have done it by now."

"He's right," Dr. Tom confirmed. "Don't worry. He'll be back in a few minutes. You can take a seat and wait," he said before turning and pointing me into his examining room.

Behind the closed door, the doctor gestured for me to sit on the metal bed in the middle of the room.

"Have a seat," he said before pulling up a chair in front of me.

I sat and looked at him awkwardly.

"So, you're a wolf shifter. That wasn't Glen's guess. He was thinking you were a Fae."

"What's a Fae?" I asked quickly cutting him off.

"That's what both Glen and I are. It's a being that is more attuned to the magic surrounding us."

"The magic surrounding us?" I said more doubtfully than I meant it to sound.

"Yes. Magic is what created creatures like you and me. I like to think of it as secret code to the universe. Fae, like myself, can sometimes hack into it. You might have noticed a difference when you entered the town."

"You mean the dome or barrier, or whatever it is?"

"It's a protection spell."

"What is it protecting you from?" I asked hesitantly.

"There are a lot of things out there that we would prefer to remain hidden from. A lot of things that would sooner kill us than live in peace."

"You mean like dragons?"

Dr. Tom looked at me suspiciously. "Yes. So you know about dragons?"

"I've run into one before. In fact, it's what led us here."

"They said you were here looking for someone. So, it was a dragon, huh?"

"That doesn't surprise you?" I asked after his casual response.

"Very little surprises me anymore. Although, I would say, if you can, you should avoid those types. They're greedy, hording, fowl tempered things. They would sooner kill someone like you than let you walk away knowing what they are."

"That sounds like the one I met," I confirmed. Although, it didn't describe Cage at all.

"What brought you in contact with it?"

Should I tell him about Cage? Considering what he thought about dragons, maybe it was better if I didn't.

"Bad luck. So, have you met any people like me before?"

"Wolf shifters? Yes."

A wave of heat flashed across my body. I felt like I was going to pass out… or shift.

"I thought I was the only one."

"Why would you think that? Don't you have a mother or father? Didn't they have a pack?"

"No. My father is a geneticist. He created me by accident."

As soon as I said it, a light flicked on behind the older man's eyes.

"You're that wolf shifter. The one the world is fascinated by."

"That would be me," I said feeling the weight of it.

"You have been a surprise," he admitted.

"How so?"

"I always thought that if the outside world knew about us, they would come after us with pitch forks. Yet, here you are still alive. There was a time when you wouldn't have been. It's not that long ago."

"Well, it's not like my life has been easy."

"I imagine it hasn't. Wolf shifters have a strong pull to be with others of their kind. They even have what they refer to as fated mates."

"What's that?"

"A fated mate is someone they're uncontrollably bound to. To be apart from them can be anything from unpleasant to incredibly painful for both involved."

"Is it possible to have that with a human?" I said immediately thinking of my feelings for Cage.

"Not as far as I know."

"I think it is," I told him.

"I have yet to see it happen. And, I'm not as young as I look."

I looked at him again. "How old are you?"

"I'm 149 years young," he said with a tight-lipped smile.

I was blown away. I thought he was going to say 65. Even that would have been a stretch considering the only hint to his aging was his speckled beard.

"That's incredible! How long do wolf shifters live?"

"Not that long, unfortunately. Most meet a violent end early. Like I said, there are lot of things out there that will hunt your type down and kill them. Hence the protective spell."

"Wait, so are you saying that there are wolf shifters in this town?" I asked suddenly unable to breathe.

Dr. Tom leaned back and crossed his arms.

"There are."

I let out a gasp.

"Where? Who?"

"There is only so much I can tell you."

"How come?"

"It could be dangerous. And, we've only just met. I might have already told you more than I should have."

"Please, I need to know more. You don't know what it's like growing up thinking I'm the only one."

"The problem is that now that I know who you are, I know the baggage that comes with you. The reason everyone was being so welcoming when you first arrived was because we suspected you were a Fae. We could tell there was something magical about you. But, wolf shifters your age aren't usually so... composed after they've started shifting. And even when Fae don't know what they are, they are able to tap into their abilities and often end up as trackers."

"I said I was here looking for someone," I remembered.

"Yes. And, Fae are even more vulnerable than wolf shifters. So, we were hoping you would stay with us. There's safety in numbers."

"So, is everyone in this town a Fae or wolf shifter?"

"No, there are human allies here too."

"Dr. Sonya?" I said suddenly recognizing the difference.

"She's human."

"Titus?"

Dr. Tom looked at me blankly. "Here's my dilemma," he said ignoring my question. "I have a spell that can make you forget everything I've told you. For the safety of the town, I can use it."

"Is there a second option?" I asked suddenly feeling like I was going to shift.

"Yeah. I can trust that you won't betray our community. It's always good to have allies."

"We'll go with option 'B'," I said with my heart pounding.

"Perhaps. But first you're going to have tell me everything you know about this dragon you're tracking."

I stared at the creature sitting in front of me wondering if he could read my mind. I didn't know what a Fae was. I didn't know what they were capable of.

I couldn't forget the way I felt when Cage's father's eyes turned black at the hospital. It felt like it was searching my thoughts like files in a cabinet. Could Dr. Tom do the same?

At the same time, there was no way I was going to betray Cage. Even if it meant having my mind wiped of all of this, I wasn't doing that to him. I couldn't put him in that type of danger.

"I was at the hospital visiting a friend and he pushed me into a room and threatened me. He told me he knew what I was and said he would kill me if he saw me again?"

"I see. Dragons are known to nest far away from others. Usually they're only threatening when they're protecting their property. Does any of that fit with what happened to you?"

It fit perfectly. But I couldn't tell him that without revealing more about Cage.

"I don't see how it can."

"Huh," he huffed staring me in the eyes.

"And you followed him here?"

"Not exactly. Cage, and I later found him when we were driving in the woods looking for him. He was dead or comatose or something"

"Cage is your friend out there?"

"Yeah. He was in dragon form but I could tell it was him from his smell. We decided to follow his trail to find out where he came from and it led us to the road leading into town. The trail suddenly stopped after that."

"That's the protective spell. It dampens the scent of anything within it."

"Is that why my wolf can barely smell anything since we got here?"

"That would be why. Otherwise, who knows what would come looking for us after it caught our scent on the wind."

"I see. And the wolf shifters here are okay with that?" I asked knowing how much dimmer life felt without my wolf's enhanced ability.

"It's better to lose your sense of smell than your life."

"I guess," I said wondering if this Fae knew how much his protective spell stole from a wolf.

"Believe me, if you knew what was out there, you would do the same."

"Maybe. So, do I keep my memories?"

Dr. Tom evaluated me one last time. "For now. But, don't make us come looking for you."

"I won't. But, do you think you might be able to introduce me to a wolf shifter? I mean, I've never met another one like me."

Dr. Tom stared not saying a word. When he was done, he turned his attention to the files behind him.

"Have you had the chance to meet many people in town?"

"We've met a few. But I'm guessing you already know who they are."

"Yes, well. There's no one whose confidence I can break. But there are a few interesting characters in town. Nero is someone you might find entertaining. He's a little rough around the edges but he's a good kid."

"Nero?"

"Yes. Is there anything else medical-related that I could help you with," he said ushering me out.

"No. Thank you. Who do I pay for the visit?"

"Don't worry about it. You had nothing wrong. It's on the house," he said looking at me with a forced smile.

I was about to go when I thought of something.

"Actually, there might be one other thing that I'd like to discuss."

"What's that?"

"You're married?"

"Yes."

"To a man?"

"Yes?" The doctor said worried about where I was going with my question.

"I'm here with my boyfriend."

"Okay."

"We might be doing something for the first time later. I'm aware that there are things you can use to make such things a little easier... you know when they slide in."

Dr. Tom turned, grabbed a small tube out of a cabinet, and handed it to me.

"Thanks," I told him. "Nero, right?"

The doctor gave me a tight-lipped smile.

"I'll take that as a yes."

I left his office and joined the two guys.

"Is everything okay?" Cage asked concerned.

"Oh yeah. Everything's fine," I said turning to Titus wondering what he was.

"Should I drop you back at Dr. Sonya's?" Titus asked vulnerably.

"Yeah. That's probably best," I told him to his disappointment.

"Will you be sticking around? Or…?"

"We'll probably be grabbing something to eat and then heading home," I told him deciding it might be better to limit what I told him.

Returning to Titus's truck, he drove us back to the bed and breakfast.

"I'm sorry it ending like this," Titus said genuinely saddened.

Not being great with social stuff, I didn't know what he was referring to. So, ignoring it, I was about to get out of the truck when something hit me. "By the way, do you know someone by the name of Nero?"

"Yeah, sure. What about him?"

"Where would we find him if we were looking?"

"I think he does a couple of shifts at the diner."

"Wait, as a busboy?"

"Yeah. Why?"

I looked at Cage who was looking at me as curiously as Titus was.

"I was just wondering. Listen, thanks for showing us around."

"Of course. And maybe I'll see you at East Tennessee next semester," he said with a smile.

"Maybe," I told him before ushering Cage out of the truck and inside.

"Why were you asking about the busboy from last night," he asked me as we crossed the living room?"

"How was your tour?" Dr. Sonya said crossing from the kitchen. "Oh, what happened to your shoes?"

"There was an incident at the lake," Cage said offering a vague explanation so I wouldn't have to.

"And you lost your shoes?" She asked me.

Dr. Tom had told me that she was human. But wasn't she also one of the people Dr. Tom had been using to figure out what I was? Didn't that mean she knew that Fae and shifters existed?

After Answering her question with a shrug she looked at my wet pants knowingly.

"I have something warm you can wear if you need it. Also, Cali and I are about to have dinner. Would you like to join us?"

"Thank you, but we have plans," I said interjecting.

Cage looked at me confused.

"Yes, unfortunately, we have plans," Cage confirmed.

"But, I will borrow a pair of shoes until we can pick something up at the store."

"I'll get them."

"Thanks," I told her before pushing Cage toward the stairs.

"I'll leave them in front of your door," she told us before we were gone.

"Do we actually have plans? Because, I have to tell you, I'm pretty hungry. I'm definitely gonna need to eat first."

"We are. We're just gonna eat at the diner... after I pick up some new clothes."

I told Cage everything Dr. Tom had said to me and what I thought it meant. Cage was as startled by it as I was.

"So, this other world has always existed."

"He said he was like 150 years old."

"I can't believe it. And my dad is a dragon shifter. Did he say what we were supposed to do with his body? Like, is there a special ritual or something? And, how are we supposed to tell if he's... you know, dead?"

"I'm sorry, I didn't get the chance to ask him any of that. He was throwing a lot of information at me. I was more concerned about hinting that you might be one too."

"If I am one, then he said I would be dangerous."

"Cage, I know you. You're not."

"What if I am? What if some people take longer to shift and then once they do, their personality changes?"

"I shift. Does my personality change?"

"But you've been a shifter your entire life. If I'm what my father was, then who knows what will happen to me?"

He was right. I knew less about dragon shifters than he did. At least he saw his father growing up. All I knew was what it was like having a wolf fighting to get out of me.

"Let's not worry about it. If it happens, then we'll deal with it then. But, the way he described dragons perfectly fit your father and didn't fit you at all. It's possible that you're just human."

""Just"?" He said taking issue with the way I said it.

"You know what I mean. And, it doesn't matter what you are. You're the one I can't stop thinking about. You, whatever you might be," I said offering him a smile.

Relenting, he smiled back and gave me a kiss.

"So, you think that little bastard is a wolf shifter, huh?"

"That's what Dr. Tom implied."

"Well, I'm sure he'll be in the mood to share his greatest secret with us after we got him docked a day's pay."

"We didn't do anything to him. He was the one who said something to us."

"And, I'm sure he'll see it that way."

"Sarcasm?" I confirmed.

"Yes, sarcasm. He's not gonna wanna talk to us. And, I'm not sure I'm gonna be able to keep my cool talking to him. There's something about that guy that rubs me the wrong way."

"Then I'll do the talking."

"I don't think he's gonna wanna talk to you either."

"Let's hope he does because I think he might have a lot of answers, and not just about what I am. He could know stuff about dragons and what you are."

Cage didn't fight me after that. Taking a few more minutes to rest in our room, I collected the boots Dr. Sonya had placed in front of our door and headed to Glen's.

"Tom told me about what happened at the lake. I thought I would be seeing you here," he said with a smile. "Here, I found a few things in your size," Glen said handing them to me.

"He told you I'm not a Fae, right?" I asked wondering why he was still being so nice to me.

Glen's eyes bounced towards Cage.

"Don't worry, he knows. I told him about me and he can be trusted."

"I see," Glen said apprehensively. "Well, what I gave you isn't new. When you live in this town, having a spare set of clothes at hand is kind of a necessity."

"So, there are a lot of wolf shifters here?"

Glen's eyes shifted to Cage again. "I'd prefer not to say."

"I told you, he can be trusted. Just think of him as one of us."

Glen shrugged.

"And Dr. Tom already told us about Nero."

"Did he?"

"In fact, that's where we're going next."

"Good luck with that," he said offering me a genuine smile and walking away.

"I guess he's met him," Cage said sarcastically.

"We should get this over with," I told him before getting dressed.

"You're not gonna buy new clothes?"

"These are fine. I just want to get out of here," I said leading him away.

Leaving the general store and crossing to the diner, we entered finding that it wasn't as empty as the night before. There was a greying couple at one of the tables, and a balding, creepy-looking man sitting in the corner picking at his food with his fingers.

"I'll be right with you," the stout cook said from the kitchen.

We took our previous booth and sat scanning for signs of the busboy. Neither of us saw any. The cook appeared to be doing everything by himself. And when he handed us our menus he added, "Tonight we're out of everything but the chicken dinner, the burger, hotdogs, and I have some pie left."

"I'll take the chicken dinner," Cage said not looking at the menu.

"Fried or baked."

"Baked."

"Fries or mashed potatoes?"

"Mashed potatoes. And a Coke."

"I'll get the same with fries, thanks," I told him.

The man took our menus and got us our Cokes. After, he went to the kitchen and started preparing everything.

"Why give us the menus if he's out of half of what's on it?" Cage asked me with a smile.

"Habit?" I said wondering the same thing.

"I guess. Although, it looks like this place has been here a while and it's the only option in town. I don't think anyone else here needs the menu to know what they want," Cage pointed out.

"True," I agreed. "I don't know."

"By the way, how are you feeling?" Cage asked squinting his eyes at me.

"I'm okay. But I'm still a little cold."

"Really?" Cage asked reaching across the table.

I grunted my reluctance to hold hands here after what had happened the night before.

"No. I won't let you get self-conscious about us showing affection in public. If I was with a girl, no one would think anything about it. I'm not gonna act differently because you're a guy."

I relaxed my crossed-arms and he took my hands.

"Quin, I'm proud to be with you. I want everyone here to know that I got you and they didn't. If they have a problem with the fact that we're two guys, then they could meet me outside. But I won't let it change us. I'll fight for that," he said lifting my hands to his lips and kissing them."

My heart thumbed hearing his declaration. How could he be so confident being with me? How was Cage, a guy who had only dated women until me, more comfortable showing his affection in public than two men who have been madly in love with each other for twenty years?

Although I couldn't explain it, knowing the difference made Cage that much more irresistible. He was everything I could ever want in a guy. It didn't matter whether he was a dragon shifter or a human.

The only thing that gave me any pause was what he said about wanting to settle down and raise a family? I mean, that sounded incredible. And the idea of creating a family with him felt wonderful and right.

But, I couldn't escape who I was or what I needed to do. I had to find a cure from being a wolf shifter. I could only do that in a genetics lab. And that meant moving back to New York and working with my dad after I graduated. I couldn't live in a small town like this.

Pushing that out of my mind, I focused on something more immediate.

"I don't think Nero is here tonight," I told Cage.

"I don't think so either."

"What do we do?"

"What do you mean?"

"Tomorrow's Monday. We have class in the morning," I pointed out.

"Did you want to head back?"

"Shouldn't we? I mean, I want to talk to him even more than you do. But, don't you have to work?"

"I can find someone to cover my shifts."

"But, don't you need to work? I've waited twenty years for answers. I can wait a week more. You're what matters to me. We could always come back next weekend."

Cage looked away saddened.

"You're right like always. It was just that answers to both of our questions were starting to feel so close. What do you think Nero would be able to tell us?"

"I can't even guess. It could be anything. But he's not here and we don't know if he'll be back tomorrow or ever."

"You're right. We should go. After we eat, of course," he said firmly.

"Of course," I said with a chuckle. "I think I've starved you enough for one day."

I stared into his eyes losing myself. I had to touch him. So, freeing one of my hands, I brushed his cheek with my thumb. He was so gorgeous and perfect. I wanted to be his. I wanted the two of us to be one.

When dinner came, we ate, Cage a little faster than I did. The big guy barely had anything to eat all day.

"Interested in a little pie?" The cook asked when he cleared our plates.

Cage looked at me clearly wanting me to say yes.

"Sure, what type?" I asked.

"It's blueberry. Two slices or one?"

"Just one. I only need a bite," I told Cage.

"Just one, thanks," Cage told the cook.

"You want it warmed up?"

Cage looked at me and I nodded. "Sure."

"Ice cream on the side?"

"Absolutely," Cage said not needing to consult with me.

The cook brought out the steaming hot pie with two forks and we ate it in silence. I wasn't talking because all I could think about was climbing into his arms naked. I had seen the outline of his manhood. He was big. What would that feel like pushing into me?

Dr. Tom had given me lube. It was what I was hinting at. I could only imagine him smearing it between my ass cheeks and massaging my hole with it. Would he push in a finger to open me up first? I got hard thinking about it.

It had to happen at some point, right? Maybe I'll stay over at his place tonight. Maybe he'll walk me to my room when we get back to the university and then follow me in. My skin crackled in anticipation. I felt like I was going crazy waiting for it.

"Should we go?" Cage asked when the pie was gone.

"Okay," I said with a smile still thinking about what could happen next.

I went to the cash register and paid the bill and then joined Cage as he walked towards the door. He reached for my hand and I slipped it in his. It felt so right. We were about to let each other go and climb into the truck when someone drew our attention.

"Guys!"

We turned seeing Titus. He was with a woman who looked like an older, female version of himself. She, however, looked like she took life more seriously than he did.

"Titus," Cage said gripping my hand making sure I didn't shy away from his grasp.

Titus led the woman over and genuinely looked happy to see us.

"Cage, Quin, this is my mom. Mom, these are the two guys I gave a tour to today."

"Nice to meet you," we both said.

"Nice to meet you. Titus hasn't been able to stop talking about you two. He tells me he's going to East Tennessee University now."

We looked at Titus who turned red.

"Come on, Mom. I just mentioned that I gave them a tour and said I was going to look into attending some classes. Quin was telling me how it might be able to help the town."

"The town is perfect just the way it is," his mother said firmly. "I don't know why you think things would be better if we were more exposed. Any old thing could just wander in." She looked at us. "No offense."

"No offense taken," Cage said politely.

"It's not about exposing us. It's about…" Titus glanced over at us. "It's about us being able to be live up to our full potential."

"Your generation and your focus on what you want instead of more important things."

Titus laughed. "Like what, Mom?"

"Like the community and the lives of everyone in it."

"I'm not saying we should put anyone at risk. I… You know what, this is not the place we should be having this conversation. Let's just drop it."

His mother huffed. Titus looked at us and shrugged his shoulders frustrated.

"Anyhow, did you two just have dinner?"

Cage replied. "Yeah. We had the chicken."

"It's Sunday, so it's what's on the menu. And another thing, Mom, if we opened up a little, maybe more money would start flowing through the town and Bill could have more than one option on Sundays."

"I've never heard you complain about his Sunday meals before."

"Well, consider this me registering my complaint."

"Noted," his mother said displeased.

"Anyway, you guys headed back to the bed and breakfast?"

"Yeah. And then we're driving back," Cage explained.

"Oh! Because I was going to tell you that I know where to find Nero tomorrow if you're still looking for him."

"You do?" I asked perking up.

"Yeah." Titus looked at his mother who was watching us talk. "He has this thing he hosts on Monday nights. It's just a little social club event. Nothing special. But I was going to say that I could take you if you wanted to go."

"Oh!" Cage said looking at me.

I didn't know what to say to him. I was as interested in talking to Nero as he was, maybe more. But, we both had classes and he had to work.

"Can we get your number and text you about it?" I said knowing Cage and I had to consider this.

"Sure," Titus said before we exchanged numbers and went our separate ways.

In the warmth of the truck, we watched Titus go inside and settle at a table with his mother. His mom smiled for the first time when the cook came to the table. They were both smiling. There was clearly something more going on between the two.

"So, what do you think? Do we stick around and try to talk to Nero at his "social club event" tomorrow?" Cage asked turning to me.

"We could also drive home and come back tomorrow after you get off of work?"

"We could. But that's two hours there, two hours back here, and then two more hours getting home. I could think of a few better ways to spend our time," he said with a smile.

I got hard as soon as he said it. He was right. I could think of several better things we could do with our time as well.

"It's up to you, Quin. It's your money. But, if you wanted to stay another night, I might be able to make it worth your while," he said sending tingles whipping through my body.

"Oh, yeah? How?"

Cage slipped his hand behind my neck and pulled my lips to his. I was weak in his grasp. The heat of his lips melted any resistance I had about staying. With his undulating on mine, I parted my lips and invited in his tongue.

As our tongues danced, my head swooned. His kiss was a warm breeze on a cool day. Everything felt so good. And, when he released me from my trance, I was willing to do anything to start it up again.

"I think that would be worth staying over for," I told him doing my best not to climb on top of him right there.

Cage smiled. "Good. I'm glad you think so," he said with a sparkle in his eyes.

I couldn't not touch him as we drove back to the bed and breakfast. I slipped my hand onto his thigh rubbing his muscles. Everything about him was so big. It didn't take me long to move my hand up his leg to his crotch. His cock was the first thing I touched. I couldn't avoid it. The thing was huge.

His sweatpants didn't hide anything. I couldn't wait any longer. I had to see it. I needed to hold him in my hands. So, as he drove, I leaned over into his lap, gripped the band of his pants, and tugged them down.

Cage helped me by shifting up allowing his pants and underwear to slide to his thigh. His cock was so big that it got caught as his pants went down. His thick shaft was the first thing I saw. But, having to slide my hand onto it and help it along, I got a full look at it as it sprung out inches from my lips.

I had never held a dick before and the feeling sent my heart racing. I couldn't encircle it with one hand. The most I could do was hold it still while I lowered my head and slipped the tip of it into my mouth.

He groaned as soon as my hot breath encased him. I had never done this before, but I was a fast learner. I knew what he had done that had driven me wild. And sending my tongue to work on the ridge of his tip, I felt the truck slow down.

Putting the truck in park but not turning it off, he stretched out his legs giving me easier access. As he did, he revealed some of his buried length. Wow!

Wrapping a second hand under the first one, there was still space for a third. Feeling his bulging veins pressing against my palms, I pushed the tip of him as far into my throat as I could. It wasn't very far.

Turned on as much as he was, I twisted my head pulling it back before returning it to the boundaries of my throat. As I did, I stroked him with both hands. His legs squirmed.

When he placed his hand on my head, I knew he was close.

"Ahhh!" he moaned.

Hearing that, I did more. Slapping my tongue back and forth across his head, I tightened my grip on his cock. Gliding across the curve of it, I finally flicked my tongue against the base of his head causing him to explode.

Not removing it from within me, I caught all of it in my throat. I didn't know if he would want me to or not, but I wanted to know everything about him. I wanted to know what Cage's cum tasted like.

Swallowing all of it, it was tangy. He was silent as it kept coming. When it stopped was when he fought to catch his breath and inhaled.

"Oh my god, you're so good at that. How did you get so good?" He asked inspiring me to sit up and release him.

I didn't want to let go of his sturdy manhood. I could have held onto it forever. It was thicker and more impressive than the truck's gear shifter which was a foot away.

I couldn't get over that I was looking at Cage's cock. It was my boyfriend's dick and it was the most beautiful thing I had ever seen.

He reached over and perched my chin on his finger. Leaning forward he kissed my lips.

"Seriously, how are you so good at that?"

"I guess I was inspired," I told him proud that I had been able to bring him so much joy.

Cage lowered his hand and laid back.

"I don't think I can move. Seriously, I think my legs are paralyzed," he joked. "I may never be able to walk again."

"Oh, no! Your football career!"

Cage laughed.

"That's what I'll do. I'll blame my quitting on my boyfriend's blow jobs. They were so good that I lost the use of my legs. I'm sure sports media would understand that."

"I would," I confirmed with a smile.

We both sat quietly as Cage gathered his strength. We were less than 20 seconds from the B&B coming into view. Finishing the final drive there, we parked out front and slowly made our way inside. I was still wearing Cage's jacket so he crossed his arms trying to escape the cold.

Entering we looked around hoping we wouldn't have to talk to anyone about where we were. No one was there. Instead, we found my clothes folded on the living room coffee table in front of us. Hanging beside it was my jacket. Pinned to it was a note.

'I didn't know if you were going to stay another night. So, either, it was great meeting you and I hope to see you again. Or, I'll see you for breakfast in the morning.'

"We should leave a note telling her that we're staying, shouldn't we?" I asked unsure of what was expected.

"Either that or she'll just see my truck."

I looked out the window to see the truck illuminated by the living room lights.

"I guess you're right. And she has my credit card number. There's no need to leave a note."

Grabbing my clothes, we headed upstairs and retreated to our room. The bed had been made. I couldn't wait to mess it up again.

"I think I need a shower," Cage said looking very relaxed.

"Should I join you?" I asked wondering if it was a part of my boyfriend-ly duties.

"No. With this thing it's more work than play," he said referring to his cast.

"Then, I could wash your back for you."

"Thanks, but I got it. Did you want to hit the shower first? I'll probably be a while."

"I guess," I said still wanting to wrap my hands around him. But instead, I grabbed my folded shirt and entered the bathroom, closing the door behind me.

Stripping down, I couldn't stop thinking about how Cage's hard cock felt in my hands. I was starting to think that I would never touch a cock other than mine. And for it to be Cage's, I vibrated with excitement.

There wasn't a moment when I was in the shower that I wasn't completely hard. I was so aroused I felt giddy. After getting out I considered putting my clothes back on, but what was the point? Instead, I wrapped a towel around my waist and rejoined Cage.

"God, I can't stop looking at you," he said washing his eyes over me. His attention caused my hard dick to twitch. He saw it and smiled.

"I'll be back," he said replacing me behind the bathroom door.

I didn't know what to do with myself waiting. Although it wasn't cold in the room, it wasn't warm enough for me to sit around naked. That was a problem because I didn't want to get dressed.

On top of that, I didn't know how long Cage would take. The best option had to be to get comfortable under the covers. I desperately wanted him to think of sex with me, though. So, what could I do to accomplish that?

What I decided was I would put the tube of lube that Dr. Tom gave me on the bedside nightstand closest to the bathroom, and get into the other side of the bed. To make sure he wouldn't miss it, I turned off all of the other lights except the bedside lamp that featured the lube like a spotlight.

If he still missed it after that, I would say something. I wanted him so badly that I was shivering with anticipation. I slipped my hand under the sheets and pressed my dick when the pressure within it got too much.

The minutes felt like hours waiting for him to come out. I was sure I was about to snap in two from tension when, to my relief, I heard the shower turn off and he returned to the bedroom.

He approached the bed like a man out of the shadows. The way the towel rode his hip looked way better than the way it had rode mine. His tapered naked torso resembled that of superheroes' in movies. I could see every ripple of his bulging muscles. But there was only one bulge I cared about. That one didn't disappoint.

His hard cock stretched across the front of him eventually being buried in the ripples from the towel's tuck. I couldn't wait to feel it again. When he approached the edge of the bed and looked down at the nightstand, he chuckled. I was pretty sure his laugh meant I would see it soon.

"Did you bring this with you?" He asked picking up the lube and examining it.

"No. I got it from the doctor."

"You're always one step ahead of everyone else."

I was curious what he meant by that but didn't want to break the mood.

"Have you ever used lube before?" I asked him knowing that I hadn't.

"Once or twice. Not like how we're going to use it, though. I can't wait to try that."

"Me neither," I told him wanting him to get into bed immediately.

Dropping his towel allowing this hard cock to spring out, Cage returned the little bottle to the nightstand and joined me under the sheets. I pressed my forearms against my chest and slid to him face first. With his arms easing around me, I drank in his body heat.

"How do we do this?" Cage asked.

"However you'd like," I said shaking.

"You're cold," he said pulling me tighter.

I loved being in his arms. The sensation made me drunk. Needing to kiss him, I pulled back my head looking up at him. He had been waiting for that because as soon as I did, he leaned down and met my lips.

Facing him, our hard cocks touched. We both felt it. When he suddenly kissed me harder, I knew that it had turned him on as much as it did me.

Without thinking, I tilted my hips rubbing his cock against my belly and mine against his leg. Quickly he started to do the same. I had never imagined how good doing this could feel. And when he moved his hand to my ass and sunk his fingers between my cheeks to pull my body closer, my hips moved uncontrollably. I wanted him to fuck me. I needed him to know that I did.

Briefly letting go of my ass cheek, Cage reached back retrieving something from behind him. I would have barely noticed if I hadn't heard a snap and a blurping sound that got me excited. And when his hand returned and his fingers tested my hole, I lifted my leg giving him full access.

Cage kissed me as his lube-covered fingers pushed into me. The pressure was almost too much. It caused me to stop kissing and groan. Responding, he pulled his finger away. Quickly returning his fingers to his target, he pulsed the pressure until, like a balloon, my hole popped.

Cage's thick finger was inside of me. Cage was inside of me. With it came a flash of pain that quickly retreated. The sensation became fantastic. Moving to again kiss him, he then slowly fucked me with his finger before adding another one and stretching open my hole.

Cage's fingers felt glorious, but there was something I wanted even more. So, hoping he wouldn't get the wrong impression, I pulled away from his lips. Rolling over, he didn't remove his fingers until I had completely turned around. With them out, I pushed my back onto his chest and found his cock with my ass cheeks.

I knew I couldn't just lie there now that I knew how it felt to have him inside me, so I rubbed my ass against him. When he didn't move, I lifted my hips sending my opening in search of his tip.

With his head between my flesh pushing above my hole, he took over. Moving his tip to my target, he clutched the side of my hip. All I could do was take a breath preparing to receive what I had dreamed about for so long.

Unlike his fingers, the head of his cock was overwhelming. As much as he had stretched me, when he thrust forward, I realized that it hadn't been nearly enough.

He kept testing me, pushing himself harder. Each time I flinched and then quickly relaxed. I could tell he was getting further with every pulse. Finally, when Cage gripped his large hand around my side and locked me into place, he pushed his cock unwilling to relent.

As much as it ached, I didn't want him to stop. Did it hurt or did it feel good? I couldn't tell. What I did know was that I wanted Cage's cock in me and then, as if I had been reborn, he popped in sending a wave of agony that was quickly followed by a sea of pleasure.

"Yes!" I moaned needing more.

As soon as I said it, he pushed harder.

"Ahhh!" I groaned.

He was too much, but I wanted more. I wanted him to keep pushing until the two of us were one. Eventually he hit a point when he couldn't go in any further. That was when he retreated and then thrust back in. His cock was strumming me like a fiddle. As he did, my sight went dark and my legs fell limp.

If I were given a hundred years I would still never have imagined how good Cage's cock felt. My head was spinning. He was fucking me. Cage Rucker's cock was inside of me. And as he thrust into me faster and harder, I felt a knot building on the inside of my thigh that slowly crawled to my balls.

I was coming from his fucking alone. How was this possible? I hadn't touched myself. Neither had Cage. Yet, my balls tingled and I felt a growing ache.

I clenched my jaw hoping I could do something to stop it. I couldn't. So, losing control of myself, my toes clenched, my muscles clamped, and I exploded into orgasm.

I grunted as I did, but that was drowned out as Cage moaned. He moaned louder than I had ever heard anyone in my life. We were cumming together.

I moved my hand on top of his as it dug into my hip. I was growing lightheaded. I wanted to stay with him experiencing every moment, but everything was too much. His cock, the way I felt about him, the events of the day, it was all coming to a head.

As it did, I took a final deep breath. Releasing it, my vision darkened. I was in the throes of the greatest feeling of my life and losing myself in it, I slowly blacked out.

Chapter 14

Cage

Sex with Quin was what I always thought sex was supposed to be like. Sex with Tasha and the other girls was fine. No one had any complaints. But with Quin, I felt like a man on fire.

Being with Quin did something to me. I felt complete when I was with him. Holding him I had thoughts about white picket fences and kids running around in the yard. He was my other half. I was sure of it. There was no question that I was in love with him.

I held onto him all night. After I drifted off to sleep and rolled over losing contact with him, I woke up long enough to reach my hand back in search of his body. It wasn't until I found it that I was able to again fall asleep.

In the morning, I opened my eyes to find him cuddled in my arms. I could smell his hair. There was a hint of strawberry in it. I could have lied there forever and we almost did. We didn't even think about getting up until after 11. By then, we were both hungrier than anything else.

"What should we do today?" I asked him as he reluctantly peeled away from me.

"Get something to eat?"

"And then for the next 10 hours before going to Nero's book club or whatever it is?"

"I don't think it will be a book club," Quin said taking me seriously.

"I'm kidding. Yeah, something tells me that Nero doesn't get his kicks from a well-constructed sentence," I joked.

"Probably not," Quin agreed with a smile.

God, did I love to see that man smile.

The two of us took turns in the bathroom getting ready and then we headed downstairs. Dr. Sonya was hovering.

"Well, good morning," she said blushing.

It was pretty clear that she knew what we had been up to the night before. Staring at her, I tried to remember how loud we were. I hadn't been quiet. I looked around wondering about the thickness of the walls. They probably weren't very thick. Whoops!

"Good morning," I said embarrassed.

Quin seemed to miss her playful ribbing.

"It's closer to good afternoon," he corrected.

"I know. And I figured you two might have built up an appetite."

"We're definitely both hungry," Quin said seeming to miss Dr. Sonya's suggestion.

"Good! Because I went out and got you a selection of pastries. I was hoping they wouldn't go to waste. Let me get them," she said heading back to the kitchen. "Have a seat."

Quin and I sat at the round table in the breakfast nook and got comfortable. Dr. Sonya returned with a selection of croissants, sweet buns, and fruit. The only thing that could have made it better was bacon. But bacon made everything better, so that wasn't saying much.

"What are your plans for today?" She asked hanging around as we tried her treats.

"We're not sure yet," I said pulling a croissant apart and popping it into my mouth. "This is really good."

"They're made locally. We have a budding pastry chef on our hands. I've been doing everything I can to nurture his interests."

"They are very flaky," Quin volunteered.

"They're excellent," Dr. Sonya concluded before changing the topic. "Can I expect your wonderful company another night? Or, will you be heading back today?"

Quin answered. "We're meeting up with Titus tonight. But, we're going to be heading back afterward.

We have classes and he has work," he said deciding for the both of us.

It was what we had discussed, but I thought we were going to play it a little more by ear. This place wasn't cheap, so I could see why he wouldn't want to stay another night. But, the way he said it made me think that us having to get back had more to do with me than him.

The guy was brilliant. Him missing a class or two wouldn't matter on his grades at all. I was the one who had to struggle with everything. I was pretty sure that he wanted to get me back so I wouldn't fall behind.

It's very sweet of him to look after me like that. It is the first time in my life anyone has. But, at the same time, I was liking it here. Even after what Quin told me about this being a town full of magical creatures, there was something about it that made me feel like I belonged. I was hoping Quin felt the same way.

"Well, it was my pleasure hosting you two. Hopefully, I'll see you again. Cali's going to be disappointed he missed you. He was quite taken by the two of you. I told him that if he wants to see you, he should apply for East Tennessee University. He's been dragging his feet on it. But meeting you two might have given him the push he needed."

"It's a great school," Quin said. "If he decides he wants a tour, I'd be happy to give him one."

"That would be wonderful. I'll let him know. He would love that."

I couldn't help but get a flash of jealousy listening to Quin offer his tour guide services. Maybe he was attempting to push out of his comfort zone, but I couldn't help but remember how much the kid was crushing on Quin. I had told Quin so he was definitely aware of it. Now it was with him that Quin was choosing to go out of his way?

On second thought, I was probably looking too much into it. Quin was a great guy and great guys did nice things for people. Helping Cali get excited about college was a nice thing. I just didn't want to think about my boyfriend with anyone else. I wanted to be the one to take care of him for the rest of our lives.

"Yeah, let us know. We can give him a tour," I said making sure Cali knew not to be too excited about it.

"Wonderful! I have your number, Quin. I'll pass it along. I have a few errands to run. But here is my card. Feel free to give me a call if you need anything else," she said handing it to Quin.

"So, what are we going to do until tonight?" I asked reaching for a slice of cantaloupe.

"We could drive around."

"I think we've seen everything there is to see. But, we could text Titus to see if he has any suggestions."

"Do you think he'll mind?" Quin said with a smile.

"Why would he mind?" I asked already taking out my phone and texting him.

'Any suggestions for what Quin and I could do today,' I typed and sent.

It took less than ten seconds for my phone to ring.

"It's Titus. Who responds to a text with a call?" I asked surprised. "Hello?"

"Cage! I was hoping to hear from you two! Remember how I said that this town has a pretty good high school football team."

"I remember."

"Well, that was me bragging a little because I'm the coach."

"You coach the team?"

"I do. It's just something I do to keep the program going. Coach Thompson, the guy who coached our team, died last year."

"I'm sorry to hear that."

"Thanks. And, not wanting to leave the guys without a coach, I volunteered. But, I was thinking, how great would it be if you with your experience came and gave them a little talk? You know, nothing formal. I think it would be thrilling for them. Maybe you can inspire them to get their asses in gear.

"And, honestly, I don't know what the hell I'm doing. I'm trying but, I could always use the feedback.

What do you say? You have any interest in coming over and talking to a few talented kids?"

"I would love to," I said looking at Quin. "I'll have to talk to Quin about it, but I think we can swing by."

"Would you? That would be incredible! I'll text you the address. And if you get here around two, I'll give you a tour of the school. It has a rich history."

"I'll talk to Quin."

"Great! I'll see you soon," Titus said ending the call.

"What did he say?" Quin asked having not taken his eyes off of me.

"He wants me to come by and talk to his high school football team."

"You agreed?"

"It's not like we have anything else to do," I told him.

Quin didn't disagree.

Over the next few hours, we lounged around, made out a little, and took back the crutches Glen had lent me.

"Were they useful?" Glen asked.

"Definitely!" I said having barely used them at all.

"How did your meeting with Nero go?"

"He wasn't at the diner. But Titus is taking us to see him tonight," Quin replied while I attempted to make myself invisible. "Is there anything we should know before we do? The first time we ran into him, it didn't go well."

"That doesn't surprise me. He's always been a little prickly. I've known him from when he was a kid and he hasn't changed much since then."

"Is it because he's a wolf shifter? Are all wolf shifters angry?"

Glen stared a Quin with his mouth open trying to decide what to say. He had clearly been reluctant last night, but staring into Quin's vulnerable eyes he softened.

"Are you asking me if there is something about shifting that makes you angry?"

"Kind of."

"No. There is nothing about shifting that turns you into something you wouldn't have become otherwise. Again, I'm very hesitant to say much, but I've met some wonderfully kind people who shift. Nero has problems he has been dealing with for years."

"What do you mean?"

Glen's eyes met mine before I turned my attention to the clothing rack in front of me.

"Nero has issues at home. But, he's not a bad kid. I got to know him a few years ago when he had adopted Tom as his father figure."

"What happened to his father?" Quin asked.

"Not sure. I don't think he ever knew him. It's tough growing up without one."

"It can be tough growing up with one," I said unable to help myself.

Glen looked at me. "It can be. When parents disappoint you, it has a way of leaving a mark."

"I know a little something about that," I said turning to Quin who grew up with at least one parent who wasn't an actual monster.

Quin bought new clothes returning what he had borrowed and I picked up a few snacks. After that, we headed to the high school. The place looked like a converted warehouse.

Pulling into the parking lot, we spotted Titus in his truck waiting for us. When we parked next to him, he got out. His broad smile was as big as ever. He certainly had a way of making people feel welcome.

Titus's tour began in the school's main building. It was where they used to store their moonshine after bottling it. In the 50s, the town got a few more kids and they converted it into a school. The building's square footage has been growing ever since.

I had thought that my high school's locker was lacking. It turns out it was professional grade in comparison to what this town's team had. The field wasn't much better either.

"It's not much, but it's about the grit of the players and not the quality of the field. That's what I always tell them," Titus said showing us around.

"You're right," I said sincerely.

"There are guys on the team who have real potential, too. If we had better equipment… and a better coach," he said with a self-deprecating laugh, "some of these kids could go far. Some might even be good enough to get a scholarship to East Tennessee. You would know something about that, right? Maybe you could talk to them about it."

My heart melted at his request. "I would be happy to. Anything I can do to help, just let me know."

Titus's smile in reply was genuine. He cared about the kids. There was no question about it, he was a good guy.

"Are you Cage Rucker?" One of the kids asked me when he came onto the field for practice.

I looked at Quin. Quin smiled.

"Yeah," I said suddenly liking being recognized.

I had been recognized a hundred times over the years. But this was the first time in a long time that it affected me. I wasn't sure why.

"Cali, you're on the football team?" I asked when he joined us on the field in uniform.

He blushed staring at me.

"Yeah. I'm the kicker."

"He has a golden foot, that one," Titus said encouragingly.

Cali turned red and then peeked over at Quin to see if he had heard it. Quin had. Cali was crushing on my boyfriend hard.

Cali was a smaller guy with a style that hinted at emo. To see him on the team, surprised me.

It made a little more sense to find out he was the kicker. You didn't have to be built like a linebacker to kick a football 80 yards. And, sure to show off for Quin before the beginning of practice, that was exactly what Cali did. He was unquestionably good enough to play for a school like East Tennessee. A few of the kids here were.

To my continued surprise, Titus didn't just have me speak to them, he roped me into running practice. It ended up being fun. Something about it felt right even though I was sure that Quin was bored out of his mind.

"I appreciate you doing this for the kids," Titus said as we headed back to our trucks.

"Seriously, it was my pleasure."

"Cage was in his element," Quin told him.

I didn't think Quin would notice that, but he was right. This was definitely what I wanted to do with my new life.

"Would you guys allow me to take you to dinner to thank you? We could head to Nero's thing afterward."

"That would be cool," I said not giving Quin a chance to weigh in.

The truth was that working with the kids had given me a high and I wasn't yet ready to come down from it. Heading back to the diner, both Quin and I looked around for Nero when we entered.

"He's not here," Titus volunteered. "He helps out with the rush on the weekends," Titus said making fun of how few people it took to be considered a rush here.

"Do you know Nero well?" Quin asked putting back on his investigator's hat.

"We went to school together. He was a year under me but he was in a couple of my classes. We did play on the team together, though."

"Football team?" I asked.

"It's the only team this town has," Titus said self-deprecatingly. "We can only afford one extracurricular activity here. So, I hope no one's interested in women's basketball."

"Oh, that sucks!" I said feeling for the girls.

We finished dinner and chatted a little longer before we eventually settled the bill. Even though Titus had offered to pay, Quin insisted. Titus fought him on it until I stepped in.

"Just let him. Trust me."

Titus was hesitant but conceded. I couldn't tell what Titus was thinking, but it was obvious that he was used to being the big man. Perhaps I should have told

Quin to let him do it, but the truth was that it felt unfair considering what I knew about Quin's family's wealth. Besides, it was something Quin wanted. I had a hard time not giving my boyfriend what he wants.

"So, what is this thing that Nero's doing?" I asked as we walked to the trucks.

"It would be better if you just saw it," Titus explained.

"Okaaaay," I said looking over at Quin who was holding my hand.

Quin didn't say anything about it until we were alone in the truck following Titus on narrow roads leading through the woods.

"Yeah, this is definitely not a book club," he said watching the trees as they went past the window. "Do you think this is a good idea?"

"Do you think we should go back? I can still turn the truck around."

"Do you?" Quin asked me. "We're only going because we want to talk to Nero. We could easily come back next weekend or the one after that. You heard Titus, Nero works the weekend rushes, and... Woah!" Quin froze overwhelmed by something.

"What's the matter?" I said panicked.

"It's back! I can smell again. At least, my wolf can."

"Are we outside of the protective spell?"

"We must be. Wow! Having it come back all at once is… a lot."

"Are you okay?" I asked concerned.

"Yeah, I'm fine."

"Do you think it's a coincidence that Nero's holding his book club outside of the barrier?"

"It's definitely not."

Quin cracked open his window and stuck out his nose.

"There are other things out here."

"Other things like what?" I asked scanning for somewhere I could turn the truck around if I needed to.

"I don't know. But they aren't human."

"Do we say, "Screw this?""

"No keep going. I think we'll be okay," he said with a puzzled look on his face.

"Quin, if anything happens, I'll keep you safe. I promise you. Okay?"

Quin looked at me. "Okay."

He didn't just say he believed me, he acted like it. Having earned his trust, there was no way I would betray it now. No matter what happened or what was out there, I was going to protect Quin. I was ready to die trying if I had to.

When we finally pulled up in front of a glowing barn, things didn't feel any safer. There were several trucks parked out front and the light within flickered.

"Are you sure it's okay that we're here?" I asked Titus feeling the aggressive focus I did before a big game.

"You wanted to see him, right? He'll be here."

"That wasn't an answer," I clarified.

"I'm sure you'll be fine. You look like you can handle yourself."

"Why would Cage need to handle himself?" Quin asked bringing up a good point.

"You want to see him or not?" Titus asked staring at us.

I looked over at Quin. I knew that no matter what happened, I could fight my way out. But, what about Quin. Was it worth putting him in danger?

"This is our chance to speak to him," Quin pointed out. "He could have the answers to everything. I say we risk it."

I smiled. I would not have thought less of him if he had said we should go back. But, here he was thinking of me, not himself. I was definitely falling in love with him if I wasn't in love with him already.

"Okay. Let's go in," I said to Quin. "This better not turn bad," I said threatening to tear Titus apart if it did.

I didn't know what to expect, but as soon as we stepped through the barn's doors, everything made sense. There were about 20 people there. All of them were facing a circle drawn on the ground where two wolves were tearing each other to shreds.

It was dogfighting but with wolves. There was a thicker more vicious one that was bleeding from its ear, but his wild eyes said that there was no way he was going to lose. That was the one everyone was cheering for.

Its eyes didn't lie. Its quick movements allowed it to get its teeth around the other one's throat. In moments, it was shaking the other one like a rag doll. It probably would have killed it if someone hadn't stepped in and pointed at it as the winner. As soon as that happened, the thicker one let the other go and turned to us.

Its narrowing eyes seemed to recognize me. My heart pounded. Heat washed over me making my skin burn. I couldn't move or breathe. What was happening to me? Frozen at the worst possible time, I watched as the wild beast shot across the barn in two moves and leapt into the air headed for me.

I braced myself for the weight of it when it never came. Attacking it mid-flight was a wolf I had seen before. It was Quin. He was protecting me from it. I shouldn't have brought him here. I couldn't protect him. And it was as I realized that I felt a familiar feeling. I felt my leg break.

It wasn't just one leg it happened to. It was both. It was also my arms. What was going on? My body felt like it was on fire. But, when the sensation eased, I came out of it with a singular thought. I needed to protect Quin.

Without thinking, my body reacted. It found the wolves rolling on the ground beside me and took control. It was like I was only along for the ride. The thing steering me knew which wolf was which and dug its teeth into the thicker one causing it to yelp and pull away.

With Quin's wolf retreating, the other repositioned itself and stared at me. It was eye level. Why was it eye level? And why could I now smell everything. It was like I was awake for the first time. I had never felt more alive.

Although I was sightseeing, it felt like whatever was in control was murderously focused. It did not like the wolf we were staring at. It wanted to take him down and kill him if it had to.

I could tell that I was bigger than it and the other one saw it too. More than that, I had a clarity of purpose that wouldn't allow me to quit until I had what I wanted.

I bent down about to attack when I heard, "Stop!"

The sound was deafening but I recognized the voice. It was Quin, but I couldn't let him distract me. I was in this.

Charging the beast in front of me, the wolf snapped its jaws in retreat. I had a hold of it and didn't know what to do. I let go of its limb to grab its throat again. I had him.

"You have to stop! He's your brother!"

I froze. What did he say?

That was when the other wolf turned the tide. Within its narrow opening, it snuck in gaining the advantage. It was on top of me with its teeth and claws latched on. It was going to kill me before another wolf jumped in. I didn't recognize this one, but its scent was familiar.

Between the two of us, we held off the first wolf and placed ourselves between it and Quin. With its eyes bouncing between the two of us, it calmed. That was when it looked like it was about to puke. It shifted instead.

In a moment, Nero was who was kneeling in front of me. He looked at the wolf beside me. That was when it shifted. It was Titus.

"Cage, can you hear me?" Quin asked as he stood over me putting on his clothes. "Cage, you have to calm down. You can't shift back if you don't."

Shift back? What was he talking about? I looked around again.

Yes, that was what happened. I had changed. But, I wasn't what I saw lying dead in my kitchen. I was... what Quin is. I was a wolf. How was this possible?

"Cage, come back to me," Quin implored.

"Is this his first shift?" Titus asked Quin.

"I think so. We didn't even know he was a shifter until now."

"Okay, then he's gonna have to let it work its way through him naturally. There's nothing he's gonna be able to do about it."

"Why did you say he was my brother," Nero said approaching Quin as he buttoned his pants.

I growled not liking how close he was getting to Quin. He got the picture and stopped a few arm lengths away.

"Alright!" Nero said turning to me.

"I said it because you are," Quin confirmed.

"How would you know that?" Titus asked.

"I can smell it."

"No one can smell something like that," Nero declared.

"I can. Right now I smell everything. I could tell what both of you had for dinner last night. Titus had the fried chicken at the dinner and you had macaroni and cheese."

Nero and Titus looked at each other.

"Is something like that possible?" Nero asked.

"He's not from here. What have I been saying for years about Dr. Tom's protective spell? It's robbing us of who we are. Maybe we would all be able to do that if we didn't have to live life with our noses cut off. I'm telling you, it needs to come down."

Nero ignored Titus's rant and turned to Quin.

"Look, I don't know you. I don't know him. And, I don't know what you're trying to pull. But if you think you're gonna mess with my head or something…"

"We came here because we found out that Cage's father — or, at least the guy who called himself that — we found out that he was a dragon shifter."

"A dragon shifter?" Nero said looking at Titus.

"Yeah. Apparently that's something else that exists. And, we would have asked him what was going on, only we found him dead, or comatose, or sleeping, or something. And since he wasn't talking, we followed his trail back to here."

"Why would he have come here?" Titus asked.

"We don't know. We were hoping to find out. But instead we've found Cage's brother."

"We don't know that," Nero shouted defensively.

I growled not liking his tone.

"Look, that sounds like a good story and everything but if you think I'm gonna let some wolf shifters I've never met talk to my mother…"

That was when it happened. My wolf retracted and I painfully reemerged. Still kneeling on the ground panting, I asked, "Your mother's still alive?"

"Yeah, she's alive. What about it?"

"My father, he said my mother died during child birth."

"Well, mine's still alive."

"Could she be my mother too, Quin. Can you tell?"

Quin kneeled and pushing his fingers through my hair. The gentle look in his eyes filled me with love.

"I wish I could tell you that. I could barely sense you two are related."

Quin helped me to my feet. When he did, I noticed something was different. I looked around and found my cast a few feet away. On top of that, my once broken leg felt perfect.

I turned to Nero whose eyes bounce between Quin and me. I stared back slowing getting dressed. When I finally found my voice, I asked,

"Did your mother ever talk about having a kid before you? Did she ever talk about someone like me?"

Nero's eyes narrowed. "Why'd you come here?"

"I told you. We came here because I followed a scent to this town," Quin repeated.

"No. I mean, why did you come here tonight? You tellin' me that you just showed up here by accident?"

"We came looking for you," I told him.

"I figured that. Why?"

I looked over at Quin.

"Because Dr. Tom told me that I should talk to you."

"Dr. Tom?" Nero said suddenly rattled.

"Yeah. I saw him yesterday. I was asking to meet another wolf shifter and he mentioned you. When we asked Titus about you, he brought us here."

Nero looked up at Titus who said, "Dr. Tom asked me to find out what I could about them and I gave them a tour. I didn't know about any of this. But, you know with Dr. Tom, nothing is a coincidence."

"I asked you if your mother has ever talked about someone like me," I said feeling anger bubble up knowing he had ignored my question.

"You're not meeting my mother!" Nero said looking like he wanted to shift.

Titus put himself between us and took grip of Nero's shoulders.

"Nero, you gotta relax."

"He's talking about meeting my mother. I'm not gonna let him do that. You know she can't handle that."

"What's wrong with your mother?" I asked.

"She's not... well," Titus explained.

"Your mother's sick?" I said feeling the empty feeling of a rug being pulled from under me.

"No. I'm not saying a god damn thing more. Prove to me this shit is real. Prove to me you're who you say you are."

"You want to see our I.D.s?" I asked.

"I don't want to see your fuckin' I.D.s. I want you to prove to me that anything you said is real."

"How are we supposed to do that?" I asked him hoping he would be reasonable.

"I know how," Quin said grabbing our attention.

"You do? How?" I asked.

"We could test your DNA. I have an uncle who works in genetics. I was named after him. He would help us figure this out. The test would be able to tell us if the two of you are related even if it's just cousins."

Nero looked at Quin suspiciously.

"No. I'm not doing this. You people are making this up. It's all bullshit."

Titus turned to Nero. "What if it isn't? I've spent the last two days with them, and they're decent guys. What if he is your brother? I know that if I had a brother I would want to know. What if they're telling the truth, Nero? Imagine that. And, with his wolf's strength…"

Nero turned to Titus. "This is a lot, you know. It's a lot."

"I know, but what if? How would you feel if you do have a brother and you pushed him away?" Titus said putting his hand on Nero's shoulder.

Nero softened as his thoughts swirled. He looked tortured before looking resigned.

"Listen, I didn't mean all of that fag stuff. It's just that when I saw you two sitting there looking so happy, I thought, 'what about me?' You know? Why does everyone but me get to be happy? I didn't mean anything against you."

I looked over at Quin for his reaction. I wasn't sure I was willing to forgive him.

"That's okay," Quin said being the good person that he is.

"Yeah. You're forgiven," I confirmed. "But, don't ever say shit like that again. You hear me?" I said meaning it to be a threat though I wasn't in a threatening mood.

"No. I won't. It's not me. Ask Titus."

Titus shrugged not taking a side.

"Anyway, I didn't mean it. You two seem like okay people. But, I can't let you tell my mom any of this. Not until there's proof. She couldn't take it if you're wrong or lying or something. She's not like that, ya know?"

"So, you'll do the test?" Quin asked.

"I'll do your test."

I stared at the disheveled, shirtless guy in front of us. He was no longer the wild wolf or the angry guy from the diner. He was vulnerable and scared.

Was this who he always was? Was this guy my brother? I couldn't believe that after feeling alone for so long, I could have a real family. What was it called with wolves? A pack?

Jesus, I was wolf shifter. What did that even mean? All of this was insane.

"How do we do this, Quin?" I asked pulling myself together. "Do we have to spit in a tube or something?"

"I mean, we could do that if you wanted to do one of those ancestry tests."

"You mean like in the commercials?" Nero asked.

"Yes. But they take weeks. If we got blood samples, I might be able to get the results in a couple of days."

"How?" I asked Quin.

"My father owns a genetics lab."

"Right. Then, let's do that," I told him.

"Yeah. Days sounds better than weeks," Nero confirmed.

"Okay. The only question is, how do we get your blood samples here?"

"Dr. Tom," Nero suggested.

"Do you think he'll do it?" Quin asked.

"Dr. Tom and I are cool. If I asked him, he might," Nero said.

"When?" Quin asked. "Because we're heading back to school tonight."

"Quin, I think we can stay over one more night if it means getting blood samples."

Nero interrupted. "No. He might do it tonight."

"Really? Then, give him a call," I told him.

"Nah. If I called him, he would tell me to come by in the morning. I have a better idea," Nero said retrieving his clothes and getting dressed.

When we all returned to our trucks, we caravanned out of the middle of nowhere back into town. Things took a while to look familiar. When they did, we were pulling up to the house we had visited the day before. In the back was Dr. Tom's office. In the front was a beautiful two-story home that glowed.

"Someone's still awake," I told Quin. "Do you think this is a good idea?'

"Which part?"

"All of it. Any of it. Honestly, my mind is a swirling mess right now. I can't decide."

Quin slowed down and looked at me with caring eyes.

"How are you feeling by the way? This must be a lot to wrap you head around."

"You know, as weird as it sounds, me getting mad and turning into a wolf? It feels like I always knew. I mean, I didn't. But, meeting you... Finding out you were one... Finding out I'm one...? It feels all kinds of right.

"Now, the fact that Nero could be my brother and that my mother could be alive? I didn't see that coming. That part's a lot."

"Do you want to keep going with this? We don't have to do the test if you don't want to," he said reaching across the truck and putting his hand on mine.

"I want to. I really want to. What if I have a family, Quin? What would that even mean?"

"I don't know. But there is only one way to find out," he said squeezing my hand.

I could have kept staring into his eyes forever if Dr. Tom and Glen didn't exit onto the porch wearing robes.

"Nero, Titus, is that you?" Dr. Tom asked as we approached. "What's going on?"

They didn't reply. When Dr. Tom saw us, they didn't have to.

"I see you found Nero," he said to Quin stoically.

"I did. But not before Cage shifted into a wolf and the two of them tried to kill each other," Quin told him.

"Huh. And, what are you doing here?"

"We need a blood test to see if they're brothers," Quin explained.

"I see," he said casually. "Come back in the morning."

"Did you know that I could have a brother?" Nero asked Dr. Tom.

He didn't answer.

"You did," Nero said shocked. "After all of those things I told you were going on, you couldn't tell me that my mom might not be crazy?"

For the first time, Dr. Tom's stone face cracked. Regret washed over him.

"No matter what else I am, I'm also a doctor. There are things I can't disclose to anyone no matter…"

"That's bullshit!" Nero injected. "I was a kid crying to you about all the crap that was going on and not once did you even suggest that this could be a possibility."

"That's not true. I hinted. I told you that sometimes things aren't what they seem."

"And that was supposed to mean something to a ten-year-old? That was just a bunch of adult garbage to me. How was I supposed to know that you were telling me that I had a brother and that my mother wasn't nuts? No. You're a fuckin' asshole."

Dr. Tom regained his composure.

"Fine. I'm a fucking asshole. If that's all, you can all have a good night."

"Wait," I said stopping him from going. "Look, I don't know you. And, I definitely don't understand how any of this stuff works. But, I do understand family.

"For 22 years I've been without one. At least, one that cared about me. And if you take 20 minutes of your time, you might be able to cure me of that. Whatever else you are, you're saying you're a doctor, right? Then, help me."

Dr. Tom's eyes bounced between the four of us yet he didn't budge.

"Just do it, Tom," Glen said moved.

"There are things going on, Glen."

Glen put his hand on his husband's shoulder and spoke to him kindly. "Just do it."

The doctor melted looking into his love's sympathetic eyes.

"Fine. Follow me to my office. But, I don't know where I can get a genetic test done."

"I can arrange it. My father has a genetics lab and…"

"Right. Because you're Quin Toro and your father has a genetics lab studying wolf shifters!"

Dr. Tom stopped and whipped around to stare at Quin. "Your father's studying shifters, isn't he? That's why you're here. That's why you want Nero's blood?"

"What? No. No! We want a blood sample to find out if Cage and Nero are brothers. Why would you think that?"

"Because you're Quin Toro, and…"

"…And I can't be trusted?" Tears immediately filled Quin's eyes. "So, the human world doesn't trust me because I'm a wolf shifter freak. And, now you won't trust me because my father is human? Really?" Quin turned to me with pain in his eyes. "Really?"

I hadn't understood. But, I was starting to get what it was like being him. He had grown up with everyone looking at him suspiciously. And, hadn't his wolf killed his mother? Wouldn't that make him suspicious of himself? No wonder he had said that he was looking for a cure for shifting. I couldn't imagine living a life like his.

"Look, it's my job to keep this community safe," Dr. Tom told him. "I can't give you their blood if there's even a chance that you'll use it to harm them."

"I'm not. I just want to help them," he insisted.

"I trust him, Dr. Tom," I told him feeling it deep inside. "You can too. He's never done anything to betray my trust. He's only ever been good and moral. He's only ever helped people. If there were ever anyone you could trust, it would be him.

"I don't know why you didn't tell Nero that he might have had a brother. I'm sure you had your reasons. But this is your chance to make up for it. And you can't do that without Quin's help. You can trust him. We all can."

Dr. Tom stared at me and then looked at everyone standing around him before settling on Nero.

"Do you want this, Nero?"

"I need to know if he's my brother. You owe me that."

Dr. Tom's eyes dipped before he quickly gathered himself. "Let me get you what you need," he told Quin.

Drawing a small vile of blood from Nero and me, the doctor labeled them and handed them to Quin.

"This should be more than enough. Don't make me regret this," he said composed.

"Thank you," Quin replied.

"Yes, thank you," I said before looking over at Nero. Nero looked away still pissed at the bearded, Latino man.

Standing in front of our trucks, Quin turned to Nero.

"We'll let you know as soon as we find out anything."

"Okay."

"Can I get your number?" I asked him as nervous as I would be on a first date.

"Yeah. What's your number I'll text you it."

I told Nero and a few seconds later my phone buzzed.

"I got it," I told him.

"Cool."

"So, I guess we're heading back," I told them.

"Okay," Nero said hesitant to say goodbye.

Instead of walking away, Nero threw his arms around me pulling me close. I thought he was hugging me. He was instead pulling my ear to his mouth.

He whispered, "Seriously, I'm really sorry about what I said. It's not me. Alright?"

"Alright," I assured him.

"It's not me," he repeated.

"That's cool, Nero. A fresh start."

Nero pulled away and smiled. "Yeah. A fresh start."

I saw it. He was as covered in dimples as I was. If Dr. Tom hadn't practically confirmed it, I would now have no doubt. I was looking at my brother.

"Quin, it was good to meet you," Nero said offering him his hand.

"Good to meet you, too," Quin said politely before both of us got into my truck and pulled away.

Most of our two-hour drive back to school was in silence. The last three days had been a lot. Not only had things happened between Quin and me, but I had found out that I was a wolf shifter and that I might have a family.

On top of that was what Quin said he wanted to do with the rest of his life. He wanted to move to New York to cure himself of his wolf. I understood why he wanted it, but neither of those things was something I wanted a part of.

With my leg healed, I could pick back up where I left off and play for the NFL. But I had given that up for a reason. All I ever wanted was a small life surrounded by people I love.

Was that the wolf in me? This was all new so I had no idea. But, whatever the cause, that had always been my dream even if I didn't realize it until now. And that didn't include moving to the big city to help my boyfriend get rid of the thing that made us perfect for each other.

What we wanted for our lives was starting to feel very different. But I didn't want to lose him. There had to be some way to convince him that he didn't need to get rid of his wolf to have a good life.

I considered all of this as I drove him to his dorm. When we arrived, we sat in the truck with the engine running.

"This weekend was…" Quin said trailing off.

"It was something," I completed.

Quin laughed. "Yes."

"Now that I'm back, I'm probably going to have to make up a few shifts at work. But, I want to see you."

"I want to see you, too," he said with a smile. "After all, you are my boyfriend."

"Yeah, I am," I said having forgotten.

With that, I leaned over, slipped my hand behind his neck, and pulled his lips to mine. The kiss was electric. The heat between us billowed. Having him in my hands again made my body tingle.

"Cage!" I heard someone say.

I pulled away from where I most wanted to be to see Tasha staring into the truck. She looked shocked.

Behind her was her best friend Vi, because, of course, she was. With her mouth still hanging open, she ran to the door of their building.

"I take it that she isn't okay with the breakup?" Quin asked.

"She should be. She's the one who broke up with me. Although, I was gonna do it if she hadn't. I didn't need to know that I was a wolf shifter to realize we were meant to be together."

Quin blushed. "Did you want to come up?" he asked with the cutest shy smile.

"Thanks for the invitation, but I should go home. I have class in the morning and it was a long drive. I just wanna shower and pass out."

Quin was disappointed. "Okay. When am I going to see you again?"

I thought about that. There was a part of me that wanted to go to his room with him and never let him out of my sight for the rest of my life.

"I'll text you tomorrow. By the way, when do you think you'll get the results from the blood test?"

"I'll call my dad in the morning and then send it as soon as I can after that. I assume I'll have something by Friday?"

"Wow, that's fast."

"My crazy life comes in handy sometimes."

Quin settled in my eyes. "I'm already missing you," he told me.

"Me too," I told him knowing what I was going to have to get him to give up if we were going to be together.

I smiled, kissed him one more time, and then watched him walk away. He was the sexiest person I had ever seen. I couldn't believe that someone like him wanted to be with me.

As I drove home I thought about the magnitude of what I had discovered about myself. I was a friggin' wolf shifter. That's... crazy. I couldn't even begin to understand what that meant.

And, how was it that my father was a dragon shifter? Could dragon shifters have kids that were wolf shifters? Or, was how Dr. Tom had described dragons true. Was the man who raised me a hording, greedy, thief?

I couldn't deny how much that sounded like him. So, if you add in how different my father and I looked and acted, didn't I have to take his drunken comments as truth? Had he just stolen me from someone who might have loved me?

Why would he have done it? How much different would my life had been if he hadn't? Could Nero be my true family? Could I actually have a mother?

By the time I had arrived back at the cabin, I had worked myself into a rage. I had a plan and I was going to use an axe to get my father out of my life for good.

Piled outside, I was then going to burn his remains to ash.

Unlocking the cabin's front door, I pulled it open with a singular purpose. What I found threw me back as hard as seeing it for the first time. The dragon was gone. Where did it go? Did this mean my father was alive?

Preparing myself for anything including a life and death fight, my heart raced. Scanning everywhere, I slowly explored the cabin. It looked like how I had left it on Friday just with the dragon gone.

My father's bedroom door was still partially open. If he had shifted back into himself, there was no way he wouldn't at least have closed it considering how obsessed he had been with keeping it locked. And, when I confirmed that the place was empty, I grabbed my phone and called Quin.

"It's gone," I told him.

"What's gone?" he said responding to my panic.

"The dragon. It's just gone."

He didn't respond.

"Did you hear me, Quin?"

"Do you think it's coming after me?"

"I don't know. I don't know anything except that it's not here. Neither is my father. Do you want me to come and get you? I can come and get you."

"No don't," he said seeming to calm down.

"It's not a problem. I could be there in thirty minutes."

"But you just drove for three hours."

"I'd drive all night to keep you safe. You gotta know that, Quin" I told him knowing it was true.

"Thank you. But, I don't think it's necessary. Wherever he is, he probably has more to worry about than getting revenge on me for stealing you away."

"You didn't steal me from anything. You're the one who always had me, even before we met."

"I can't explain it but I feel the say way," he told me.

"I wish I could shift on command like you do. If I did, I could get his scent and find out what happened to him."

"I could teach you how. Why don't I go home with you after you're done with work tomorrow? I could see what my wolf knows. And, I could start teaching you how to control your shifts."

"You can do that?"

"Of course. I can't have you wolfing out in the middle of class and killing everyone, can I? They would not let you graduate if you did that," he teased.

"And all of your tutoring would be for nothing?"

"Exactly!" he said smiling.

I laughed. "We wouldn't want that."

"No, we wouldn't. So, I'll meet you at the activity center after your shift… I mean, when you're done with work?"

I chuckled. Yeah, being a shifter was going to come with some rewording.

"Sounds like a plan," I told him before telling him good night and ending the call.

I slept uneasy that night. The slightest sound woke me up. But, when the sun rose and neither the dragon nor my father returned, I relaxed and was able to get in a few hours uninterrupted.

I could barely think of anything else during my classes and at work. So when Dan asked me how my leg was and reminded me that I no longer had a cast, I didn't know how to reply.

"It's feeling better," I told him.

"Does this mean you can come back to the team soon?" He asked excitedly. "We need you, man. It's been rough without you."

I considered it. I could definitely play. And tapping into my new abilities, I could probably sniff out a play better than I ever have. It wasn't that I hated football. I just didn't want everything that came with going pro.

As a top prospect returning to the field from what seemed like a career ending injury, how could everyone else's expectations for me not return? Not to mention, what if after a dirty tackle, I shifted and tore the guy to bits?

No. I couldn't be trusted on a field. At least, not yet.

"Sorry, Dan," I told him feeling like I was letting the team down.

"Don't worry about it. We'll figure it out. You just figure out how to get healthy. That's all that matters," he told me with a smile.

I appreciated him saying that. I had allows thought of him as one of the guys trying ride my coattails as the star quarterback who would go pro. But, I had underestimated him. He was a real friend. If there was anyone I would tell the truth about what I am, it was going to be him.

Ending work at 7, I met up with Quin and we headed to my place. He brought a bag telling me that he was intending on staying over. I liked that. I had missed sleeping with him in my arms.

When we arrived back at the cabin, he shifted and got right to work. His wolf sniffed every inch of the space before he reemerged naked and looking as sexy as hell.

"You're right. He's gone. There's not a trace of his scent anywhere. It's like he vanished into thin air."

"Is that something that dead dragon's do?" I asked confused.

"Your guess is as good as mine," he admitted.

"You know who might know?"

"Dr. Tom? Yeah, I was thinking about that. But, I'm not his favorite person."

"Maybe Nero or Titus knows something about it. By the way, did you send your dad the blood samples?"

"I overnighted it. It won't be long now."

With Quin still walking around naked, I grabbed my phone and shot Nero a text.

'He sent it off. Not long now.'

'Cool,' he texted back immediately. 'When do you think you will know?'

'Quin guessed Friday. Btw, know anything about dragon shifters?'

'No. Why?'

I debated telling him. Something told me to wait until after we confirmed that he was my brother.

'Just tryin' to figure everything out,' I wrote instead.

I didn't hear back from him after that. I wasn't sure why.

"So, do you want to learn how to do this?" he asked standing in front of me looking incredible.

"Yeah."

"Then, get naked."

I looked at him suspiciously. Was he just looking for us to have sex again? If he was, I was up for it. And by that I meant that I was starting to get hard.

"Maybe, I'll start like this."

"Suit yourself. But, you're going to have to tap into your inner wolf to let it happen."

"What does that mean?"

"It means, you have to let yourself go and let your instincts and raw emotions take over. Watch," he told me before closing his eyes and gritting through his breaking bones to become his wolf.

After staring at me for a moment, he shifted back.

"Doesn't that hurt?" I asked him remembering the agony I felt.

"You get used to it. And, like I said, it's like child birth. You get a rush of endorphins to help you forget the pain when it's done," he said with a smile.

"I don't remember that part of it. All I remember was hearing things snap."

"Yeah. There's that too," he conceded.

Just like how he had tutored me in 'Intro to Childhood Education,' he tutored me in shifting. It turned out that his overnight bag included charts and a lesson planner. I would never have guessed that turning into a wolf could be so clinical, but Quin had made it that.

I wasn't able to shift that night… and we spent hours trying. Nor could I do it the following night. But on Wednesday, I did even though I couldn't control it.

It just kinda slipped out. One minute he was telling me to think of something my father had done that had pissed me off. I thought about him threatening Quin. Seconds later, I was floating behind my wolf's eyes.

It took all night to return to my human self, but when I did, I fucked Quin like an animal. It was primal. I had gripped his hair pulling it back while stretching his hole open with my throbbing cock. It was like I was still part wolf and he was my mate.

After we had both cum multiple times, we laid together with him buried in my arms. I couldn't get enough of him. I hadn't realized how good he smelled until that night. His scent could only be described as jasmine mixed with black licorice. Who would have thought the two would smell so good together, but, god damn did it do things to me.

The following night we continued working until I was able to shift back within an hour. And when we both decided that I could control things to a reasonable degree, he took his training to the next level.

"I haven't shifted this much since I was 14," he admitted. "I had been trying to avoid it for so long."

"Feels good, doesn't it?" I asked him hoping he would see his wolf as a good thing.

"It has it perks," he said reluctantly. "So, do you think you're ready for this?"

"And, what happens if I take off?"

"Then you ride it out. And when you shift back, you walk home. I don't think that will happen, though. You've caught on a lot faster than I did."

"Well, you didn't have such a good teacher."

"I didn't have any teacher. All I could do was figure things out as I went. I mean, my father did his best, and I'm grateful to have had him. But, it's not like having someone who's gone through it."

"I'm lucky to have you," I said feeling a connection with him that almost brought me to tears.

"Okay. So, if you want to shift first, I'll open the door and then I'll join you. And, don't worry. You have this," he said confidently.

I appreciated the faith he had in me even though I didn't know if I deserved it. I was still inconsistent with my shifts. And, as much as my wolf yearned to run free in the woods, I questioned whether I would have any say once he was out.

Looking into Quin's eyes a final time, I undressed and focused. Knowing it was getting what it wanted, I never shifted so quickly. It stared up at Quin waiting anxiously. When he opened the door a crack, my wolf pushed into it and was gone.

Cutting through the trees, I realized why I had enjoyed playing football so much. It was my wolf begging to be free. The feeling of the breeze on my fur, smells that were layered all around me, there was nothing about this that I didn't like. And when Quin's wolf caught up to me and we ran together, my heart hurt with joy.

Quin and I ran until our bodies couldn't take it anymore. I was, of course, a lot bigger and faster than he was. But, unlike me, he knew how to run like he wasn't an excited puppy with a new toy. While my tongue flapped as I fought to catch my breath, he cut through the air like a silver bullet. He was amazing.

When I couldn't run anymore and he slowed to be with me, our eyes caught and I knew what I wanted next. I shifted into a human as quickly as I had a wolf. And when he joined me and again looked into my eyes, the two of us attacked each other and made love in the moonlight.

Lost in the middle of nowhere, I met a side of Quin I had yet to. As aggressive as I was being, he was more so. Tossing me onto my back, he took my cock into his mouth. It was only enough to get me flinching because what he really wanted, he claimed next.

Climbing on top of me, he grabbed hold of my dick and lined it up with his opening. As if I were half my size, he threw himself onto me. Not ready for it, he howled feeling me enter him. Whatever pain he felt, he took it out on my chest.

With his nails digging into my pecs, he slapped his dripping cock on my stomach. He was a wild man. And the way his head rolled, I had to wonder if he was possessed.

Possessed or not, I wanted it all. Gripping his small chest in my large hands, my thumbs pressed his nipples. That didn't stop him from using my cock like a jackhammer.

When we finally came, it was together. I screamed as the pleasure ripped through me. Perched on top of me, Quin arced his back and literally howled at the moon.

Staring up at his silhouette in the night's light, I was sure that I saw his wolf appear. It didn't last. He was back to his full self for when he fell forward and collapsed into my arms. It had been the most erotic experience of my life. My mind swirled processing it all.

What do you say to someone after something like that? It was beyond words. All I could think of was how Quin could want to get rid of his wolf knowing that it allowed him to have such experiences. It seemed unthinkable.

"I have something to tell you," he eventually said breaking the hollow silence.

"What's that?"

"My father sent me the test results."

My heart sunk hearing Quin's words. It wasn't like I had forgotten about it. But, I hadn't expected to hear it now.

"And?"

"Are you sure you want to know?"

Did I want to know whether Nero was my brother and if I had a mother? Of course, I did… I think. What would knowing change? Probably everything.

I didn't even know what it would mean to have a family. The man who had raised me wasn't what family was supposed to be. I had always known that. What if I could have that other thing with Nero and… my mom?

"I wanna know," I said preparing myself for anything.

Chapter 15

Quin

I wasn't sure what I was doing with Cage. I mean, I knew. I was in love with him more than I thought possible. I thought about him constantly. He was like a drug for me.

What I wasn't sure about was what I was doing with him tonight. My mind had been swirling ever since my father had called me this morning. As soon as I heard the results, I could see the end of us. But I was going to do anything I could to hold onto him.

Did I think he was ready to let his wolf run in the woods? Not really. I had it on my lesson plan for much later. But I thought he needed to feel the rush of it. And I wanted him to feel it with me first.

Then, I guess, with everything going on in my head, it opened a door for my wolf to take the reins. The thing riding him like a sex-starved cowboy wasn't me. That didn't mean I didn't enjoy it. It was fantastic. It was just that I wasn't the one in control.

But it was now time to tell Cage about the results. With Dr. Tom's suggestion playing on my mind, I had only told my father that the blood was from two friends looking for a favor. That left no room for doubt about what my father told me. I kinda wished there was.

"I wanna know," he said as his body tensed under me.

I swallowed and braced myself.

"You and Nero are brothers," I told him.

"We're brothers?"

Cage looked at me and sat up. That forced me off of him. I found a spot on the soft ground next to him and stared.

"Yes."

"That means I have a mother."

"You do."

"Oh my God. I can't believe this."

"There's more."

"What?"

"You're not just brothers. You're full brothers. You share the same mother and father."

Cage stared at me stunned. His mouth hung open trying to process it all.

"I need to tell him. We need to go back," he insisted as he stood up.

Following his lead, I got up. "We could walk if you aren't up for shifting again so quickly," I told him wanting to spend as much time with him as I could before everything changed.

"No. I think I can do it," he said closing his eyes and quickly shifting.

I wasn't that surprised. Shifting had a lot to do with motivation. Clearly he wanted his new life to begin. The question was whether I was going to be a part of it. I hoped so, but if he wanted a life with them, didn't it mean that he wasn't interested in being a part of my life?

I shifted and was ready to follow him when I realized that he hadn't yet figured out how to track his own path back. That made sense. As quickly as he was catching on, there was still a lot he didn't know.

It took me years to figure out as much as I knew and even with that, I hadn't been able to shift back and forth on command until a few weeks ago. Part of that was because of all of the work my father and I had done to stop me from shifting. Another part was that, before the day I had met Cage, it had been years since my last shift.

There was something about him that drew my wolf out of me. And it was only because of Cage that I have embraced my wolf as much as I have. I was still going to get rid of it, though, no matter how much harder it was becoming. Because as friendly as he had been with Lou and Cage, I couldn't forget that he was a wild animal and could turn on someone I loved at any moment.

Leading Cage back to his cabin, we entered the still open door and shifted back. The first thing Cage did was put back on his jeans and grab his phone. Knowing that I had lost him for the night, I got dressed and got comfortable on the couch.

"Nero, we got back the results... Yeah. We're... brothers," Cage said with tears forming in his eyes.

There was a long pause before Cage spoke again. Tears streamed down his cheeks as he listened. Cage turned to me and mouthed, "He's crying."

"Yeah," he said returning his attention to the call. "I would definitely like to meet our mother... What about tomorrow? I could drive up... Okay. Then I guess I'll see you, and mom, then... I know, right," Cage said with a smile.

Cage ended the call and stared at his phone.

"I'm going up tomorrow."

"Can I come with you? I mean, if you want me to. I can get us a room for the weekend in case you want to stay over," I told him wanting to be a part of what was going to be the most important moment of Cage's life.

"Of course you can! None of this would be happening if it wasn't for you. I want you there," Cage said sincerely.

Relief washed through me knowing that he wanted me there. I was sure that he would hear that he had a brother and mother and things would immediately be over between us. I could never compete with that. Going with him at least gave us a shot.

In spite of what I thought it meant for us, it did warm my heart to see Cage as happy as he was. He seemed equally excited and nervous.

I couldn't sleep thinking about what was going to happen when he was introduced to his mom. I hadn't met another shifter until Nero, but even I knew the importance of a pack to a wolf. How could his family not be his new pack? Where did that leave me in his life?

Driving up the next morning, it was pretty tense in the truck. Neither of us was saying a word. Nero had suggested that we meet at the diner since nowhere in town showed up on a map. Approaching it, I asked Cage if we should check in with Dr. Sonya and drop off our bags before we met up. Cage didn't see the point. I agreed, so we headed right over.

"You guys hungry?" Nero asked when we entered.

He looked like a different person than the one we had first met. For one thing, he had a smile on his face. Everything about him looked lighter.

"Are you going to join us?" Cage said as happy to be with Nero as Nero was to be with him.

"Yeah, I'll join you," he said enthusiastically.

"You're not off yet," the cook yelled from the kitchen.

"Is there anyone else in here? I'll get back to work when someone comes in," he said with bravado. "You guys want burgers? I'll ask him to fix us a couple of burgers. Pick a seat," he said before heading back to the kitchen.

"He seems happy to see you," I told Cage.

As nervous as Cage had looked before we arrived, he was now glowing. I was an only child so I didn't know how the two of them felt. Was this the way it was when you had a sibling or a pack? It must be nice to have someone you can count on to have your back.

I had always thought that was what a boyfriend was for. But, I guess when you grow up alone and thinking you are the only one of your kind like I did, that was as much as you can imagine.

Once Nero rejoined us. I couldn't do much but sit back and listen to the two talk. Every so often Nero would direct a question at the both of us. He even asked me a few questions directly. I tried to keep my answers short, though. I knew why we had come, and I wanted this to be as little about me as possible.

Once we were done with lunch, the look on Nero's face changed. A weight took over him.

"So, did you want to meet our mother?"

"Yeah," Cage said with the innocence of a ten-year-old.

Getting up, I reached for my wallet to pay.

"I got it," Nero said.

"That's fine. I have it," I said not wanting to put him in that situation.

"No, I got it," Nero insisted.

I was about to object when Cage cut me off.

"Nero, says he has it!" he said abruptly.

It startled me. I had clearly upset him. But, at the same time, I couldn't let him pay for me. It would be unfair. Nero might not have known it. And, Cage might not have realized how unfair it would be. But I knew, so I couldn't let it happen.

"Can I at least leave the tip?"

"The tip?" Nero asked confused.

Cage growled. He was not happy.

"For the cook," I clarified.

"If he wants to tip the cook, let him tip the cook," the cook yelled from the kitchen.

I didn't realize that he could hear us.

Nero laughed. "Alright, you can leave the tip."

I pulled out enough to pay for the meal and left it on the table. I tried to do it so Nero didn't know how much I was leaving, but he did. His eyes flicked up at me amused by what I had done. Thankfully he let it go.

"Do you want to leave your truck here and ride with me, or follow?" Nero asked.

Cage looked at me.

"Whatever you want to do," I told him not wanting to upset him any more.

"We'll follow you," Cage said getting into his truck.

The drive to Nero's place turned out to be long. They lived 25 minutes out of town. It was outside of Dr. Tom's protective spell and it was a relief to not have to deal with its limitations. I looked over at Cage wondering if he noticed a difference.

"How are you feeling?"

"Nervous. Scared. What if she doesn't like me?"

Either the other things on his mind made him not notice, or he wasn't yet connected to his wolf enough for the change to register.

"Cage, she'll love you," I reassured him. "Everyone does. I just hope she likes me."

Cage didn't reply. Did that mean that he was worried about the same thing? I was sure that I wasn't the type of wolf shifter a person who grew up around shifters would want their kid to bring home. Who wanted their son to be with a boy who couldn't fit into either world?

I shouldn't have come. I could see that now. But it was too late for him to drop me off at the bed and breakfast without making things worse between us. So I instead chose to keep my mouth closed and be as invisible as possible.

Cage was meeting his mother for the first time. I just wanted him to be comfortable. He seemed to be having a hard enough time as is. He didn't need all of the complications that I brought along with what he was already going through.

When Nero's truck pulled over, it was into a sparsely populated trailer park. I didn't know what I was expecting but I wasn't expecting this. I looked over at Cage to judge his reaction. He didn't have one. I could tell that he was on edge, but it probably didn't have to do with where we were.

Following Nero to an aging mobile home that reminded me of the office on a construction site, we parked next to Nero's truck and joined Nero in front of it. Nero looked at Cage with sympathy in his eyes. He looked like he wanted to tell Cage something before he invited him in. He didn't.

"Come," he said nervously before leading us up the wobbly stairs to the front door.

Waiting at the bottom of them, I put my hand on the railing. Paint chips stuck to my palm. Subtly brushing them off, I waited my turn to ascend and enter.

Inside was worn, but tidy. The linoleum floors, floral wallpaper, and wooden kitchen cabinets had all faded to the same shade of beige. It was also very small. To the right of the door was the kitchen. To the left was the TV room and past that was a small hallway with three doors.

I turned to Cage. His eyes were locked on the woman sitting on the couch in front of the TV. With her dark, graying hair, angular features, and distinct wolf shifter scent, there was only one person she could be. She had clearly been as beautiful as Cage was handsome. But time, and a hard life, had caught up with her. Not having turned when we had entered, Nero called to her.

"Mama?" Nero said getting her to turn around.

Seeing Nero, Cage's mother next turned examining us. She looked confused.

"Mama, remember I said that I was going to bring some friends by?"

She didn't say anything but her eyes bounced between the three of us.

"This is Cage and his boyfriend Quin," Nero said speaking slowly.

"Nice to meet you," Cage said stepping forward. He lifted his hand to shake hers, but when she didn't move, he abandoned the gesture.

"Nice to meet you," I said questioning if I should be here.

"Mama, I found out something about Cage that you should know."

Her eyes turned to Nero.

"Cage is… my brother."

Her increasingly confused look said that she had understood.

"Your brother?" she said slowly.

"Yeah, Mama. Quin took our blood and everything. He's my brother."

"Your brother?"

"Yeah. Our blood says that we share the same father… and mother."

She looked extremely confused after that. As she fought to wrap her thoughts around what Nero was saying, Cage stepped forward.

"Mama, you know how you say that they took your baby away from you and told you that he had died? Mama, this is your son. He's your baby," Nero said getting emotional. "You were right, Mama. He was alive. This is him."

"Nice to meet you," Cage, said again.

She stared at his face from the couch.

"Augustus?" She said squinting at him.

"My name's Cage," he told her.

"I named you Augustus," she said slowly melting into tears. "They took you from me and told me you had died. I knew you hadn't died. I told them to show you to me. They couldn't. They couldn't," she said reaching up for Cage overwhelmed.

Throwing himself into his mother's arms, both held each other crying. I couldn't imagine what Cage was going through. But it felt good to know that I had helped do this for him. It had to be the most fulfilling thing I had ever done.

Soon, Nero joined them on the couch and embraced the two. The three cried and held each other not saying a word. I couldn't escape the moment. Tears rolled down my cheeks as much as they did theirs.

This was their private moment, though. I shouldn't have been there. Without any of them noticing, I slipped outside and made my way to the truck. Getting in, I bundled up and thought.

I had grown up surrounded by wealth and humans. This was a different world than anything I could have imagined a short time ago. I knew that it wasn't just wolf shifters who lived like this. But, did being a wolf shifter mean that this was the life you were forced to have?

Nero and Titus were the only ones I had met. Clearly Titus didn't live like Nero and his mom did, but he still lived in a struggling town. Is that what you had to do if you wanted to embrace being a shifter? Were you forced to scratch out an existence on the fringes of the human world? And, even if I were willing to keep my wolf, could I live like this?

I sat thinking about this for thirty minutes before Cage came out and joined me.

"You left," he stated.

"I wanted to give you all some privacy."

Cage's eyes dipped down without him responding.

"You did this. You and your wolf found my mother. All I can say is thank you."

"Of course," I responded not knowing what else to say.

"It's not "of course." My entire life I've wondered what she looked like and what it would be like to hear her voice. You gave me that. And, I don't think anyone else in the world could have."

I responded with a tight-lipped smile. I didn't know what I was supposed to say.

Cage's eyes left mine as he measured what he would say next.

"I want to spend some more time with her… with the both of them. But, I don't want you to feel like you have to sit out here. Do you mind if I drop you off at the bed and breakfast? It would probably be more comfortable than sitting in this cold truck. Maybe you could call Titus. I'm sure he'd want to hang out."

I didn't know what I was expecting Cage to say, but it wasn't this. Maybe I thought he would encourage me to come inside. Maybe I thought he would want to bring me into his moment. But, thinking about it, that was probably just a fantasy.

Cage had just met his mother for the first time. He had so many questions for her. What would I do except sit there? He was right, it was better that I go somewhere else instead of being the awkward guy sitting in the car during the most important moments of his life.

"I wouldn't want you to have to drop me."

"Well, you can't exactly call an Uber," he said with a smile. "I'll drop you and come back."

"Okay," I agreed feeling Cage slowly pull away.

Cage headed back to the front door and Nero came out to talk to him. Nero looked back at me as Cage spoke. I hated being the asshole breaking up this amazing moment. I felt awful.

Both Cage and he walked back to the truck. As Cage got in, Nero circled to my door. Withdrawing his hand from his pocket he knocked and stepped back. I took that as a sign that he wanted me to come out. When I did, he threw his arms around me.

"Cage said that you were the one to bring us together," he whispered into my ear. "Thank you. Thank you!" he said before slapping my back and pulling away.

"You're welcome," was the only thing I could reply.

I couldn't truly understand what this moment meant to them. How could I? I had grown up with more love and family than I knew what to do with. But the moment wasn't completely lost on me. Would I ever in my life accomplish anything greater than what I had done for them? I didn't know.

Cage and I didn't speak much on the drive back to town. He was deep in thought. The selfish part of me wished that a few of those thoughts were of me. It was probably too much to ask for, though.

Pulling up to Dr. Sonya's bed and breakfast, Cali quickly came outside to greet us. Standing in front of the door on the porch, he looked at us with a light in his eyes. Before I got out, Dr. Sonya joined him.

"It looks like I'm leaving you in good hands," Cage said staring at the two.

"Don't worry about me. Go. Spend time with your family. You deserve this. I'll be fine," I told him.

"I love you," Cage said leaning over and kissing me.

"I love you, too," I told him before grabbing my bag and leaving the truck.

Walking to the veranda, Cage didn't wait for me to get there before driving away. I turned to watch him go. I got the sense that he didn't look back. I couldn't know that for sure, but it certainly felt like it.

"Welcome back!" Dr. Sonya said enthusiastically. "It's good to see you," she said putting her arm around me and leading me in. "Will Cage be coming back?"

"I don't know," I told her honestly. "We found his mother."

She looked at me confused. "I thought you came to the town looking for a red headed man?"

"We did. But we found Cage's mother instead," I said with as much enthusiasm as I could manage.

"That's incredible! Had she been missing?"

"In a way. He had never met her."

"That's amazing!"

"It is. It's quite wonderful."

"Well, we'll have to do something to celebrate," she concluded making me feel as if I were a part of her family.

I dropped my bag in my room and lied in bed thinking about everything again. Once it started making me feel worse than I already felt, I decided to head downstairs.

"Did you have dinner plans? Would you like to join us?" Dr. Sonya said from the kitchen.

"I don't think I have plans. I haven't spoken to Cage, though."

"Then how about you join us, and if you have to run off, you do?" She suggested with a smile.

"Sounds great. Thank you," I told her before joining Cali in the living room watching TV.

I could feel Cali's uneasiness as I sat there with him. Always having been the shy one, I knew how he felt.

"How long have you been playing football?" I asked him causing his cheeks to turn bright red.

Cage might have been right. He did seem to have a crush on me.

"Since freshman year," he eventually squeaked.

"That's cool. Are you thinking about attending East Tennessee?"

"I was thinking about it."

"It's a good school. I think you'd like it there. If you ever want a tour, let me know."

Cali didn't respond, but he did turn beet red at my suggestion. I was going to have to be careful with what I said to him. The last thing I wanted to do was hurt him or lead him on.

Bringing up Cage many times, I spent the rest of the night with my two hosts. After dinner, Dr. Sonya suggested a game of Scrabble.

"I have to warn you. I'm pretty good," Dr. Sonya said proudly. "There's a group of us in town that play and I haven't lost a game in two years."

I nodded politely and then beat them by 50 points.

Dr. Sonya stared at the board shocked.

"We need to play that again," she announced.

We did and the results were similar. But, more importantly, it was fun. It took my mind off of Cage. So, when he texted saying that he was going to sleep there, it stung less.

Heading to bed alone and waking up alone, I tried not to let my imagination get away from me. The only reason Cage hadn't returned was because he wanted to spend time with his family. That made complete sense. It had nothing to do with me or how he felt about us. He needed this time and I was going to give it to him.

I didn't hear from him until nearly 11 A.M. when he told me that he would come by around 7 P.M. to pick me up.

'Are you having a good time?' I texted in reply.

It took him 30 minutes to text me back. 'Definitely! I'll tell you all about it later.'

I was trying, but it was getting harder not to take this personally. No matter what I told myself, I couldn't shake my insecurity.

To take my mind off of it, I texted Titus. It took less than a minute for him to call me back.

"Quin! How the hell are you? I was just thinking about you two."

"I was texting you because I'm in town."

"Seriously! Let's get together! When are you two free?"

I explained to him where Cage was and what they were doing, so he instead suggested that we do some ice fishing.

"You already made the hole," Titus joked.

Although I had never gone ice fishing, I had done plenty of shallow water fishing during my summers in the Bahamas. Most days it was the only thing to do.

After a day out on the ice, we didn't end up catching anything. Titus said it was because they weren't biting. My guess was that it was his non-stop talking.

That was fine with me, though. What was I going to do with a fish other than throw it back? And Titus was interesting to talk... I mean, listen to.

He had ideas about a lot of things, most of which involved growing up in a town cut off from the outside world by a spell that dampened a wolf's senses. He claimed that it robbed shifters of half of who they were.

He also explained Nero's wolf fights. Although Titus said he never participated in them, he said he understood the desire to let go and completely embrace the wolf.

"When did you first shift?" I asked him as I began to notice a pattern in his stories.

"When I was 18. Around the same time as most people. Why? When did you first shift?"

"About 5 minutes after I was born."

"Wow! That's incredible. So, you have always known life as a shifter?"

"Actually, being in this town feels like the first time I've known it."

"I don't understand."

"I thought I was the only one."

Titus stared at me and then laughed. "You thought you were the only wolf shifter in existence?"

"Yeah, that's what I was told."

"By who?"

"By everybody. You don't know what it's like living outside of this town."

Titus became more serious. "You're right. I don't. And, I shouldn't laugh. I'm sure it was a challenge."

"It was near unbearable."

"Well, I'm sorry to hear that. But, as a person who wishes he knew life outside of this bubble, what you're describing doesn't sound so bad."

"Have you given any more thought to coming to East Tennessee University?" I asked him deciding that he would fit right in.

"Yes, I have. The way Dr. Tom always talked about the human world made it seem like a shifter would die the minute he stepped foot in it. But, knowing you and Cage have lived your entire lives out there has inspired me. I will be filling out an application for next semester," he said with a smile.

"That's awesome!"

"Yeah. And, maybe when I'm there, I'll find myself a great guy like you did," he said with a knowing smile.

I stared at Titus not wanting to express my surprise. I really shouldn't have been. The one thing I should have learned from the people I grew up with was that you didn't have to look or act a certain way to like someone of the same sex.

"So, you're... gay? Bisexual?"

Titus's head bobbed around as he answered.

"Let's say, I'm open," he said with another of his brilliant smiles. "I haven't said that to anyone before."

"Thanks for sharing it with me. If you come to E.T. I'll have to introduce you to my roommate, Lou. I don't know that many people at school like us... I don't know any other people at all, really. But, he'll be able to tell you all of the places to meet guys. That's kind of his specialty."

"He sounds like a great resource."

"He's a great person," I said not able to say enough about Lou.

The rest of our day was spent discussing when we each realized that we were into guys. I certainly would have preferred to spend the day with Cage. But the day I had with Titus was pretty good.

Overall, the weekend ended up being better than any I would have had if I had stayed at school and allowed Cage to come up by himself. I liked Titus, Dr. Sonya, and Cali. When Cage came to pick me up, I promised that I would come back and hang out with them again.

"You're always welcome," Dr. Sonya told me as I left.

"How was your time with Nero and your mom," I asked Cage as soon as I entered the truck.

"It was pretty amazing," he confirmed.

Cage looked different. The tension that had enveloped him as we drove up was gone. He seemed calmer and more settled.

For the next hour and a half, Cage filled me in on what he learned about the mystery surrounding his birth.

"I couldn't ask all of the questions I wanted to. She's not fully there, mentally," Cage explained. "Dr.

Tom thinks she has some type of dementia. She has an unusual set of symptoms, though, which for a while made him think that it was magic induced. He goes back and forth on it now. And the longer I was there, the better she got. Nero said that he hadn't seen her this clear-minded in years. That's why I decided to sleep over and spend today. The longer I was there, the more she was able to tell me. I didn't want to risk leaving and losing the momentum."

"That makes sense. I'm glad you were able to spend so much time with her."

"Yeah," he said letting the conversation drop.

"That makes sense. I'm glad you were able to spend so much time with her."

"Yeah. And last night, Nero and I shifted and ran the woods together. It was pretty amazing" he said flatly.

Not knowing how to respond, I let the conversation drop. As we drove in silence, it became clear that there was something else on his mind. Everything about it filled me with dread.

Even though I wanted to ask him what he learned about his biological father and how he ended up with the man who raised him, I didn't dare bring it up. At this point, I just wanted to get home without a disaster happening. I thought I had made it until Cage parked the truck in front of my place and turned the engine off.

"Did you want to come up?" I asked hoping it was the case.

"Actually, we need to talk."

The blood rushed from my face hearing those words. I was a deer in headlights.

"About what?"

"I told you that the more time I spent with my mom, the better she got, right?"

"Yes."

"I think I'm gonna move there and stay for a while."

My fingers tingled and there was a hollowness in my throat that made me want to shift and run.

"What about classes? Are you gonna drive back and forth? That's a long drive."

"I think I'm going to drop out of school for now."

"But you're so close. This is your last semester?"

"My mother needs me. Nero needs me. He's been taking care of her alone all this time. It's been hard for him. He said that she isn't always as in control as she was this weekend. He needs help and they're my family… and my pack."

My next question caused heat to flash across my face.

"What about us? Will you be coming back to see me?"

Every second Cage didn't answer sucked the life out of me. I thought that was painful until he spoke.

"I'm not sure if we should be together."

"What?" I said starting to sweat. "But, you said you loved me."

"I do. You don't have to question that. I do."

"Then, what?"

"You are an incredible guy, the most amazing guy I've ever met. But, we want different things."

"What do you mean, I want you? Don't you want me?"

"I do. I absolutely do. And if you tell me that you can accept your wolf and be a part of our pack, then I will commit to you forever. Tell me that you won't spend the rest of your life trying to "cure yourself" of the thing that makes us perfect for each other, and I'm yours."

I looked at him silently. My heart was breaking.

"That's what I thought. As long as you can't accept yourself, you won't be able to accept me or my family. And, let's say you do discover how to kill your wolf. And, let's say that it gets out and the rest of the world finds out about us. What would happen then?"

"I would never let anything happen to you, Cage. Don't you trust me?"

"How do I trust someone who doesn't trust himself?"

There was nothing I could say to that. All I could do was stare at him, because he was right. My father had opened Pandora's box by telling the world about me. And I couldn't guarantee that anything I did in my father's lab wouldn't get out. I could do my best to bury any discovers I made, but if I use it, its formula will always exist within my genetics.

He shouldn't trust me. Dr. Tom shouldn't trust me. No one should, least of all myself. All I would ever do to Cage and his pack is put them at risk. My soul burned realizing it.

"Cage, I love you," I told him no longer able to hold back my tears.

"I love you too, Quin. I do. Tell me you can live your life with me as a shifter. Please. Please, Quin, just tell me that," he pleaded.

The tears flowed down my cheeks knowing the answer.

"Cage, you can't imagine what I've gone through."

"And, with my pack, you can't imagine the responsibility I now have," he said his eyes filling with tears.

"Is this it?" I asked him desperate for him to say that it wasn't.

"I guess so," he said shattering my heart.

I knew I should have said something after that. Anything. But, I couldn't. The pain I felt disconnected me from my body. I floated somewhere over the two of us looking down. I was sad for the boy crying his eyes out in the passenger seat of Cage's truck. But I couldn't feel him. It would have been too much.

I was grateful when he opened his door and stepped into the cold. Anything was better than watching him suffer. Now, he just needed to make it inside and to his apartment before his legs gave out from under him and he collapsed.

Wishing him forward step-by-step, he ascended the stairs. When he took out his key and attempted to put it into the lock was when I couldn't hold it back anymore. Suddenly drowning in pain, the world around me spun. Luckily I didn't have to open the door. A friendly face opened it and now it was looking back at me.

"Are you okay?" Lou asked. "Quin, are you alright?"

I wanted to say I wasn't. I wanted to tell him that Cage and I had broken up and that we weren't getting back together. I couldn't. All I could do was step to him and fall into Lou's arms.

"He hurt me," was what I said. "I don't know what to do," I explained before spending the rest of the night suffocating on my tears.

What I went through as the weeks passed approached unbearable. It was clear I wasn't made for this. Lou went through guys like popcorn. None of them even left butter on his fingers. Yet, I dated one guy, and breaking up with him left me catatonic. Maybe I was just weaker than everyone else but, there was no question about it, I wasn't made for love.

Lou did his best to get me out of bed and at least attend classes, but I couldn't do that either. Part of me knew that no matter the subject, I could probably cram it a few days before the exam and pass. The other part was that I didn't see the point in school anymore.

What was the point of anything? Why should I leave bed except to eat and go to the bathroom? With all of my smarts, I couldn't figure that out. So, instead, I lied there, I cried, and I allowed my thoughts to endlessly spiral around Cage.

One second I loved him. The next second I hated him. But every moment I cursed my wolf for destroying everything I cared about.

"Quin, you have to get out of bed!" Lou said insistently. "If not for you, for me. There is a smell coming from here that's making the guys I bring home think I'm using the room to store dead bodies."

"Sorry," I said not wanting to be the burden I was.

Lou sighed and then crawled into my bed wrapping his arms around me.

"Come on, Lamb Chop, you gotta snap out of this. There are other guys out there. Believe me. And a hot guy like you would have your pick".

I hadn't told him about Cage being a shifter. It wasn't my secret to share. So, Lou still just thought that he was a hot guy I was crushing on and not that he could have been my soulmate if I hadn't been cursed by being who I was.

"You just need to go outside. How do I get you to leave this room?" Lou asked me with gentle caring.

"I don't know," I told him honestly.

"Okay, maybe that was too much to ask for. How do I get you to leave this bed?"

I didn't respond.

Lou suddenly popped up and looked around.

"Okay, that's it. I was trying to be nice but you've given me no choice. Where is it?"

"What?"

"Your phone."

"Don't call Cage."

"You think I wanna call Cage, that stinking, rat-bastard? Oh no. He needs to burn in hell for what he did to you."

"He was doing it for his…"

"If you tell me he had to do it for his sick mom, I swear to god I'm gonna lose it. You don't get to defend him until you're capable of standing long enough to take a shower. Do you hear me? I said, do you hear me?"

"Yes."

"Good. Now, where's your phone?"

"In the drawer."

Lou looked at the nightstand and found a charger cord preventing it from closing. I didn't feel like explaining how it got that way and he didn't ask.

Instead, he took it out, grabbed my finger, unlocked it, and searched the contacts.

"Who are you calling?" I asked realizing that I had a few numbers I wouldn't want him to call.

"Hello, Mr. Toro? Hi, you don't know me, but this is Quin's roommate... It's nice to meet you, too."

My head popped up. "You called my dad? Low blow!" He wasn't even on my radar of people I didn't want to face. I turned over and buried my head in my pillow.

"Listen. I'm calling because I'm having a bit of a situation with Quin..."

"You called my dad?" I groaned.

"Yes. I can't get him out of bed," Lou said to my father. "Why is it? It's because some guy broke his heart."

"What? Noooo!" I exclaimed reaching for the phone. Lou jumped out of the way.

"I know! They're the worst, aren't they? ...Anyway, I was wondering if you had some way to get him up to at least take a shower or something? ...Yeah, it does smell rather rank in here."

"Noooo!" I said mortified.

"Okay. You got it," Lou said lowering the phone. "Quin, I have your dad. He wants to talk to you."

"I hate you!" I told him meaning it.

"But, I love you," he said handing me the phone with a smile and leaving my room.

I looked at the phone and took a deep breath. It wasn't that I didn't want to talk to my father about this. It was just that it was humiliating. He and I had worked so hard to get me to be able to live around others that I wanted him to think that I could. But, I had failed. Not because I couldn't control my wolf, but because I couldn't control my humanity.

"Dad?" I said doing my best to sound composed.

"Quin, I'm sorry. I'm so sorry, Quin."

That was when I lost it. Retching pain waft out of me as snot drained down my face.

"It just hurts so much, Dad. Why does it have to hurt so much?"

"Because that's love. Sometimes it hurts."

"But why?"

My father went quiet on the other end.

"Okay, that's it. Get out of bed, get dressed. I'll be there in four hours."

"What?"

"Your roommate caught me on the jet flying back to New York. I'm making a detour to see you. We're gonna go get some dinner and we are going to talk this out."

"What are you talking about?"

"I mean it. Get out of bed. Get dressed. I'm gonna be there in four hours."

As much as I didn't want to, after the call, I dragged myself out of bed and into the shower.

"Hallelujah!" Lou yelled from the living room.

"I hate you," I mumbled with the shower droplets drowning me out.

I didn't hate him. Lou was the best friend I'd ever had. I might have starved if it wasn't for him because there was no way I was walking to the front door to get my food deliveries.

He also cared about me in a way that I had hoped that Cage would. Lou deserved more from his college experience than having to take care of me.

Returning to my bedroom clean, I smelled what Lou had talked about. My room smelt like a tomb. I cracked a window. I didn't want my dad to see me like this.

My dad had always imagined great things from me. Yet, here I was unable to feed myself after having my heart broken by a guy. I wasn't as special as he thought I was.

I sat on the edge of my bed in my towel for a long time. It had taken a lot of energy to take a shower. I needed to rest. When I received the text from Dad saying he had landed, I forced myself to get dressed.

"He emerges!" Lou said when I entered the living room.

I gave him a resentful glare. That didn't stop him from running over and throwing his arms around me.

"And you smell good! I had my doubts about calling your dad on you, but look at my Lamb Chop now."

I wasn't resisting his hug. It felt really good, actually. But when the intercom buzzed, he let me go so I could reply.

"Hello?"

"Quin, it's Dad."

"Coming down."

"You're not going to invite him up?"

"Why would I?"

"So, I could meet him. Any tree that you fell from has got to be… yum!"

I gave him an annoyed look and headed for the door. The truth was that my whole life I have had people tell me how good-looking my dad was. I didn't need Lou having fantasies about him and then telling me about it. Ewww!

I tried to leave Lou behind, but when I left the room, he did too.

"What are you doing?"

"Just making sure you get downstairs alright," he said with a devilish smirk.

"Whatever," I said not having enough energy to fight him.

Lou followed me downstairs with a smile on his face.

"Dad," I said looking at my father just past the door.

Lou gasped. He didn't need to tell me that I would never live up to my father. It was obvious. My dad went from being so poor that he and his mother couldn't afford heat during Wisconsin winters, to having a billion dollar genetics company. On top of that, he looked like the guy sailing the yacht in cologne commercials.

No matter what I did, I could never measure up to him. And now Lou knew it too.

"And, who's this?" Dad asked.

"This is my roommate, Lou."

"Nice to meet you, Lou," Dad said with one of his charming smiles. Lou giggled, and then pulled himself together and offered Dad his hand.

"Nice to meet you too, Mr. Toro."

"Thank you for looking after my son. He needs some looking after."

"Dad!"

"Of course. Anything for my Lamb Chop… I mean Quin."

"And thanks for giving me a call. It looks like I came just in time."

I looked at him confused and then looked down at myself. I thought I had done a good job of pulling myself together.

"Shall we go? Again, it was good to meet you, Lou. The next time I'm in town, we'll all have to go out to dinner."

"I look forward to it, Mr. Toro," Lou said blushing.

Yea, I was sure he was.

Walking away, Dad put his arm around me. It felt good to feel him there. Though, he might have done it so that he could fix my hair.

"What are you doing?"

"Did you look in the mirror before you came outside?"

"Not everyone cares about looks as much as you do, Dad."

The truth was that I had forgotten to. And although I had managed to get dressed, it had completely slipped my mind to brush my hair. Baby steps.

As he always did, Dad took me to the best restaurant he could find. Considering we were in East Tennessee it wasn't like the ones in New York and Los Angeles, but it was nice. For some reason, I could barely taste the food, but that probably had more to do with Cage than the chef.

"So, tell me, what's going on, Quin? Who's this guy who broke your heart?"

Despite whatever faults he had, he always listened closely. As he did this time, he seemed to genuinely feel my pain. But, I wasn't still the boy who thought that was enough. I had seen too many things. I now needed more.

"How did you create me, Dad?"

He froze.

"I told you that I don't talk about that."

"You don't talk about it to others. And, that's for the best. But, you can't keep it from me anymore. I need to know."

"Honey, I swore that I would take that to my grave. I can't risk what happened to you happening to others," he said with empathy. But I wasn't going to accept that.

"When did you know there were others like me?"

"What?"

"When did you know? Was it when I was a kid? Was I still a baby?"

"Other's like you how?"

"You know how, Dad," I insisted not giving an inch.

"Quin, I'm telling you that I don't."

I stared into my father's eyes. He really didn't seem to know. Did that mean that I could still trust him? What if what Dr. Tom said was true? What if he has been experimenting on shifters this whole time?

"Son, did you find others like yourself?" He asked hesitantly.

I didn't know what to say. Never had I doubted that I could trust my father. He had always been the only one I thought I could believe in. So, what had changed? Why was my faith in him so easily shaken by Dr. Tom's words?

"Tell me how Mom died," I said when it popped into my head.

"Your Mom?" He leaned away going on the defensive. "Why would you want to talk about that?"

"Because you don't. You never do. All I know is that when I was a wolf, I attacked her and you found her covered in her blood. That's all you've ever told me. I need to know more, Dad. You owe me that."

"Quin, it's my job as your father to protect you."

"Well, I don't need your protection now. What I need is your honesty. I've hated and resented my wolf my entire life fearing that at any moment it could attack someone I love. It's been destroying me slowly. How could I trust anyone if I can't even trust myself, Dad? I need to know whether or not I can trust myself."

My father stared at me until his gaze fell to his plate. He sighed painfully.

"You're right. Maybe you don't need me to protect you anymore. Maybe you're old enough to handle the truth."

It was my turn to freeze. I was just hoping to get a fuller sense of what happened. I hadn't considered that he was covering something up with a lie. Heat washed across my face considering what it could be.

"Yeah, Dad. I can handle it."

He looked up into my eyes with sadness.

"Your mother didn't accept what you are as easily as I did. In fact, she couldn't accept it at all. She would barely ever hold you. When she did, she would look at you with something dark in her eyes.

"As time went on, she become increasingly cruel towards you. When you shifted into a wolf, she would sometimes shave you. She said that she did it hoping that your fur wouldn't grow back. It always did the next time you shifted and that angered her even more.

"She would clip you ears back with clothes pins threatening to cut them off. She would threaten to cut off your tail. In fact, I think she did once. She never told me about it, but there was a time when that particular threat stopped. I wondered why and then saw the terror in your wolf's eyes the next time you two were in the same room together."

"Oh my god, Dad," I said not able to believe what I was hearing.

"Your mother terrorized you, Quin. And then, one day, I think she went too far. I don't know what she was planning or what she did. But after finding the nanny I had hired to make sure that you two were never alone together, without you, I raced around the house looking for you.

"I found you two in the attic. You were crying your eyes out five feet from your diaper, and she was dead. I didn't know what to do, but clearly I had to report her death.

"That was when I made the decision to tell the world about you. I thought that if you hadn't been a secret, your mother wouldn't have tried whatever she had attempted to do. And, I needed a cause of death.

"If I thought I could take the blame, I would have. But me being locked away would mean that you would grow up alone. So, I told everyone.

"And, when you grew older and started asking about your mother, I had to decide if I was going to let my sweet little boy grow up thinking that the person who was supposed to love him most, hated him. Or, if I would just blame it on the thing that we were already trying to get rid of."

"So, you blamed it on my wolf?" I asked in a daze.

He shook his head.

"I've thought about that decision every day since. I still haven't come up with what I could have done differently. I wanted my son to grow feeling loved. I wanted that for you."

"And I got it at the expense of loving myself," I realized.

"What could I have done differently? You now know the truth and you're old enough to have an answer. So tell me, if you had a say in the matter, what would you have wanted me to do? Did I make a mistake?" My father asked with tears in his eyes.

I thought about it. What he had told me had rattled me to my core. My mind swirled.

"I don't know, Dad. I don't know," I said with wet streaks lining my cheeks.

"I'm sorry this happened to you, Quin. I wish I could have been a better father. I tried. I tried so hard."

"I know you did, Dad. You did everything you knew how to do," I said reaching for his hands.

I was right. I could trust him. Maybe how he had handled it was a mistake. Maybe it wasn't. It was going to take me a lot longer than a night to figure it out. But, I knew that what he did, he did thinking it was in my best interest. What more could I ask from him than that.

"I'm not the only one, Dad," I told him unable to look him in the eyes.

"What?"

"There are others like me."

"How? I never told anyone about the genetic codes I switched to make you. Not even your mother."

"Wolf shifters have been around for a long time. And, they aren't the only things out there. There are dragon shifters, Dad. I've seen one. And there are Fae."

"Do you mean fairies?" He asked looking at me as if I was crazy.

"I don't know. I just know what he told me. He said that magic exists and I've seen it."

"Quin, I'm a scientist."

"And so am I. But, I'm also a wolf shifter who was attacked by a dragon shifter and who's visited a town with a protection spell cast around it."

"Any sufficiently advanced technology is indistinguishable from magic," he said quoting his favorite author.

"There are more things in heaven and earth, Horatio, than are dreamt of in your philosophy," I said quoting mine.

"You are truly a wonder, Quin," he said with a smile. "Does anything of this have to do with why your roommate can't get you out of bed?"

As hard as it was to find out the truth about my mother, at least it took my mind off of Cage for a moment.

"Yes," I said feeling the pain come rushing back.

"Is he the dragon shifter you talked about? The Fae?"

"No, he's like me."

"A wolf shifter. That's amazing. So, what went wrong?"

I told my father the story from beginning to end. When I was finished he considered it all.

"I might be a little biased because I will always be on team Quin, but there is something that every relationship needs to last."

"What's that?"

"You need a partner who will always choose you. When it's easy, and when it's hard," he said empathetically.

"He didn't choose me," I said putting it into words.

"You didn't choose each other. But even if you had chosen him…"

"He chose someone else."

My father gave me a tight-lipped sympathetic smile. It hurt me to realize it, but my father was right.

"Do you really want to find a cure for your wolf?" He asked me curiously.

"I think I do," I told him thinking about how much pain it has brought me, including the pain I felt from losing Cage.

"If you do, you know that you don't have to be here to learn how, right? I have a lab and I think it's safe to say that I'm the world's leading expert in wolf shifter genetics. Why don't you just come and work with me? I could teach you everything you need to know.

"I never pursued a cure for you because I didn't think there was anything about you that needed curing. You're perfect the way you are. But, if you don't want it, as the person who did this to you, I'll help you get rid of it."

My Dad's words danced through my head.

"Do you think it's possible that my wolf was just protecting me when it did what it did to Mom?"

"It's possible. But it's also possible that it would have done what it did anyway. The question you should ask yourself is, do you think your wolf will bring you more pain or happiness? And, do you think that being a wolf shifter will make it easier for you to find love?"

It only took me a second to answers his question. I knew what I needed to do.

I'm coming home, Dad. I'll work with you on a cure."

Chapter 16

Cage

Sitting at the table eating lunch with Nero and my mother, I again thought about how lucky I was. The man who raised me wasn't a father. He didn't treat me like family. This was what having a family was supposed to feel like.

After a tense conversation with Dr. Tom, he told me what he thinks happened. He was working at the hospital where I was born. It was one that serviced a lot of shifters. And when they came in with problems that other doctors couldn't figure out, he would take their case ensuring that their magical origins wouldn't get out.

The hospital has since closed but while it was open it serviced all types. At the time of my birth there was a dragon shifter there. The night after I went missing, so did the dragon shifter.

The humans there couldn't explain my disappearance, nor could they pin it on the man Dr. Tom knew was a dragon shifter. A part of the reason was because they didn't know how he could have gotten away with the baby. The maternity ward was on the second floor and there was a camera pointed at the stairwell and elevator.

Since the hospital was already struggling to stay open, the people running it decided to cover up my disappearance. Calling it "The greater good", they told my mother I had died.

My mother said she never believed it. She said she kept asking to see my body and they said that she couldn't. Eventually, they told her that it had been accidentally cremated and tried to give her money to go away.

She didn't take the money, but in the end, it didn't matter. My mother was a nobody from the middle of nowhere. No one was going to believe her over a bunch of people with 'Dr.' in front of their name.

I get the sense that that was what broke her. Nero told me that she acted crazy for most of his childhood. Her behavior was that of a tortured woman.

According to Nero, eventually, she stopped her erratic behavior. Nero said he was relieved when it happened, but that was also when her decline began. Each day she became further disconnected from reality until she stopped going to work at all and they were about to be kicked out of their home.

That was when Nero stepped up and took care of both of them. At 13, Nero got his first job. It was a crap job that didn't pay much, but it was enough to keep a roof over their head. And, ever since, he has done whatever he has had to to make ends meet.

I didn't have a job in town yet, but I was asking around for one. Nero needed help and I was going to give it to him. Right now I was doing it by watching over our mother while he did what he had to do during the day. But, things were going to change as soon as there was a job opening anywhere.

I cleared the table when everyone was done eating. Washing off the dishes and setting them to dry, I could feel Nero staring at me.

"What is it?" I asked knowing that he often had to be prompted to say what was on his mind.

"You think we could go for a run?"

"Of course," I told him feeling uneasy.

I had only been living here for a few weeks so everything between us was still new. But this was the first time he had suggested we let our wolves run during the daylight. It made me think of the last time I had spoken to Quin.

It took everything I had to not think about Quin. Most times I failed. The only thing that prevented me from calling him was that I deleted his phone number. I had to. I wasn't strong enough to simply not call him. I needed to put a mountain of obstacles between us to stop me from running back to him. Deleting his number was just the first.

Finishing up what I was doing, Nero and I went outside and got undressed.

"There's a place I used to go when everything would get too much for me as a kid. Want to see it?"

"Yeah," I told him feeling a wave of guilt that I wasn't here to take care of my little brother until now.

I was getting pretty good a shifting on command. Quin had done a great job of teaching me. And, when my brother and I were both wolves, we disappeared into the woods.

We ran for what felt like 45 minutes. When we stopped, we were at the edge of a valley. I followed Nero's lead and shifted back.

"This is it," Nero said looking out at the waterfall below. After a long winter, it was thawing. I tried to imagine how beautiful it looked when it was warm and flowers covered the valley. This town really was breathtaking.

"It's nice. It's quiet," I told him appreciatively.

"Listen, I wanted to talk to you about you staying here…"

"You have a problem with me staying here?"

"No! Absolutely not. You being here has been the best thing that has ever happened to me."

"Thanks! Me too," I said feeling rewarded for the tough decisions I had made.

"It's just that you're here all the time."

"You want me to find somewhere else to live."

"No! I'm getting this wrong. What I'm trying to ask is, don't you have classes? When you first got here I thought you were taking a couple of days off. But, it's been weeks. Don't you have to go back soon?"

"Oh! Yeah. I dropped out."

"You dropped out?" Nero asked startled.

"Didn't you say this was your last semester and that you just had three classes left to graduate?"

"Yeah. But, I need to be here with you. I need to help with Mom."

"And I appreciate that. I really do…" Nero stared at me measuring what he would say next. "It's just that, I thought that school was important. I mean, I never used to think that. But after I met you and Quin, I…"

He trailed off.

I wasn't sure what was going on. Nothing Nero had told me about himself had led me to believe that he had valued school. So where was this coming from?

I wouldn't want to push him in any way, but it was clear that if he went to college it would change his life. Nero wasn't the dumb thug I thought he was when we had first met. He was thoughtful, vulnerable, and pretty ingenious. If he was exposed to the outside world, there was no telling who he would become.

"School is important," I told him taking the opening.

"But, you only had three classes left and you dropped out. If it's so important, and you were so close, why did you leave?"

"I left for you and Mom."

"Huh. Okay. And, I appreciate that. It's just that I thought it was really important."

"It is really important! It's just that you two are more important."

Nero didn't respond to that. I obviously didn't clear things up for him. And, honestly, I could see why. It was a matter of priorities and responsibilities. But, at the same time, I didn't realize that I might be setting an example for my younger brother. I was new at this.

"Why hasn't Quin come to visit?"

"What?" I asked caught off guard. As his question echoed in my mind, I felt a tightening clench around my heart, and waves of pain shot through me.

"I said, why hasn't Quin come to visit?"

"Oh! It's because…"

As I began to say it, I realized that I hadn't said it aloud before. It took everything in me not to fall to my knees at the thought.

"We broke up."

"What?" Nero asked shocked. "I liked him!"

"I did too," I admitted feeling it for the first time.

"What happened?"

"I have responsibilities now."

"Wait! You broke up with him because of us?"

"I mean…" I didn't want to say it.

"No!" He said turning to me angrily. "Just no!"

"What are you talking about, no?"

"I liked him. He was really good for you, Cage. You two were cute together. It was clear that he was your fated mate," he said distressed.

"There's more to being with someone than how you look together. But, what's a fated mate?"

"You gotta know what a fated mate is," Nero said dismissively.

"Nero, just tell me what it is," I said feeling my wolf growl.

"It's the person a wolf shifter is meant to be with. It's a magic thing. There's one person for all of us. When you're with them, it sometimes feel like you can't breathe. When you're apart, it could feel like hell.

"I was sure that Quin was yours. Was I wrong? Is he not your fated mate?"

"I…" I said caught off guard.

Yeah. From the first moment I met him, I had the sense that there was something powerful pulling us together. I needed him. Nero was right. It sometimes felt like I couldn't breathe. And now that we had broken up, it took everything in me to stand upright every day.

This time with my family should have been the greatest time of my life. But, I constantly fought the feeling that I was being torn to shreds. I needed Quin like I needed air. I was slowly going insane without him.

"You don't understand. Quin didn't want this life. What he cared about most was curing himself of his wolf. I could never be with him because he didn't want to be with someone like me."

"You said he grew up thinking he was the only wolf shifter and that I was the first one he had ever met."

"Yeah."

"Cage, I grew up my entire life knowing that one day I was gonna shift. Yet, even though I had a pack around me, when it happened, I still felt a certain way about it. He had none of that."

"You had a hard time accepting you're a shifter?"

"Most people do."

"But, it felt so natural for me."

"And, I don't understand it. How is it that it comes so easy for you? That first fight we had, there was no way you should have been able to get the upper hand on me like that. No one should be able to. I've fought a lot of wolves. No one can."

"Yet, I did?"

"You did. You're special somehow, Cage. And if someone takes a little longer to get to where you are, you gotta give them the time."

"But he chose getting rid of his wolf over being with me."

"Then you convince him. You fight for him. That's what I would want someone to do for me...

especially my fated mate. And you can't use your pack as an excuse to ruin your life."

My mind spun thinking about everything Nero had told me. It was too much. I needed the spinning to stop.

"I thought I was supposed to be the wiser, older brother," I said hoping being light-hearted would relieve some of Nero's pressure.

"Then act like it, bro. Fight for Quin. Go after the man you love!"

I couldn't deny it. Everything he said was right. There was something I couldn't control drawing me to Quin. And, I shouldn't have given up on him. What was I thinking giving up on Quin without a fight?

"What have I done? What do I do?"

"Go after him!" Nero insisted jolting me into action.

I knew Nero was right. Without a word, I shifted into my wolf and sprinted back to the trailer. As I did, my thoughts swirled. I didn't have his phone number. I had deleted it. I needed to find someone who had it. I needed to get to my truck.

Feeling like I was back on the football field, my strides were long and strong. Jumping over streams and across ravines, I arrived back in a fraction of the time it had taken to get out there.

Shifting back and getting dressed, I raced inside in search of my keys.

"Why are you in such a rush?" my mother asked drawing my attention.

"Mama, I love you, but I made a huge mistake I need to correct."

"Did you finally come to your senses about your boyfriend?"

I looked back at her shocked.

"How did you know?"

"I'm your mother. A mother knows these things," she said with a smile. "Now, go get him."

I smiled unable to love her more.

Hurrying to my truck, I put my foot on the gas racing to town. My first thought was to go to Dr. Sonya's. I knew she had his number. But the closer I got, the more I realized that that couldn't be the plan.

It had been too long. A phone call wouldn't do. I had to see him. I had jerked him around too much already. He had to see that I was serious.

He didn't deserve what I did to him. And, I didn't deserve him. But, deserve him or not, I was going to let him know that I didn't want to live without him. He needed to know that I was going to do whatever I had to do to keep him whether he was a shifter or not.

My lead foot got me back to campus in the half the time it usually took. As I approached his place, my heart pounded with fear. What if what I had to say wasn't enough? What would I do then?

Whatever I have to do, I am gonna do it. Quin is my man. He is the love of my life and, no matter the consequences, I'm gonna fight until my last breath to be with him.

Not finding a parking spot, I pulled my truck onto the sidewalk making my own. I didn't care. What I had to tell him couldn't wait another minute. So racing out of my truck with the engine running and the door open, I approached the front door of his building and lunged for the intercom.

The timing of it all couldn't have been worse… or maybe better. Because as I stood there waiting for the intercom to light up in reply, a face appeared on the other side of the glass in the door. It was Tasha. Of all people, why did it have to be her?

"Please, open the door. I know things didn't end well between us, but I have to go see Quin. Please!"

I was half expecting Tasha to turn around and walk off pissed. Instead, she popped open the door. As I stared at her, she smiled. I wasn't sure why until I saw who was standing behind her. It was her best friend, Vi. Vi was smiling too, and I didn't make the connection until I looked down and saw that they were holding hands.

"Go get him," Tasha told me not needing to say anymore.

"Thank you!" I said rushing past her and bounding the stairs three at a time.

Arriving in front of Quin's door, I was exhausted and crackling with excitement. I didn't know how I had managed to stay away from him for so long. I knocked on the door trying to calm myself. As soon as I did, it flung open. A very pissed face stared back at me from within.

"Lou, where is he?"

"Gone! He's gone because of you!"

"What? Where? When?" I asked pushing past him and seeing that half of the living room furniture was missing.

"You hurt him. He decided to leave school because of you."

"What? No! When did he go?"

"An hour ago."

"An hour ago?"

"His family came and packed him up. They're probably flying away right now. I guess you're too late."

"No! This can't be happening."

"What do you care? You just want him so you can have someone you can hurt again."

I looked at Lou devastated that he would think that. But, he was right. All I had done was hurt Quin. Quin was probably better off without me. ...But maybe "better off" wasn't always better.

"Lou, I know you hate me. And you have every right to. I didn't treat Quin how he deserved to be treated. But, he is the most special person in the world to me. And, even if I have to spend the rest of my life making it up to him, even if I have to follow him around the world to do it. I will.

"I love that man. I love him more than I thought possible. So, if there's anything you can tell me, anything that will allow me to tell him how much of a fool I've been, I will owe you forever. Please, Lou. Please!"

Lou's gaze was ice-cold, until in an instant when his tension melted and tears pooled in his eyes.

"Why can't a guy ever say those things about me?" Lou said overwhelmed. "Okay, let's go."

"Where are we going?"

"To the airport. They might not have left as long ago as I said. But they're taking a private jet so if we don't get there soon, they'll be gone."

Lou didn't have to say any more. Hurrying back to my truck, we climbed in and raced to the airport. It wasn't the one my team flew out from when we traveled for games, it was the one for private planes. I had never been there and knew nothing about it.

Pulling up, I found an open spot next to the entrance of the building. Sprinting out, I entered the terminal and looked around. The place was much smaller than I ever imagined it. I could see everyone in the open space in one sweep. Taking a second scan to be sure, Quin wasn't here.

"There!" Lou said pointing to a door marked 'Exit'.

He didn't have to say anymore. Running to it, someone yelled, "Hey!"

Exiting the terminal, I stepped onto the tarmac. Still, there was no Quin. Had they gone? Was I too late?

No. There was only one place he could be. It was on a plane circling the tarmac and heading to the runway. I ran after it.

"Quin! Wait! Stop! Don't go! I have to talk to you!" I yelled.

It was no use. I could barely hear myself over the roar of the engine. All I could do was sprint towards the runway and hope he saw me.

Racing as if for a touchdown, I leaped everything in my way and spun around the things I couldn't. I was two hundred feet away as the plane raced past me. I couldn't stop it. But as it crossed in front of me, I saw a familiar face in one of the windows. It was Quin. Our eyes met.

It wasn't enough, though. Nothing I had done had been enough. With the force of a rocket, the plane approached the end of the runway and took off. He was flying away. Quin was gone. I had waited too long. It was over.

Watching his plane disappear into the air, I slowed down giving up. The second I did, I was taken down by a linebacker. Maybe he wasn't that big. Maybe it was just that I hadn't seen the hit coming.

Whatever it was, my face was now pressed against the ground. A man was kneeling on my back. All hope was lost.

"Do you realize how illegal it is to run onto a tarmac? It's a federal crime? You're going to jail for a long time," a large, angry, out of breath man yelled into my ear.

If I wasn't going to be with Quin, what did it matter if I was in jail? I was realizing that, without Quin, nothing mattered. He was gone and it had all been my fault. I didn't care what happened to me now because I had let the best thing in my life slip away. From here on out, I deserved everything I got.

When another man joined us, they grabbed my arms and pulled me to my feet. I didn't resist. I was going to let them do their job. My fight was gone. My will to go on was gone... until I heard something I hadn't expected.

The plane that had taken off with Quin in it was circling and heading back down.

"Wait, look," I told the guys turning their attention to the landing plane.

The three of us watched it. As soon as it touched down and came to a stop, the door opened. Someone raced out. It was Quin Toro, the love of my life, and he was running towards me.

Two freight trains couldn't keep me from him after that. Pulling from my captors and running to Quin, I didn't stop until I was right in front of him. He leaped into my arms.

"You're here! I didn't want to leave without saying goodbye," Quin declared.

"Why are you going? Please don't go."

"Why shouldn't I? I have nothing to stay for."

"What are you talking about? You have Lou and school. But, more than that, you have me. I love you, Quin. I was crazy not to do everything I could to be with you."

"But, what's changed. I still don't know if I want to be a shifter. You still have your responsibilities with your mom and your pack. We can't deny that."

"No, we can't. But I'm willing to do whatever I have to to have you in my life. I'll go wherever you need me to go and do whatever you need me to do. If you don't want to be a shifter, then I'll love the human part of you twice as much. All I ask is for you to love me."

"I would never want to take you from your pack, Cage. I couldn't do that to you."

"But, I want you to be my pack. You're just as important to me as Nero and my Mom are. It's because of you that I have them. I love you, Quin Toro. I want to love you for the rest of my life. Please, be with me," I said with a smile.

"I don't know, Cage. I want to. I want to more than anything in the world, but…"

"Quin, what are you doing?" A voice said from behind him.

We turned to see the most James Bond-looking guy I had ever seen in my life. But, the resemblance was unmistakable. He was Quin's father.

"The man's telling you he's choosing you. Quin, you have to know when you've won."

"But, what if…"

"The only thing you have to decide is, are you willing to choose him. Are you, Quin? When things get hard, are you willing to keep figuring out a way?"

I turned to Quin who looked back at me.

"What do you say, Quin. You want to figure out a way?"

His smile lit up my heart.

"Yes, Cage. We'll figure out a way. I love you. I want to be with you no matter what it takes."

That was when I leaned in and kissed him. His lips had never tasted sweeter. Lost in the wonder of his touch, I knew that Quin and I were about to live the rest of our lives happily ever after.

Epilogue

Quin

Unpacking the plane turned out to be a lot easier than packing it. It was probably because Cage was there doing it with me. It gave him a chance to meet my father. Cage was the first other shifter he had met. He liked Cage immediately as I knew he would.

Moving back into the apartment with Lou, my dad and I agreed that I would finish up the semester before making a decision on whether I was going to work with him to find a cure. The arrangement would allow me to join Cage on the weekends when he visited his family and for me to experience life with a pack. If I still wanted to find a cure after that, my father told me he would help me.

But the more time I spent with Cage and the other wolves, the harder it got to imagine my life any other way. My life with them became an adventure. There were still so many things Cage and I didn't know about being a shifter and our new world.

A part of that mystery had to do with Cage and Nero's biological father? Even as their mother became more coherent, she wouldn't say who he was.

"You have no idea?" I asked Nero as we sat together at Cage's graduation.

"I'm not sure," he responded in hushed tones.

"Wait. That's not what you said to Cage. You told him that your mother forbid you from asking about him."

"That's true. She did forbid me. But that hasn't stopped me from looking into stuff."

"So, you think you know?"

"I might. And, since you were able to find us in a town that wasn't even on the map, I was thinking maybe you could help. I don't know how much time I'm gonna have while taking classes next semester, but…"

"Wait, are you going to be taking classes here next year?" I asked shocked.

Nero looked at me and blushed.

"I was thinking that with Cage helping out and my mom doing so much better, I might give it a shot. I might even try out for the football team. I was pretty good in high school."

"Pretty good?" Titus said leaning over from the seat next to Nero. "This guy set the record for most yards run in a season. This one is lightning on the field."

Nero blushed.

"I might have run a few yards," Nero said humbly.

"Trust me, Quin, this school won't know what hit them," Titus said with his usual salesmanship.

"Hey Quin, do you know who that is?" Nero said staring at someone standing under the oak trees past the chairs.

I turned to look. It was a guy with shaggy dark hair, a thin frame, and round glasses. He was cute.

"No. I've never seen him before. Why do you ask?"

"It's just that I thought I saw him look at me."

"Oh."

I turned back to the guy. As I did, he looked at us. I couldn't tell who he was looking at. But as the three of us stared at him, he smiled. I looked back at Nero. Nero couldn't take his eyes off of him.

Wait. What was going on? Was Nero into guys? My mouth dropped open.

"Cage Augustus Rucker," a man said over the P.A. system.

I turned to see Cage step onto the stage to collect his diploma.

"Oh, he's getting it," I said tearing Nero's attention from the guy.

Once the scroll of paper was in Cage's hand, everyone in our little group, which included Lou and Cage's mother, stood up and cheered. The love of my life was graduating from university. I loved him more than I had ever loved anyone and I couldn't be happier for him.

The next chapter of our lives was about to begin. Would it include Nero and the guy he still couldn't take his eyes off of? Would it include finding out who their father is and solving the mystery behind Cage's birth?

I didn't know. But, whatever it included, I was all in. So was Cage. And as long as we had each other, I knew that anything would be possible.

The end.

Thinking about rereading this book? Or, do you have a preferred genre? Consider reading this series as a sexy male/male contemporary romance series starting with 'Serious Trouble', a male/female wolf shifter romance in 'Son of a Beast', a male/female sexy sports romance in 'My Tutor', or a wholesome romance in 'I Don't Date My Tutor'.

*****

Sneak Peek:
Enjoy this Sneak Peek of 'Grumpy Boss Trouble':

Grumpy Boss Trouble
(M/M Romance)
By
Alex McAnders

HIL

As I pull into Snow Tip Falls, there is nothing about it that makes me want to stay. It's a beautiful small town, but if you stop running, your problems have a way of catching up with you.

But then tragedy strikes, and suddenly I find myself wanting to help. And when the person needing help is a chiseled football player with brooding eyes, dimples, and an endless desire to protect me, I'm reminded of the other purpose of my trip, to have a one night stand that finally rids me of my gay v-card.

I know why I haven't lost it yet. Guys confuse me. Cali isn't confusing, mostly because he doesn't say much.

Maybe he'll be the one. And if I get his rippling, jock body wrapped around me, it will totally be worth the heart break that will follow when he finds out who I am and what I've done.

CALI

You know how some people are rays of sunshine that light up a room? That's Hil. Man, it's annoying. Annoying or not, it's not like I can refuse his offer of help if I want to stay in university, or on the football team.

It's not that he's hard to look at. That guy makes me think dirty thoughts.

And, it's not like he isn't the sweetest, kindest guy I've ever met...

Wait, am I falling for the stranger who showed up out of nowhere wanting to fix my life?

There's a reason I like to keep to myself. And as hot as Hil is, I'm not sure my heart can take being hurt again.

*****

Grumpy Boss Trouble

Reaching down, he took my hand. His warm flesh against mine sent a tingle that rippled through me. I wanted him. I'd never been more turned on in my life. But I also wanted to respect him. I didn't want to do anything that he wasn't ready for.

Because of that, I reeled in my desire. It nearly broke me, but I did. Still holding his hand, we entered the room. It was weird seeing Hil's stuff scattered around my familiar space. I liked it. I couldn't have guessed how much.

"Do you have to head back to campus in the morning?" Hil asked as he hovered around his travel bag. "Yeah. But I'll be back early to help Mama settle in."

"I'll make waffles."

"I would like that. I think Mama would enjoy that too," I said, starting to relax. "We should probably head to bed. I'm thinking it's going to be a long day tomorrow."

"Of course," he said nervously.

Seeing how nervous he was, only made me want him more. I wanted to hold and take care of him. I wanted to protect him. And whether or not I admitted it, I wanted to slowly push into him, listening to his light moans as I did.

I turned away when I began to throb. I didn't know how I was going to do this. It was taking everything in me not to race across the room, scoop him into my arms, and throw him onto the bed.

"What's the matter?" he asked, lightly wrapping his fingers around my bicep from behind.

I could feel his body heat. My heart thumped needing him. Did he know what he was doing to me? Could he know what his touch was about to unleash?
Read more now

Sneak Peek:
Enjoy this Sneak Peek of 'Best Friend Trouble':

Best Friend Trouble
(M/M Romance)
By
Alex McAnders

'He slipped his hand between my legs. I froze. I was pulsing. What would happen if he touched it?'

Imagine if you asked your straight best friend to pretend to be your fiancé and one night while sharing a bed, his naked body reacted to your touch.

————

LOU
I know it shouldn't matter what people say about me. But when my parents told me that I would never find love because I liked guys, I was willing to do anything to prove them wrong.

So, when the most romantic guy ever asked me to marry him, I had to show him to them immediately. Was I moving too fast? Because as soon as I scored him an invitation to one of our obnoxious family get-togethers, he called things off.

Now, I need a fiancé to replace the one I thought I had or my parents will think they were right about me all along.

TITUS

I can't tell you why Lou has dated so many guys, but watching him do it has torn me up inside. Now he needs someone to pretend to be his fiancé for a weekend. I'm his best friend. Of course I'm gonna do it.

Will it be weird pretending to be engaged to the man whose naked body makes me want to break headboards? Yeah, especially since he doesn't even know I like guys. But while I'm getting his parents to like me, maybe I'll tell him how I feel.

That would have been the perfect plan if Lou's rich, hot, openly gay quarterback ex didn't suddenly show up wanting to win him back.

Every day not telling him rips my heart out. But even if I could confess my feelings to Lou, would it be enough to make him choose me over the perfect guy?

My aching heart hopes so. I don't have a lot of time to find out.

*****

Best Friend Trouble

"Roll over," he said ordering me onto my stomach.

I complied.

"What are you doing?" I asked open to anything.

"I'm gonna give you a massage."

"Yes, please," I said with a smile.

With my head turned to the side, I watched as Titus climbed on top of me. He sat on my ass and pushed his large hands across my back. His two hands spanned the whole thing at once. I felt small in his grasp. The feeling took my breath away.

"How's that?" he asked.

I couldn't answer.

"Do you want me to stop?"

"No," I chirped terrified he would. "No," I repeated calmer. "It feels good."

Titus's fingertips pushed into my muscles relaxing them. My thoughts swirled bathed in the sensation.

Losing myself, I felt his hands find the bottom of my shirt. His fingers touched my flesh. It was electric. I struggled to breathe.

"Do you want me to stop?"

"No. Don't stop," I begged.

He didn't. Pushing his hand up my back, he lifted my shirt higher and higher.

"Don't stop," I repeated.

When my shirt pressed against my neck, he pulled it off of me. With his hands sliding against the back of my arms, he leaned down and kissed my back.

His was a trail of kisses. Each delicate and seductive.

Finding the canal of muscle down my spine, his lips entered. Spilling onto my lower back, they slowly climbed the gentle slope towards my ass.

"Do you want me to stop?" he asked breathlessly.

"I don't want you to stop," I said offering him the final permission he would need before I lifted my hips and he reached under me unbuttoning my pants.

I was hard, very hard. His hand found it. Caressing it through my pants, his hand returned when my pants were off.
Read more now

*****

Printed in Dunstable, United Kingdom